My Liberty

A fight for freedom

by

Andrea Mells

Eloquent Books

This work is entirely fiction. The people, places, times, and dates are fictitious. Any resemblances to actions or incidents in this book are coincidental and in no way a reenactment produced by the author or publisher.

Eloquent Books
An imprint of Strategic Book Group
P.O. Box 333
Durham CT 06422
www.StrategicBookGroup.com

ISBN: 978-1-60911-415-2

Special Thanks

Having a dream is something most of us have known. Having that dream come true is something many of us never realize.

I send a special thanks to Kim for being for me the kind of friend Kathy was for Mrs. Liberty. I also sent special thanks to Aunt Barbara because she has been my sounding board and an encourager. Thank you for being my Patricia.

CHAPTER ONE

It is an early January morning, just before nine. Normally, I have a nursing class at this time of day, so I'm not at home. I get up this morning just as I have for the past seven semesters. I cook breakfast, dress and feed the kids, pack lunches, book bags, as well as the diaper bag and get everyone in the car to make the various drop-offs before heading to school myself. But, today proves to be different from all the other typical days; I have to come back home, unexpectedly, because I don't have my homework assignment; this is something I have never done before. This day turns out to be my wakeup call.

I pull into the driveway of my tri-level brick home, which is fenced in on three sides. As soon as I pull past the front of the house, the fence hides my car and protects the side and back yards, garage, and most of the driveway from any curious onlookers. Our house sits in a small subdivision nestled in a small town called Portage, just outside of Kalamazoo, Michigan. I throw the car into park, leaving it running, jump out and run to the door. Even though it's cold outside this time of year, I leave my coat in the car; so I can move quickly. I come through the unlocked, back door which opens into the kitchen. While I rush around the kitchen table and head for my desk in the basement, I trip over one of Jonathan's stupid thermoses lying carelessly on the kitchen floor. I stumble past the phone mounted on the kitchen wall, and it rings. Instinctively, I grab the receiver. I pick it up at the same time as my husband, who is off today. The other person on the line asks for him, so

I hang up the phone and continue my quest for the missing homework. At first I don't think much about the phone call, but as I limp up the basement stairs, I can hear him talking. Certain tones in the sound of his voice catch my attention. He's using his playful, sexy voice that should be reserved for me alone. I can only hear his part of the conversation, but what I hear is enough to stop me in my tracks. Immediately, I know something is wrong.

First of all, he's never awake at that time of day, let alone in full conversation. After all, it's because of his need for rest that he insists the girls can't stay home with him while I go to school. Judging from the freeness in his tone and the volume of his conversation, he doesn't realize that I am in the house; obviously, he must not have heard me pick up or hang up the phone. He isn't whispering, but I can't hear him clearly from where I'm standing. He is upstairs in the master bedroom, and the door is wide open. The master bedroom is at the top of the stairs, down the hall, to the right. Because there is no wall at the top of the stairs going to the right, only a wrought-iron railing, I can see up into the hall and bedroom from the living room. He is lying on the bed, but from where I'm standing, only his feet are visible. Fortunately, he can't see me at all. I tiptoe to the bottom of the stairs and lean in toward our bedroom, almost lying down on the stairs, listening intently, straining to hear what he is saying. Never have I mistrusted nor spied on him; but this is different. I'm minding my own business and this suspicion seeks me out, so I can't ignore it.

"Yeah, she was all right. We talked. She seems pretty nice to me," he says to the caller. His words and the freeness of his voice sound an alarm inside me.

"Is she married? Well, how many kids does she have? You think she likes me? That's cool." He's laughing at whatever is being said. He's enjoying this conversation.

I am able to piece together from his end that he is talking to a female co-worker. She seems to be setting my husband up with another woman, a new co-worker. As I listen, my heart is pounding so loudly in my ears that it becomes even more difficult for me to hear him. I feel myself having trouble breathing. I dare not move for fear that my legs will not support me. Or worse, I'll stumble, and he'll hear and know that I'm listening. Yet, I need to move closer. I need to know.

Slowly, I unzip and peel off my boots and leave them at the bottom of the steps. I begin easing up the few steps that lead upstairs to our bedroom. Only tiny, well-placed steps will quiet the squeaking stairs. This yields me slow progress forward, and it distracts me from my real purpose. Still, I press on, carefully placing my feet toward the edge of the steps trying to reduce any warning sounds and maintain my balance. Finally, I reach the landing, but the bedroom door still seems miles away. I lay myself down at the top of the steps realizing that I must crawl slowly, painstakingly on my hands and knees if I don't want the hall floorboards to betray me, too. Moving down the hallway toward our bedroom, I lower myself, dragging my body across the carpet. I can feel the carpet twisting and tangling my top until it rises; then it burns my stomach as I slide ever closer to the open bedroom door. It's funny how when these brief moments play out in one's life, there's time to envision yourself in your mind's eye. I can see myself as a lioness, like the ones I have seen many times on those nature shows, stalking its prey, moving in slow motion, down the hallway that goes on forever. When I reach the doorway, I crouch down, catlike, outside the door and listen. None of this feels real.

Even with all this unfolding right before me, I find that I still should adhere to some code of honor. As I crouch, waiting to learn my fate, I feel like I am breaking that secret, silent code of trust as I spy on him. For some reason, my mother's words about listening at doorways pop into my head; I recall her saying something about hearing things that might hurt your own feelings, not the one you're spying on. That's an understatement. Anyway, it's too late now; I've been overtaken by the compulsion to move forward, and I can't turn back now. I feel like I have already begun unraveling a yarn that will entangle me deeply and try to strangle the life out of me.

After holding my breath and my position until I am about to explode, I hear him say goodbye as he hangs up the phone. I just stay where I am outside the bedroom door, dumbfounded. In a few moments he gets up and starts out of the bedroom. When he reaches the doorway he is smiling, feeling satisfied with himself, like when you get away with something. Then, he looks down and sees me. He is visibly startled to see me outside the door on the floor, and that confident smile leaves his face. I don't bother to change my position. He tries to hide his surprise, but he knows I heard him.

"Oh, how long you been there?" he asks with a casual, no-big-deal tone in his voice.

"I've been here long enough to know that something strange is going on." I reply in a voice so filled with hurt that I barely recognize it as my own. He marches past me, down the hall into the bathroom, and closes the door. I realize that he needs time to get his story together; I need time too. I need time to believe that I have not heard what I have. I need time to unfold my tangled body. I need time to get my heart to stop pounding and to catch my breath. When he comes out, I ask him again about the phone call.

"Ah, that was nothin'. We were just talkin' about a new girl at work." Then he turns to me and smiles his sheepish grin.

I say, "Sounds like she's more than just a new girl," sounding unsure of what I really believe.

"Ah girl, you're always thinking something silly," he replies as he passes by me again on his way back to the bedroom. I stay crouched down on the carpet, feeling stupid. I forgot about my homework that I came back home for. I forgot about class. I forgot about the running car. I even forgot about that thermos that almost crippled me. This thing has all my attention.

This whole episode of the call while I'm supposed to be out, the new girl at work, and his willingness to set himself up with a date all catches me totally off guard, but instead of dealing with it, I choose to dismiss it. I decide to use my own special brand of problem solving; I ignore it, let this incident slide. Maybe it really is nothing. Jonathan has always told me how I can get excited over nothing. Maybe he's right, or maybe I don't really want to know the truth. I have thought of ours as the perfect (all right, semi-perfect) marriage. I have been happy with our life for years. I have learned not to make waves. This is no different; once again, I decide to believe that what he said and what I heard somehow means nothing. I am able to cope by telling myself that maybe the root of the problem is me. Perhaps I should check myself. I try to remember the last time we'd been out together. It's longer than I can remember. Since starting school, my schedule is full of all the things I was doing before, and much more. I try to think about the last time we made love. It has been well over a week ago, and even then it was quick and off to sleep. Yet for years, I've come to bed in sexy nightgowns and plenty of pillow talk. I don't remember any sounds at our last sexual encounter except for a few grunts at the end. I need to find some ways to make him happier. Then maybe some girl at work won't seem so appealing.

***

I stay at home during the day, a domestic engineer (chief cook and bottle washer), and we are surviving on his income alone. I know it was I who made the decision to stay home and raise our three girls rather than to work. My decision reduced us to one income; but, according to Jonathan, most of my income was being absorbed into childcare anyway. Therefore, the loss of income was minimal. Besides, Jonathan says working for $5 or $6 an hour in the mall or at some fast food place and letting some young, insensitive, junior college graduate boss me around can be humiliating. In time, we both felt my staying home was the best decision for our girls, and for our family.

Things seemed to have been going pretty well. But after the unexpected phone call, our marriage gets bad fast. As the weeks go by, Jonathan suddenly begins building a new image: new wardrobe, contacts, and sunglasses cause another $300 to slip away this payday too. Workout sessions at the gym and hanging out with the guys turn into what looks like an obsession. When I try to talk with him, he claims it is important for him to show a higher level of camaraderie amongst his colleagues if he's going to further his career. Helpless to stop the force of the oncoming storm that is mounting, I look on knowing that I'm losing ground.

Keeping my mind on school and studying becomes increasingly difficult. I try to give Jonathan's some space while encouraging (not nagging) him to do something with me, anything. His responses are always the same: either he is too busy with the job, or I am too busy with school and the girls. My attempt to prepare some sort of career for myself is beginning to suffer in the wake of all that is going on. I want to get finished with school quickly, so I carry a heavy load each semester. I have eighteen hours this semester, and it is killing me. Concentrating on school in the midst of my drama is almost impossible. My mind keeps taking me to fears of being left unemployed, unmarried, uneducated, and unprepared to face the world alone. So, I begin moving more and more slowly. I want to quit school; life is just getting too hard. Maybe quitting school is what will make him happy with me again.

I know all Jonathan's actions are leading up to something, but I don't know what. Correction: I do know what, but I just don't want it to be true. It has all the markings of another woman, yet I continue to live in denial, praying and hoping that I am wrong or that it is just a phase. Maybe it's that seven-year itch thing I've heard some of the old folks talking about showing up a few years late. I am like a child, waiting to see what the class bully will do to me next, yet powerless to stop it. When I question him, he keeps telling me that everything is fine and not to worry. Somehow, this is not reassuring me. I know something is coming; I can feel it.

As Jonathan spends more and more time out of the house, I have no choice but to go on with life; going to school and Bible study, singing in the choir, and praying for direction. I honestly believe that God knows what we need to be a strong family, and I rely on my blind faith in Him. Looking for God to heal my situation, I get in prayer line after line. I cook breakfast every Sunday morning before getting ready for church, and I serve it to Jonathan in bed. I can't use the crock-pot and let food cook at night because Jonathan doesn't like smelling food at night. So, I make Sunday dinner the night before so that he cannot accuse me of neglecting him by putting church before him. I do all I know to do to make him happy.

***

In February, less than six weeks after the telephone call I overheard, drama begins unfolding. Jonathan announces that he is going to a co-worker's birthday party. Once again, I cannot go; it is for staff only. I watch him take special care at getting dressed: polishing his shoes, slicking back his wavy hair, splashing on his new, expensive cologne, and, finally, putting in his contact lenses. It is difficult to see him look so good and know that I won't be going along, but I accept it and keep myself from getting upset.

Once he leaves, I feed the girls and put them to bed. I try to read my Bible and find myself reading the same lines over and over again. Before long, I hear Jonathan returning. It is not particularly late, but I switch off the light, put the Bible on the nightstand, and pretend to be asleep. He undresses and gets into bed. He then reaches over me, almost squashing the life out of me, to get the telephone off my nightstand. Using the lighted receiver, he dials a number from memory.

"Hey, man," his voice is smooth and silky again.

"Just checkin' to see if you made it home OK. All right, see you later." Then he hangs up the phone. There is no apology for my temporary injuries; no goodnight, no nothing. He just rolls over away from me to go to sleep. I am a little annoyed but happy he didn't stay out late. I, too, go to sleep without saying anything to him. That night's sleep is restless; something bothers me all night.

When I awake Sunday morning, he has already left for work. He is scheduled to work every other weekend, and I am surprised he's gone because he worked last Sunday. To add to my quandary, I can't stop replaying that brief telephone conversation from the night before in my mind. I can't figure out why he needed to call another man to make sure he got home safely, especially since it had not been that late. I thought about his tone of voice. Why didn't he make the call from the kitchen before coming to the bedroom or from his cell phone? Why did he make such a point of being sure I was awake to hear his conversation? Who is he trying to fool? I begin feeling sick and angry. I can no longer rest, so I get up. I have to know, and I know exactly what I have to do. My intuition will not release me. I have to know. I reach over to the nightstand just as Jonathan did the night before, and I do it. I have to know.

7

I HIT THE RE-DIAL BUTTON.

"Hello," answers a soft female voice.

"Hello," I say, trying not to sound surprised.

"Who is this?" she snorts.

"I'm the wife of the man you were with last night. Who is this?" I retort while struggling with the fact that my intuition was correct, struggling to hold back the tears in the wake of this great disappointment, struggling with my anger.

"Your husband and I are just friends. I'm having some marital problems and he's just helping me out," is her explanation.

Before thinking, I ask, "Don't you have any girlfriends who can help you? I don't feel it's appropriate for you to be crying on my husband's shoulder when he has his own family to deal with." I suddenly realize that I am beginning negotiations to save my marriage. I hate what I am doing, but this feeling of desperation is all over me, and I am unable to stop myself.

"I don't have any girlfriends," is her sorry response.

"What about brothers or a sister?" is my next question.

I know I must sound like a complete idiot to her, but I have already dug the hole, so I might as well continue to bury myself in it.

"They wouldn't understand," she says defiantly.

"Well, you need to find someone else other than my husband to confide in because his relationship with you is causing us problems."

Darn, I didn't mean to tell her that. How stupid can I get? Here I am, acting like a fool, telling my rival that what she's doing is working. Regretfully, I spend the next thirty minutes listening to her troubles while mentally trying to assess how much trouble my marriage is in. We all know a man can become a sucker for any woman he feels he has to rescue. I feel bad for her, but if what she says about her situation is true she should also understand my situation. I offer to pray for her and her family. *I can't believe this? What's wrong with me?* She sounds grateful for the offer and thanks me. All I know is if she'll find someone else to tell her troubles to, my life will get better. I am almost convinced I have gotten through to her, and I fight to make myself believe this after our conversation. Maybe this whole unfortunate misunderstanding will

8

finally be over and things will go back to normal for Jonathan and me. *Who am I fooling?*

My husband never mentions to me the conversation I had with his coworker, so it's safe to assume she hasn't told him. It doesn't matter, though, because things only get worse. His lies become increasingly more difficult to believe, and I can feel myself falling into deep depression. Each day, making the decision to go to class and getting through my daily chores becomes more and more difficult. Lord knows I try hard to convince myself that he is telling the truth. I want to believe him, but he calls me from what is supposed to be a public place and there will be dead silence on the line, except for his voice. He says he has to work late, yet we never get any extra money. Once or twice he was supposed to be visiting his parents, but when I call, no one there has seen him. So, I know it's just a matter of time. There is no longer a storm coming; this thing had gotten much bigger. It has grown in magnitude and become more frigid. The tip of an iceberg is aligning itself to crash headlong into me.

***

Another Saturday night rolls around, and Jonathan is five hours late getting home from work. He has not called. He is normally home around 5 p.m. At about 11 p.m., I begin calling hospitals. I fear he may have had an accident and is unable to contact me. There are only a few hospitals in the area and each emergency room nurse gives me the same response. "There is no one here by that name." I check with the local police and the state patrol. After having no success finding him with the police or the hospitals, the idea to check the local motels, drops into my head. I don't know why I have that thought; maybe it's that intuition thing again, but I decide to go with it. I want to know. I am sick of being alone. I am being held prisoner, and I don't know what I have done to be deemed unlovable? Am I being betrayed? Once I find out, I will not need to ask myself these questions anymore.

I get the phone book and begin calling motels near the area where he works. My plan is to start closest to his job and work my way toward home. Even though my system is very methodical and may seem calculating, I have not considered what my response will be if I do find him. I can't. I just need to do something now. I need and want to be wrong, but after only three calls, I find him.

I dial the third number, just as I had dialed the other two, and ask for him by name. The operator asks me to hold on just like the others had. When she returns, she says she'll ring the room. In this moment, for me, time stops, and I believe my heart does too. My emotions are running amuck. I'm shocked and relieved at the same time. Then, I feel the anger. He doesn't even try to hide his little indiscretion. He has the nerve to rent the room in his own name! Did he think I wouldn't look for him? Does he think he's that good, that clever? How insulting! I am furious. Does he think so little of me that it isn't worth hiding? Use another name for God's sake! This is just too easy! Perhaps he thinks I would never know where to look, worse yet, maybe he wants me to find him. That thought is even more frightening.

I don't know what he's thinking, but it is all about to "hit the fan." My whole body goes numb. I want to know, and I am about to find out. Suddenly, panic strikes and I'm not so sure anymore about what I want. My hands begin to shake. *Maybe I should hang up. No! Take it like a woman. You said you wanted to know.* The phone rings and a woman answers.

"Let me speak to my husband," I demand.

"He's not here," is her lie.

"I don't believe you. Put him on the phone," I shout.

"I told you, he's not in the room right now. He's outside somewhere. He may have left."

I just lose it. Her voice reveals to me that she's the same bitch (excuse my French) that told me a few weeks ago that she was just telling her problems to my husband. I guess now she needs a nice quiet room with a soft bed to tell him the rest of her troubles. I begin screaming. I start calling her names over and over. My French becomes increasingly more pronounced. I'm saying things that even I do not understand. Suddenly, I slam down the phone. I simply cannot bear it anymore; I can't hear more lies.

10

I don't realize until I hang up how loudly I'm screaming; my voice seems to be echoing through my living room. My head is pounding, and I'm gasping for breath. I have to do something; I can't just sit here and let them make a fool of me. I need to do something. I get up and begin pacing the living room floor; and my brain is racing. I think about the things I can do to both of them and not be convicted by a jury of my peers. I can't let them get away with this. I need a plan.

First, I check on my three children to make sure they are asleep and that they hadn't heard me. I look at their innocent faces not knowing whether I will see them again. I don't know how the events of this night will change all our lives. My girls are all too young to be left alone. Jonita is only twelve, Jolisa is five, and Jovida is three. As much as I love them, this night, it is God who will have to watch over them. They cannot go with me, so I have to leave them in His hands.

My mind then reflects back to when I sat watching Jonathan get ready to go out. I intend to take just as much care preparing myself for this all-important date. I carefully select the right outfit to wear; I am determined not to reflect the look of the ragged housewife the way most men paint their "stay at home" wives. I slide my slim, 5' 4" body into a pair of designer jeans. I select an oversized jean shirt and a red camisole to wear underneath. I slip into a pair of low pumps and take the time to find a matching belt. I unwrap my shoulder length hair and style it where it frames my round, warm brown face, and let it cascade down on one side. I have a bottle of good perfume that my father gave me for my birthday. I bathe myself in the alluring smell. My hands begin to shake as I try to apply my makeup, but I command them to settle themselves. I tell myself that this night is important. This night is a crossroad that could change my life forever. Perhaps this is really just my sorry attempt at holding on to whatever dignity I can, but if that be the case, at least I can hang on to that if nothing else.

Once I am satisfied with myself, I rip the page with the address of the motel from the telephone book. I get my keys, slip on my coat, and quietly open the back door, trying to make as little noise as possible as I ease out. I start my car, praying that I will be able to stand the trip. Not allowing myself to think about what I'm doing, I point the car in the right direction. Each mile brings me ever closer to that iceberg, but I recklessly charge on. I am sick at heart. The disappointment of this night is almost too much to bear. As I drive, I begin to scream, and to cry, and to pray. Yes, pray! Someone is going to have to face my wrath this night. I no longer want to hold on to that good girl image, that nice girl thing, that "always do the right thing" crap. I release it all, and I feel deliciously out of control. Somehow, my mind seems clearer than it has been in a very long time. I seem to know exactly what I need to do. I want a fight. I feel like tearing someone apart. This night will tell the story. Tonight, I will face my worst fear; failure. I have always dreaded being branded as the one who is rejected and left alone with three children. I've seen it happen too many times to my family and friends. Tonight I'll find out if standing up for myself means it's my turn to be alone.

***

The streets are totally unfamiliar to me. I have an address but only a general idea of which way to go. Regardless, I continue on, determined to reach my destination. My mind tries to wander back towards home and the thought of my children awakening afraid and wondering where their mother might be. I struggle to gain control of my thoughts and focus on the task at hand. Finally, after a dreamlike journey down a dark highway lasting an eternity, out of nowhere, the sign I've been searching for appears: "Motel Cestode." Something is hurling me forward. I am like a robot following a command. Even though I realize I am not sure what I'm going to do when I get there, I keep going.

I pull into the parking lot and select a space close to the office door. As I look around, a cynical smile comes to my face. She doesn't know that it has already started for her. This hole on the side of the highway is exactly what she has to look forward to with Jonathan. There is some sort of bittersweet satisfaction in that thought. However, it is not enough. I take a quick look at myself in the rearview mirror before opening the car door. Suddenly, I realize that bringing along some sort of weapon might have been a good idea. But, this brief concern is overpowered by my anger, and I jump out of the car so fast that I almost slip on a patch of ice that lay waiting for any careless passerby. I regain my footing, slam the car door behind me, and start for the office door fighting to compose my anger before going inside. No one can suspect anything.

When I go inside the motel office, I know the desk clerk will not give me the room number. I stand for a few moments at the counter watching as the clerk works the switchboard. I position myself so that I can see her telephone console and ask her to ring my husband's room. I give her his name, just as I had on the phone some hour or so earlier. I put on my pleasant, 'nothing is wrong, he's expecting me' face. When she connects the call, the room number appears on the console. That's all I need.

I leave the lobby without saying a word. I get back into my car without incident, and as I drive around the back of the motel looking for the room, I also look around for Jonathan's car in the parking lot. I spot it, parked boldly in plain view, underneath the streetlights, right out front near the entrance. I don't know how I missed it coming in. This only fuels my fury. I remember the numbers that came up on the console. The numbers 118 burn in my mind as though it were tattooed onto my forehead. The rooms are arranged crazily. The upstairs and downstairs rooms both start with one. Somehow it all fits this night. I find the room; it's on the second floor facing the street on the backside of the motel. I park near the stairs going to the upper level. I get out and start to climb the stairs. My head is pounding and all kinds of emotions are flowing through me at once. When I get to the top, I pause. *It's not too late to turn back. No one knows you're here.* I shake off those weak thoughts and push myself forward before I lose my nerve. I stand myself directly in front of the door with the numbers 118 on it. At first I tap on the door lightly, and politely. Then, something shoots through me, and I knock hard on the door. I knock like someone who has business here. It is a knock that says *I'm coming in, like it or not.*

After a few moments, a skinny, cross-eyed, plain-looking woman peeks out the curtain. She is dressed in a "peasant look," ankle-length, cotton dress with a belt that ties in the back. She has micro braids that hang halfway down her back. She looks disheveled from head to toe. I can't help think in this instant about the great contrast between the two of us. She looks like a rag doll. But, it happens that it is this "Plain Jane" who, at the moment, has my husband with her in this room. I state forcefully who I am and demand that she open the door and let me in. I suppose she has more sense than me, or maybe it is the fire in my eyes that convinces her not to open the door. But, she yells through the glass window that Jonathan is not inside the room and that she is alone. She whips back the curtains so that I can see for myself that she is alone. I pretend not to be interested, but in reality I'm scrutinizing the entire room, including the rumples in the bed sheets. One bed spread is turned back while the other bed has not been touched. I think maybe he's hiding in the bathroom. If that were so, it is a good thing. It would mean he thinks I am worth him hiding the truth despite the dismal reality of it all. (I know this is twisted thinking.) I have to shake it off; none of that really matters. All I want her to do is open the door.

Strangely, I see her as the crux of all my problems, and I want to get her within arm's reach. When she refuses to open the door, I move to the window, clinch both my fists, and begin to pound on the glass; I am determined to break it if necessary. I want in! I can see the frightened look on her face as the noise from me beating the glass echoes through the courtyard and bounces back into my ears. I see security coming, but that does not stop me; my rage becomes more intense. I begin screaming for her to let me in. Before I can break the glass, Jonathan appears out of nowhere from behind me.

"Girl, what are you doing here?" he says as calmly as though we were at a church function.

"What are you doing here?" is what I scream at him.

"You don't understand. I'm helping her hide from her husband who has just beaten her up."

They both try to convince me of this crazy story. But, I could care less whether it's true. If I get inside, she will suffer another beating. I just want some relief from the pain I have felt for the last few months, and she is where I want to relieve it.

I scream, "I don't care what's going on. You have let this woman keep you away from your family. You haven't even bothered to call home and you show no sign of planning to do so tonight." Again, he

14

responds very calmly, "I didn't want to have a confrontation with you. That's why I didn't call. I knew you wouldn't understand, and that you'd react just like you are now." I continue screaming, "You got that part right! You're telling me that her needs come before your family's needs? Before mine?" His response is cool and unattached. "Right now, she needs me more."

I stand motionless; stunned by his words, as though he just shot a bullet through my gut. I have to resist the urge to grab my stomach and fall over from the pain. In an instant, all the fight oozes out of me. There is nothing left for me to say. I look one last time over at the window where she stands protected by the glass. For the first time in my life, I feel hatred. It isn't just toward her. I hate her. I hate him. I hate me. As she is staring her cross-eyed stare back at both of us, I suppose, all I can do is walk away. He has made his choice. So, I turn around and see the officer that Jonathan has waved off. I walk past him, down the stairs, and get into my car. As I start the car, I look up. They are all looking down at me. I feel the tears burning on the inside, but I do not release them. I put the car into gear, back out, and drive off. I hear a very quiet voice speak within me, a voice I don't recognize, like being on the edge of insanity.

It says, "They will pay. Make them pay."

As I drive down the highway, I cry! I scream! I shout!

But this time, I don't pray.

CHAPTER TWO

Ours was not the typical meeting; Jonathan was a blind date that turned into the classic fairy tale… His best friend is marrying my best friend, who graduated from high school with me a year ago, and we are planning to meet at their wedding reception/baby shower. After the introductions, I'm able to get a sneak peek at his more important features. Sitting across the room, I can secretly admire his smooth, white chocolate complexion, his tall, well-built frame, and his long, beautiful wavy locks that give him sort of a mysterious island look. He's fine and he knows it.

As he walks across the room towards me, he trips over nothing, spilling his drink on the floor, and he bends down to clean it up, putting himself in direct contact with my legs. He says I have the most beautiful legs he has ever seen. He says he became so captivated by them that he lost his balance and dropped his drink. It might be a tired opening line, and I think he has had a little too much to drink, but it was something special for a man that looks this good to come on to me.

It is clear right away that all the women at the party have their eyes on Jonathan, but he chooses me. How does a man, who can have nearly any woman he wants, end up with an average girl like me? He captivates me, but I try not to tip my hand; I play coy. Before long, he asks me to dance. When I stand up, I take my time twisting and turning in my seat, making sure that the focus is on my legs. The short dress I have on and the high heels I'm wearing give his eyes the look he says he fell for. We dance, laugh, and talk until the party is over. We enjoy each other so much that that when the party is over, we aren't ready to go our separate ways, so we decide he should follow me in his car to my house.

We get to my house and he gets out of his car and gets into mine. We sit in my car talking and watching the sun come up. It's the first time I ever watched the sun come up with anyone. It feels like we are in one of those old movies. It's so romantic that I feel like I have just met my soul mate. After that night, we become inseparable. We spend every waking moment together. And when we aren't together, we are talking on the phone. My mother jokingly refers to him as my shadow. At first, she isn't happy about us spending so much time together. I didn't know then that mothers have a type of sixth sense about men who are not right for their daughters. But at 19, who listens to her mother?

Jonathan and I often fall asleep on the phone whispering sweet words and dreams into each other's ears. Every time he comes over, he brings some sort of little trinket for me. No one, since my dad, has ever paid me this much attention. I know it won't be long before we find ourselves in love. Jonathan is becoming my Prince Charming, Sir Lancelot, and Romeo all wrapped up in one. This is the love I have been looking for, ever since my daddy left us.

After three months of being swept off my feet, Jonathan asks me to marry him. He shows up on my job with roses and candy. In front of my boss and all my customers, Jonathan gets down on one knee and he asks me to be his wife. Of course, the word "yes" is the only sensible answer. This proposal takes everyone by surprise, especially his family. They already behave strangely towards me, but this marriage proposal is the last straw. His entire family disagrees with his choice for a bride. Naturally, they assume I'm pregnant, which tickles both of us since we have not slept together. I take great delight in perpetuating that charade and make no effort whatsoever to straighten them out. In fact, I change my walk and eat strange things around them because I think it's funny. I don't think about the fact that this will only add to their dislike for me.

We are moving way too fast for them, and they call for a family meeting, which includes every adult relation within the city limits. Since most of his family has grown up in this town and still live within a five-mile radius, everybody was there and everyone had something to say. Their purpose is to sit Jonathan down and let him know that a man is no longer subject to a shotgun wedding because his girl gets herself pregnant. Jonathan thinks the whole thing is ridiculous. He's a grown man, well able to decide on his own what he wants to do with his life. He resents their meddling and trying to control his life. Their meeting doesn't stop a thing. If anything, it draws us closer together.

I later find out that their dislike for me runs far deeper than my made up pregnancy. The real problem is that his family sees me as a young gold digger. Jonathan is seven years older than me. They drop subtle little hints whenever possible, as if I have forgotten about my age. His aunt never misses an opportunity to make baby or little girl jokes, especially when there is an audience of other family members who can join in the laughter. To add insult to injury, they devise an elaborate plan to try to set Jonathan up with one of his old girlfriends, Gabby. She is much more acceptable by their standards.

First of all, she's around Jonathan's age. She works in a well-paying job at the city courthouse as a supervisor. She has known the family all her life. Her parents lived next door to them for years, and she still lives conveniently close by. Now you know this implies that I am the opposite of all that she is. Whether that's the case or not doesn't matter because Jonathan resists their interference and continues to woo me. Besides, she doesn't have my legs.

Jonathan assures me that at 26 years old he's a man, not a mama's boy, and he is committed to me and me alone. In order to prove his resolve, he asks me to go on vacation with him to California. His parents are violently opposed to our plans and another family meeting is called. My mother is not thrilled either, but she has some crazy notion that her adult child should be allowed to make her own mistakes or some foolishness like that. I don't know what she was thinking; she has never had difficulty butting in my life before. This time, however, she does not raise an objection, so Jonathan turns a deaf ear to the family council and whisks me off to San Francisco.

It is there that I truly learn love's beauty, and I fall hard. Jonathan wines and dines me at Fisherman's Wharf. He is attentive to my every need and wish. We stay in a beautiful hotel near the Golden Gate Bridge. During the day, we tour the city, eat in Chinatown, have our picture painted by a street vendor, and sample food at the Wharf. We go in shops up and down the streets, getting the biggest laugh from all the strange and different people we encounter on the streets of San Francisco. They are a great contrast to the straight-laced, plain people we're accustomed to seeing in Michigan. At night, we stand on the balcony of our hotel and watch the lights of the city while talking of our hopes and ambitions.

Jonathan has done well in the seven years he's worked for the postal service, working his way up from mail carrier to team leader. He aspires to become a shift supervisor in the next few years. He wants to start a family (of five) so that he can have his own basketball team or rap group or something. Maybe later he'll retire early and start his own business or something like that. My dreams of being a nurse seem to dissolve next to the prospect of being part of Jonathan's reality. I'm younger and have barely considered my options as an individual. I haven't even finished my first year in college. I know in today's world women should strive for high-powered careers and independence, but my secret hope is to enjoy life as someone's wife and lifelong companion, living happily ever after. I long to be like the happy families I see on television. I want to make someone happy, and I want relief from the loneliness I constantly feel. Somehow, my dream of being anybody special has disappeared, and I find myself linking my dream to Jonathan's; that's all that matters to me.

Jonathan helps me to see that his love for me goes beyond family ties or obligation, and he swears his undying love and devotion to me. We will defy all and dare to indulge in this young, underdeveloped love affair. It is here in San Francisco that Jonathan takes me in his strong arms and expresses his true love for me. He is the one who checked us into the hotel, and it wasn't until we got to the room that I discovered we only had one room. This didn't distress me once I saw that there were two beds.

We stand close together on the hotel balcony until all we can see is the orange reflection of the sun that looks as though it's being swallowed by the earth. With his arms wrapped around me, I can smell the sweet, fresh fragrance of his cologne. I lose track of time. I have never been alone like this with a man before, yet I feel completely safe and comfortable. I know that I'm falling in love, and it feels good. I no long feel that overwhelming sense of longing.

A little while after the sunset, we leave the balcony and lie down together on one of the beds inside the room. He continues to just hold me as I close my eyes and dream about our lives together. I wonder what he's thinking. I wonder if he feels the same way about me that I feel about him. This night is going just like I have dreamt it so many times. It's dark in the room, but light is coming in from the balcony, and when I open my eyes, I can see Jonathan clearly. As we lie together, passion overtakes us both. At first Jonathan kisses me on my neck. I know that at some point I should tell him to stop, but the words will not come out. I really want him to continue. I want him to make love to me. I don't know what to expect, yet I am anxious to find out. I feel like every nerve in my body is tense and standing at attention waiting for command. I have to fight the impulses that are making my legs quiver with anticipation. He's moving from my neck to my breasts. He slips the straps of my tank top off my shoulders. This exposes both of my braless breasts. Jonathan licks, sucks, and caresses my breasts until my body aches. I am wound up so tightly that I will explode at any moment. There is no doubt about it; I know I'm about to lose my virginity.

Out of nowhere, I begin to hear my mother saying, *"Make sure you protect yourself. Men only want one thing."* Nothing can kill the mood like Ma's voice. And to tell the truth, it's shocking to me that I even remember anything Ma has said to me, especially at a time like this. Unfortunately, she has left me only half prepared; there is no voice to tell me what to do when I'm the one who only wants one thing. But, I am clear on the protection issue. Jonathan is starting to remove my panties now, so I need to say something fast.

What do I say? Hey Jonathan, did you bring your rubbers? No, that won't work. It sounds stupid and immature. Oh my God, he's naked. I've never seen a man completely naked before. He is beautiful. Wow! His penis is huge. It's beautiful! "Protection! Protection! Don't let some boy get you pregnant. Save yourself for marriage." Finally I am able to speak.

"Jonathan, I'm scared." I confess

He stops and looks me in the eyes. His look suggests to me that everything will be all right.

He says, "We need to use protection."

It's like he is reading my mind. He picks up his pants from the floor, reaches into his back pocket and pulls out his wallet. I feel pretty stupid just lying naked watching him. I'm beginning to feel self-conscious; I want to pull the sheet over myself. Instead, I focus my eyes on his every movement. He opens his wallet and takes out a small square packet. He rips away one end and then he slowly removes the contents. It looks like a rolled up balloon, except I can tell by the way that he handles it that there is a liquid substance inside it. I try not to look shocked. I know most girls my age have seen this thing before, but that's not the case for me. I'm trying to look mature and worldly, but I feel stupid. As I watch Jonathan run his hand down his penis from his body outward, all my inhibitions disappear. He holds his erection in one hand and unrolls the rubbery thing down the length of his penis with the other. As I watch, I become extremely excited and more nervous, but I love him and I want him.

Right here, in romantic San Francisco, I make love for the first time. It isn't painful like my girlfriends told me it would be. It is slow, steady, and rhythmic. He guides my hands and my hips. He shows me how to move my body in sync with his. At first I am afraid, but Jonathan takes his time. He touches me everywhere, and I do mean everywhere. He gently caresses away all thoughts of the outside world, and he slowly becomes my world. I begin to feel flush, excited, wild, unleashed, and then it happens. Love spills from both of us, together as if on cue. That's when I know we are meant to be, no matter what anyone says.

***

When we return from our trip, we have two months to prepare for the wedding. The dress, the church, the hall, the flowers, the pictures— we do it all together, except for the invitations. Ma and I work on putting those together. We weren't that close before my plans to get married.

She's been busy doing her thing and I've been doing mine. It's the opportunity to put together the wedding of the century for her only daughter that really brings us together. We go to lunch to discuss to whom we will send invitations. Also, because mom and dad are divorced, we need to figure out how we will word it. We decide on this:

Mr. --------- ----------------
Father of the bride
And
Ms. --------- -----------
Mother of the bride
And
Mr. and Mrs. Jonathan Liberty Sr.
Parents of the groom
Request the honor of your presence at
The union of their children…

I'm glad I found a way to include Dad on the invitation and keep Ma happy, too. As we make out the guest list, Ma is happy to include many of her executive friends. This is her chance to recoup some of the many gifts she has purchased for their children throughout the years.

As the weeks pass and we talk and work together, I begin to sense that there is something deep about my mother, some things I hadn't noticed before. All of my life she's seemed kind of crazy, always telling me to look out for this or that in a man. She has been divorced twice, so I figure if she can't get it right, how can she tell me anything? I remember telling her so many times, "Ma that was back in the horse and buggy day," or "Was that before or after they invented the wheel?" Surprisingly, now in my adult life, I seem to have found this bright, interesting, wonderful friend. She's treating me like a responsible adult, and I'm ashamed of myself for all the rude things I have said to her and for all the times I didn't listen.

***

Before the wedding, I'm able to spend more and more time with Jonathan at his parents' home. This is where I get to know Jonathan a lot better. At first, I thought it strange that they seem to love to pile up in one room, in one bed, and talk about their troubles. They crowd around his mother, half lying on the mattress (that lay frameless on the floor) and half way on the floor until they finish talking. This is how they communicate. This is equal to the around-the-table family time to which many families are accustomed. Many times Jonathan, his mom, and his brothers and sisters leave me sitting alone in the living room while they all huddled together in their mother's bedroom. I know that the moment they invite me to grab a piece of that old, worn-out mattress, I'm in and one of the family. (Sadly, that day never comes.) I sit alone and wait. I can hear the hum of their voices and sometimes laughter. It's OK; I don't mind. It gives me time to think and reflect.

Each family member seems to do his or her own thing with little regard for the rest. His mother works nights and his father works afternoons, so it seems no one raises his younger sisters and brothers. Being the oldest, Jonathan's younger sisters and brothers adore him. It is much later when I discover that it is his sisters, not him, who have kept him looking so well groomed. They are the ones who put that razor-sharp crease in his jeans, the shine on his shoes, and the starch in his shirts. His sharp appearance is one of the things that drew me to him. I thought he must be some kind of man to keep his things so neat. I guess that is a small detail he neglects to mention (no harm done).

I further solve the mystery of, "Why me? Why did he choose me? The first time I hear his mother laugh, an eerie feeling passed through me. I have that same laugh, the same lighthearted spirit, and the same fun-loving nature as she has. The only real differences between us are our obvious age differences and outward appearances, as well as the drive I always have to go after the things I want. I know he sees her in me. I take that as a compliment.

As we near the wedding day, our relationship becomes stronger. We share most everything. Once when his vehicle is out of commission, he borrows mine. He comes straight to my house after work, and we spend the evening together until I take him home late that night. I almost don't notice the dent on the passenger side of my car. Jonathan forgets to mention to me that he was in an accident on his way over to my house.

I know it is unintentional. It just slipped his mind. He apologizes profusely, and reminds me that after all, it is an old car. I tell myself that there is no real harm done and all is forgotten.

***

The wedding is a month away and the family council tries one last strategy and drops the bomb on Jonathan. No one on his mother or father's side of the family is coming to the wedding. This has got to work because they think the wedding can't go on if they're not present. You can't stop what is inevitable, and even though it has been several months since Jonathan's family first met me, they still have not warmed up to me. But this family proclamation does not deter him at all. Besides, Ma has already put the money down on the reception hall, and you better know somebody is going to get married. We continue our plans, and I look at the bright side. There will be more food and drink for my guests. It's funny how people say what they're not going to do. It is the family council of adults who are the first to show up at the church. Surely they cannot let the event of the year, and free food and drink, pass by without the benefit of their scrutiny.

***

Amazingly, the day of the wedding starts out just fine. Ma has everything planned to the smallest detail. But you know the saying about the best-laid plans. The day before the wedding, Ma's friend was at a flower festival where they gave away all the flowers. She shows up at our house on the morning of the wedding with 100 dozen gladiolas. We have flowers in the bathtub, sinks, laundry tub, washing machine, and anywhere else we can store enough water. We run around all morning from florist to florist looking for cardboard flowerpots so that we can arrange the flowers and take them to the church and reception hall. If that isn't crazy enough, the power goes out on my block. Surely, these are unmistakable signs. You would think someone could have stopped this train wreck before it got started, but no such luck.

We get to the church on time, but we forget the video camera. (Oh well, there will be no visual record of this ceremony.) We get over that and we're ready to start. That's when we discover that the maid of honor has not shown up yet. After waiting about thirty minutes, we call her house. She is still getting ready. (Again, we do not recognize the signs.) Ma goes through the audience looking for someone dressed in our wedding colors. She finds a young woman, whom I do not know, shoves a bouquet in her hands, and positions her in the maid of honor's place. Just before we start the march, my best friend and maid of honor bursts through the door. A quick shuffle in the lineup with the last-minute replacement and we're ready to go. We're more than an hour delayed. Ma gives me one last quick inspection and finalizes things with a tight squeeze and a peck on my cheek. She signals the usher to take her to her seat.

The wedding starts and everything is beautiful. My bridesmaids are in purple dresses lined up and ready to march. The groomsmen wait inside the vestibule in their white tuxedos and purple shirts, to march the ladies down to the altar. To me, it seems as though I'm watching someone else getting married. I can't see everyone, and the double doors that separate me from the audience muffle the songs that are being sung. Through the glass in the doors, I can partially see my husband-to-be standing at the front of the church. He looks on in awe as the bridal party starts down the aisle. Maybe I just think its awe; it could be terror. It's too hard to tell from here. Oh well, it's too late for him to turn back now.

This moment is so breathtaking that it's like I'm stepping outside of myself to watch this beautiful princess dance down the aisle towards the man of her dreams. My gown fits perfectly. It is beautiful white lace and satin. The top of the dress lines my neck with tiny pearl buttons down the front of the bodice to the waist. It accentuates my slim figure. The dress has laced long sleeves with little straps that go between my fingers. The train starts with a white tiara that crowns my head and trails behind me twenty feet. The skirt of the gown has a big hoop underneath that makes the dress stand out just like I'm Cinderella at the ball. Finally, I have reached the day that I will be joined with my prince; it is too good to be true.

All of the girls and the bridal party have gone down the aisle, and the ushers close the swinging doors. It's my turn to march now. I'm standing in the church foyer waiting when my daddy enters from a side room. He's a robust man whose presence commands respect. He is handsomely dressed in his white tuxedo and shirt, white leather shoes, and a white bow tie. His smile covers his entire face. I can see the pride in his eyes. Dad walks up to me and kisses me on the cheek.

Then he asks, "Are you sure this is what you want, D?"

Daddy hasn't called me "D" in years. It makes me remember the way things were with us before he left. As we turn toward the closed doors, I can see both of our reflections in a huge mirror hanging in the church lobby. That's when, of all places, memories of Daddy and I begin to flood my mind with things I have long forgotten.

I remember when I first knew myself. I was a princess back then. I am Princess D. I'm Daddy's little princess, the fifth child born after a quad of princes. I am the perfect lady, the apple of Daddy's eye. My eyes are as black as the night and as large as saucers; my brows thick enough to catch the rain; my lips well defined and plump; my cheeks made full from an angelic smile; my hair bushy and dusty like ashes; my skin black as coal. Still, I am Princess D.

The wedding march begins.

As I glance backwards into the mirror of Daddy's rear reflection, I'm trying to remember something terrible that happened within my kingdom. In my mind, I see Daddy's duffel bag packed. He throws the bag over his shoulder and walks out the door. I watch him as he leaves. My mother closes the door and turns the big lock on it. She moves in slow motion.

"Who gives this woman in holy matrimony?"

The lock clicks again and again—louder and louder. It's a deafening sound. It's a sound that can give a princess nightmares. Yet, I am still a princess. That's when things begin changing for the princess.

"…till death do you part."

After Daddy leaves, I notice pictures in magazines don't feature my hairstyle or my features. All the beautiful people on the television look nothing like the princess I thought myself to be.

"May I have the ring?"

Daddy's princess loses her beauty along with her Daddy. I am realizing for the first time, that I am different from the rest of the world. Something is wrong; nothing fits; nothing looks like me.

"With this ring, I thee …"

I turn my head and look back at my Daddy, and it's like I'm awakening from some sort of hiding place. I realize that his little princess got her crown straight from Daddy's heart. I remember who I am. I am Princess D.

"I pronounce you man and wife. You may kiss the bride."

Oh my God, NO!

"Ladies and gentlemen I present to you Mr. and Mrs. Jonathan Liberty."

CHAPTER THREE

I suddenly stop crying and decide I have had enough pain, but I can still hear the echoes of my screams bouncing around the car in my head. The highway in front of me is swaying, moving, slithering like a snake, and daring me to run off of it. Trying to focus through my swollen, tear-stained eyes makes it almost impossible for me to stay in my lane. My mind is racing ahead of me. I can make both of them sorry; I can make them pay. They'll have my blood on their hands. I can't allow myself to think of anything else. They deserve what happens to them. I charge full speed ahead. I press the gas pedal down as far as it will go. I close my eyes, and I let go of the steering wheel. *I need to do this to stop the pain, to stop the humiliation, and to stop the betrayal. No more tears, no more prayers, nothing but death will fix this situation.* I must keep my nerve and wait for death. I am determined and will not waver. Somehow, strangely, in spite of my determination, I hear myself praying.

Father, I call you father because you are supposed to be my protector. I have spent countless hours before you glorifying your name, declaring you as author and finisher of my fate. Where were you, Lord, when my marriage was falling apart? Why didn't you send a prophet to warn me like you did David? Is that too much to ask? Why didn't you give Jonathan a dream like you did Joseph? Does anything I do matter? Have I stored no blessing in heaven? Tell me, Lord, where is my miracle? Where is my blessing? Where is my mother?

Horns begin to blow, and I can see light through my tightly closed eyelids. I try not to open them, but I cannot resist; something else wins. I open my eyes to discover that I am no longer on my side of the highway. I am barreling headlong into oncoming traffic. The late hour is responsible for there being only a few cars on the highway. Those vehicles are weaving and jerking to avoid colliding with me.

Reflex, self-preservation, God's intervention, or something makes me grab hold of the wheel. I don't know what to do first. I need to get out of the way of the oncoming traffic. Their headlights are blinding me and I am feeling disoriented. There is a 20-foot patch of grass between the opposing lanes of traffic. I take my foot up slightly from the gas and bear down hard on the wheel, pulling the car into the grass, heading back across the highway. The wheel bumps, pulls, and jerks trying to make me release it, but I hold fast trying desperately to swerve back into my lane, while slamming down on the brakes. My head snaps back and forward even with the seatbelt trying to hold me in place. Finally, the car gives up and comes to a complete stop on the shoulder of the highway facing me in the right direction. "I did it." Every nerve in my body is tense and my whole body is shaking. I whisper over and over.

"I'm saved. Thank you, God; you sent my miracle."

After praying and crying for I don't know how long, I struggle to peel my fingers from the wheel. I settle myself down and somehow I'm able to continue my drive home. I try to forgive myself for what I just attempted. I can't afford to think about it and risk more self-loathing. Besides, other thoughts of what I will do if and when Jonathan returns have already begun to flood my mind. As I drive, I try to decide what to do next. Jonathan has drawn a wedge between me and most of my family and friends. I am too humiliated to ask for anyone's help or to even tell anyone what has happened. Worst of all, what will I do if he comes home tonight? What can I do? If I tell him to get out, he'll just ignore me. If I call the police, what am I going to say?

"My husband' is sleeping with another woman, or at least I think he is. I caught them at a motel, and I want him out of my house."

I can see the folly in that plan. While they might feel sympathetic towards me, they will tell me that my only real recourse is to take it up in family court. They will tell me to divorce him. Now let me think about this rationally: Divorce. I have no job, no degree, no real skills, no parents, nowhere to go, no way out. I'm beginning to realize why this is happening to me. I am vulnerable; I am the perfect victim. What's sad is that Jonathan has known this all along, but I'm just finding it out. They must be having a good laugh at me right about now. Everybody, especially Miss Plain Jane, is probably laughing at me. Today I'm the big joke, but they won't have the last laugh.

Finally I reach home. Everything and everyone is as I left them. I look at each one of Jonathan's daughters, my daughters. All three of them have his beautiful hair; they are a pecan tan color with light gray eyes. The only part of them that resembles me is their button noses that turn up at the end. That is the extent of my contribution.

As I watch them sleep, I think about how innocent they are. I touch the tops of each of their heads and vow that they will never be as naive as their mother, nor will I allow them to suffer for my stupid mistakes. I will teach my girls how to recognize the warning signs I missed. I'll teach them how to fight back. They will not repeat my cycle. *I swear it.* I finally leave their room and decide to make coffee, get paper and pen, and sit down at the kitchen table. I need to devise a plan.

***

My worrying about what to do if Jonathan comes home tonight is in vain. By daybreak, he has not come, and I can no longer force my eyes to stay open. Sleep overtakes me and will not let go, but it is a restless, tormenting sleep. I begin to dream shadowy reminders of the past like in *A Christmas Carol*. I go all the way back to the night of my wedding. That's when I got the first signs, and I ignored them.

***

Everyone has left the reception and gone to my mother's house. Of course, I too want to go. Instead, we go directly to our apartment at

Jonathan's insistence and unpack all our gifts. Jonathan lays down the law right then and right there.

"I'm the man of this house, and we're not going to your mother's house." I try to convince him to change his mind.

"But Jonathan, everyone's there. They're expecting us. Even your mom is there." I'm thinking maybe it's about my family, knowing his family is there might help to sway him.

He raises his voice slightly. I thought then that it was because I was moving around the apartment trying to put things away, and he thought I might be out of normal hearing range.

"Well, they'll just be disappointed because we're not going."

Inside I'm crushed. My heart sinks, and right then I feel something's wrong. We have all our lives to be together alone. This is supposed to be a night of celebration. At this moment I think perhaps I made a mistake marrying him. I don't let my hurt or my feeling of disillusion show.

I simply reply, "Do you think we can at least go get some ice cream?"

He answers, "Yes."

I decide to make myself happy with that trade-off.

***

Somehow, my dreams are very different from how I saw things at the time. I had no idea how ill-prepared we were for marriage. The apartment we rent is located about halfway between both our parents. A few weeks before we got married, I began decorating it while Jonathan was living there. For some reason, it never occurred to us that the place didn't come with toilet tissue and toothpaste. For the first time in our lives, we have to go buy these things. We are totally responsible for ourselves. I don't know what he was thinking, but I had these pictures in my mind of us dancing around and singing to each other like Doris Day and Cary Grant did in the movies from the '60s. Or maybe things would be all laughs like the *Jeffersons* of the '70s. Better yet, life can be like *The Cosbys* of the '80s. Babies never cry and everyone is always happy. Of course they have problems, but the wives always have snappy comebacks, and the men eventually do the right thing.

This, however, is not nearly the way my marriage began. Aside from things costing far more than we have budgeted, Jonathan doesn't even know how to balance a checkbook. Wait, he doesn't even have a checking account. Ma set mine up at 16. He is from the school of stick the money in your pocket, pull it out as needed, and see how long it lasts. According to Jonathan, I'm the only one who has a lot to learn. But as I dream, all the scales are being taken off my eyes. I see what has happened to make me a perfect victim.

After our honeymoon, Jonathan immediately begins becoming impatient with me. My first big disappointment happens the night we get home from our honeymoon in Jamaica. My period was scheduled to start on the day of our wedding. To keep that from happening, I decided to delay it by continuing to take my birth control pills. I don't stop taking them until two days before we get home so my period will start the night after we get home.

I suppose I should have warned Jonathan about my severe cramps and heavy bleeding in the first two days of my period, but when you're dating, you try to show your best sides and keep lots of personal secrets. Perhaps my silence is partially based on the fact that when my mother took me to the doctor about the cramps in my early teens, they told her that I was faking. According to them, there was nothing wrong with me; I was probably trying to get out of going to school.

Anyway, the only relief I can get is to take eight aspirins, roll up into a fetal position, and rock back and forth until either the painkillers rendered me unconscious or the cramps stop on their own. Usually, the former is the sure remedy. This catches Jonathan totally off guard. He is somewhat understanding the first hour, but by the end of the second hour, he orders me out of the room. He tells me to take my rocking and moaning somewhere else. When I leave out of the room, the door slams behind me. I rationalize that the breeze from the window must have caught the door as he closed it. Since then, I prepare a spot for myself in the other room when it's that time of the month so as not to disturb him.

Even when I make dinner (I have grown up with four princes), if I cook too much food or if it isn't the food he likes or wants for dinner, he will insist that I sit down while he stands over me and lectures me about not meeting his needs. It doesn't matter; he is always right and I'm always wrong. I just vow in my heart to get it right next time.

***

As I sleep, I dream, and I understand. Unfortunately, my pain only intensifies. I see my face in the dreams. I remember and feel the hurt like it's happening all over again. I toss and turn, but sleep holds me in its grip. Things are coming back to me, not as I chose to see them then, but how they really happened.

***

"Honey, the fellows down on the job and I are going on a fishing trip this weekend. We're leaving right after work today, and I'll be back Sunday night," Jonathan says.

This is a strange call to get from Jonathan on a Friday afternoon just days before our firstborn is due, but I only ask him one question.

"Where will you be staying? The baby is due any day now, and I need to know how to get in contact with you if anything happens,*"* I reply.

Jonathan rattles off some vague location, promises to call later, and hangs up the phone. During the evening I have lots of free time. I decide to visit my mother for a while. She is excited about the coming of her only daughter's baby. Her sons have children with different women and some with daughters-in law. But everyone knows it's different when your own daughter has a baby. I try to enjoy the time with her and forget about Jonathan, but it is almost impossible. Instead, I find myself getting restless and watching the clock until I eventually decide to go home and wait for Jonathan's call. I fall asleep waiting, watching television; there's no call. Saturday morning, the ring of the telephone startles me.

"Hello," I say, sounding somewhat alarmed.

"Hey, what's up?" says the caller. I recognize Jonathan's voice. "Why didn't you call me last night like you promised? I was worried sick about you. I had no idea where or who to call.*"*

He dismisses my questions and tells me he is having a great time and he'll see me Sunday afternoon. Once he says this, he quickly ends the conversation. His shortness with me causes a knot in my already ballooned stomach.

I make it through Saturday and Sunday morning without any problems, but I all but hold my breath trying to get through time. Jonathan never calls back. I prepare a huge Sunday meal to welcome him home and wait. Pacing back and forth to the window does not help. He never comes home. By Monday morning, I'm frantic. I call his job, thinking that maybe he was running late and went straight to work. Wrong! I remember the name of the town where he said he was going to fish. I know he called his buddy before from the house, so I get last month's telephone bill and look for an unfamiliar long distance number. There is only one number on the bill that I don't recognize, so I call it. An older man answers and I tell him who I am looking for. He sounds very nice and tells me that Jonathan is not there. He says Jonathan might still be at his daughter's house and proceeds to give me her phone number. I am relieved but a little confused at the same time. I rationalize that he probably went fishing with the man's son-in-law, planned to leave early in the morning, and overslept. That doesn't explain why he hasn't called me, but I can find that out later. I nervously dial the number.

A woman's sleepy voice answers "Hello."

"Hello, may I speak to Jonathan?"

There is no pause, no hold on, nor any background noise; he simply speaks into the phone.

Sleepily he says, "Yeah..."

"Jonathan, what are you still doing there? You were supposed to be home yesterday."

He says, "I'm on my way." Then the phone goes dead. I try to call back but get no answer. I try not to get too upset; all I can do is wait.

Jonathan returns home late in the evening. He comes in the house, goes to our bedroom, and begins packing his things. After much questioning and pressing, he tells me he's had enough of married life and he certainly is not ready to be a father. I find myself running around

34

behind him holding my stomach trying to keep up with him, and trying to get his attention, trying to make him talk to me, not leave me.

"Do you mean to say that you are just going to forget about two years of marriage just like that?" I implore. I am terrified to hear his answer. Surely he loves his unborn baby and me. I have put everything into our marriage. He has to feel something.

He finally responds, saying, "Just like that." He leaves our unborn child and me standing at the door in shock. I guess I must have had to go to the restroom because I look down and water is running down my legs.

***

I need to wake up. I'm tossing and turning trying to force my subconscious to listen and release me. It's no use. The dreams aren't finished with me; there is more truth for me to face.

***

I stand at the front door, watching him leave me. Even though I don't feel any pain or discomfort, I know that I don't have time to deal with the pain of rejection right now. Yet, I can't resist making a last ditch attempt to hold things together, to keep me from having to do life alone. I try to lean out of the door without being seen by any of my neighbors or some passer-by and I call for Jonathan to come back. He must not have heard me because his window is up, and he continues to drives off. I duck back into the house. I am wet, water is running down my legs, and I'm making a puddle on the floor. I remember asking the doctor many times how will I know when it is time and he simply says that I will know. I guess this is the time.

I try to think what to do next. Suddenly, a sharp pain hits me in my lower abdomen. I grab my stomach and hold on to my baby. I know I have to get help. After waiting for the pain to subside, I carefully step out of the puddle and slowly work my way across the room to the phone.

"Ma, I need you. Come quick!"

There is alarm in my voice. This is her child calling. The one she thinks is old enough to make her own decisions. Why hadn't my mother been one of those meddling mothers who sees all the warning signs in a man, and isn't afraid to use emotional blackmail to make me stay home? She is really starting to get on my nerves with all that talk about young, independent woman.

"Honey, what's the matter?"

"Ma, there's water all over the floor and I don't know what to do."

She asks, "What kind of water?" I am beginning to become impatient and suddenly I scream into the phone,

"Ohhhhhhh!" Another pain hits me.

"I'll be right there, baby."

***

Jonathan and I live in our first home now. We bought it right after I got pregnant. I am relieved because we only live a few blocks from my mother. Jonathan loves my mother, and she treats him like one of her own sons. She probably sees him for what he really is, but she never says a word. She's the type that prefers to pray. I have a feeling she has some other plan in the works for Jonathan.

Ma is in her 40s, stands five-foot five, wears a perfect size 12, and has impeccable taste in clothing. She is a high-level executive for one of the major cereal companies in Michigan. She has enough pull on her job that most of her work can be done from home. This is a new work concept of the day. This also gives her time to pursue some of her many other interests from home.

What I like most about Ma is that during the past few years, she has become very spiritual. Her faith in God is strong and she is dedicated to her church. Her religion doesn't get in the way though—she isn't like those "holy rollers" of yester-year, always carrying their Bibles around waiting for a chance to hit you over the head with it. She isn't so deep that every other word is Jesus and she can't talk about anything else. On the contrary, when Ma talks about God or the Bible, she makes everything sound so real. The people come alive; they are so interesting, almost inviting. Often times I find myself almost tempted to open a Bible to see if I can find the stories that she tells. Naturally, I always find something else to do instead.

While waiting for her to come to my rescue, I begin to understand that in the midst of Wall Street, church conventions, tragedies and mishaps, and everyday life, my mother really loves me. It's funny how I never realized these things before now. It's not until I'm about to give birth to my own child that I get it. At this moment, I want to be just like her. What am I saying? Yeah! I do! I want to be like her. Man, that's going to take a lot of work!

"Ohh!" Another contraction.

"Please hurry, Ma!" Before I can get to the bathroom and get out of the wet clothes, Ma is at the door.

She asks me, "Where's Jonathan?"

That's when I break down and begin to sob uncontrollably. It feels as though the burdensome weight of continual floodwaters is being released from the dam within me. When I need him the most, he fails me, and I really don't want her to know how things are. I continue to try to dress myself and prepare to leave as I release this mournful moaning sound. I can hear it in my ears originating deep from inside me. But I press on anyway; I have to keep moving. It is clear that this baby is not going to wait on Jonathan. There's a long silence and Ma finally says,

"I love you, baby. You're not alone."

She doesn't ask me any more questions. She helps me finish dressing. Then she puts my coat on me and we start out the door. We drive the short distance to the hospital without exchanging a word.

Ma takes me through the emergency room. All my paperwork had already been submitted, so I don't spend much time getting registered. While Ma goes back out to attend to the car, the nurse wheels me upstairs and leaves me in a room to undress myself. She says she'll be back soon. The realization that this thing is going to happen and that there is nothing I can do about it is scaring me to death. I have seen all the movies and heard all the lectures, but I still cannot believe this baby is going to come from that little, tiny place. The pains are coming more frequently now. *Why did they leave me sitting here alone in this room?*

How am I supposed to reach my feet to take off my boots while trying to hold this giant baby inside, or how am I supposed to reach behind me and tie up this stupid hospital gown? This bed is up too high. If I hold on to my stomach and hop up on the bed, I can sit on the bed and unbutton my blouse and unfasten my bra. Oh my God, the nurse left the room door open. Anyone who passes by and looks in and sees my half-naked body will need therapy. Let me hurry up and get this gown on. I can't allow myself to think about what's really troubling me. OK, I have the gown on; I need to get the bottom half of my clothes off. I think I can get my pants and boots off before the nurse gets back. If I rock from side to side, I can get my bottoms off, but I can't get them over my boots. This isn't gonna work. I gotta take my boots off first. Maybe I can just pull my pants down and wait for someone to come help me. I don't think so! That would be too embarrassing. "Ooooooo!" I have to let this pain pass. I'm sitting high enough that maybe I can swing my foot up high enough to catch it and unzip my boot. Man, one of the most important events in my life and it's full of drama. OK girl, on three, swing that foot. Got it! God, I have got to be a sight, feet up in the air, gown falling off my shoulders, belly swollen like I'm harboring the great pumpkin under my gown, one boot off and one boot on, and trying not to fall off the bed. I know what Humpty Dumpty must have felt like. This is hilarious; don't laugh girl. "Ohhhh!" I'm ready now. Ah man, I have to ease down and get my clothes and boots off the floor and put them in the closet. What a draft. All I have to do now is jump back up on the bed and slip under the cover. Again I get a mental picture of what I just did and I get tickled. I begin to laugh, but the laughter very quickly turns to bitter tears.

Where has my husband gone? Where's Jonathan?

Before I have time to consider that question all hell breaks loose, literally. When the nurse returns and straps my stomach to a machine, lights begin to flash frantically and beeping noises are going off. The nurse picks up the phone and dials a number.

"Doctor, according to the monitor, the baby seems to be in distress. The heart rate is far too rapid. I think you need to come now. No, she's only dilated six centimeters. Thank you, doctor." That phone call brings me back to reality.

"What's the matter? Is everything all right?"

The nurse doesn't stop to answer me. She's rushing around the room, moving equipment. Another nurse joins her, and my mother enters the room. Apparently, she hears me ask the question and, like me, she hears no response. She reaches out and catches the first nurse by her arm and stops her in mid-step. She looks directly in the nurse's eyes and speaks in a very calm, quiet voice that mothers use when they want you to know that they mean business.

"My daughter and I would like to know what is going on."

"I'm sorry ma'am," the nurse says apologetically.

"The baby is in distress and the doctor is on the way. She is not dilated enough for the baby to come naturally, and we are preparing for an emergency cesarean if things do not change." When I hear what the nurse is saying, somewhere from within me, I get the urge to pray. Ma has often told me that I can just talk to Him like He is anyone else, right here in person.

Oh my God! What's happening to my perfect life? How did I end up here? I have already lost Jonathan. I don't want to lose my baby. Where is Jonathan? Oh Lord, please hear me. I need your help. My baby needs your help.

The contractions are stronger and more painful. I'm thirsty, but they won't give me water. Instead, they want me to suck on ice chips and that just isn't enough. The pain is unbearable. The doctor is not here and the nurses keep going in and out. I don't know why no one will help me.

I call out, "Nurse, how long will it be before the doctor comes?"

"The doctor is on his way." is her response.

"I can't wait. I need this baby out now!" I know I'm screaming, but I can't control myself.

"Mrs. Liberty, there is nothing I can do."

"Please come here. You can take the baby can't you?" I plead.

"Just cut me open and take it out. I won't tell anybody. They'll think it fell out and you can sew me up." The nurse snickers.

"What's funny? Why are you laughing? Please, nurse, come back," I beg.

Moments later the doctor rushes through the door. The nurses return and put something in my IV to relax me. They position my body down toward the bottom of the bed and put my feet in the stirrups on either sides of the bed. The doctor is putting on his gloves. He appears to be moving in slow motion. Everyone is moving slowly. I can feel myself relaxing.

"What's the baby's heart rate?" are his first words.

The nurse, whom I tried earlier to get to cut my baby out, answers. Then the doctor asks me how I feel.

"I'm ready to sleep."

"No, Mrs. Liberty, I need you awake for this one. The baby is on the way." I look around the room for Ma, and she is gone. The nurse says someone wanted her out in the hall. Just as I begin to panic, I look up and Jonathan is coming through the door.

Thank God!

He must have come to his senses. Everything is finally going to be fine. I look at him and smile a sorry smile as tears of relief run from my eyes. He takes my hand and begins to remind me to do the things we learned in the classes. The pain medication is working better than they expected, and I slowly lose all ability to feel any contractions, which eliminates my impulses to push. I am able to pull myself together to a more coherent level.

The doctor says, "You have not dilated enough, but this baby has to come now. The other problem is that the baby's head is too large to pass through without my help, and we are going to have to push for you."

My eyes are heavy and my speech slides from my lips in slow motion.

"Do whatever you want, Doc,"

He turns and tells the nurse to bring a surgical kit. He looks at me and says,

"I need to make a few cuts to guide the baby's head out."

I am not upset. I want this baby more than anything. My husband has come back and we can't lose the baby now. The doctor makes the incision and tells me it's time to push. I didn't really know how to do that. Suddenly, a pain hits me and an uncontrollable urge to make a

40

bowel movement is overtaking me. I think maybe its just gas. I hope I don't pass gas in the doctor's face. How embarrassing! This seems to be a day full of embarrassment.

"Push, Mother! Bear down!" the doctor says.

I have no idea how to push. On top of that, I am so very sleepy that I can hardly keep my eyes open. They keep saying. "Push!" So, I grit my teeth and begin to growl like some wounded animal. The doctor tells me to stop pushing. I am happy to oblige. He tells me I'm letting all the power out through my mouth. I begin again, trying as hard as I can, keeping my mouth shut and pushing that gas, but nothing is happening.

"Are you the father?" he asks Jonathan.

"Yes."

"You stand on her right and hold her knee at her shoulder. Nurse, move to the other side and hold her other knee to the left shoulder."

"Mother, I'm going to push down hard on your stomach and help you push the baby out. Are you ready?"

"Whatever you want," I say, exhausted. The second nurse is also pushing my stomach from the other side on the doctor's command.

"Mother, look in the mirror and you can watch the baby being born!"

I look, but I can't focus. It just looks like a mess of guts. I feel myself getting sick, so I quit trying to look. I close my eyes and listen. After just a few minutes, I hear it.

"It's a girl."

I can finally relax; everything will be fine. She weighs eight pounds four ounces and is 21 ½" long. She's a whopper. For some time after the baby is born, the doctor continues working on me. He tries to make a joke about dressmaking, but in reality he is trying desperately to sew me back together. I look over at Jonathan who is holding the baby. He looks so precious sitting in the chair holding our first-born. Jonathan starts talking about naming her. If he is disappointed by not having a boy, he is recovering quickly. He didn't like any of the baby names I suggested anyway. He is still determined to have a Jonathan Jr., so he proclaims the baby's name as Jonita. I'm alright with that proclamation because I know this baby is going to hold us together.

She was a hard baby to get out, and I've lost a lot of blood. By the time the doctor finishes sewing me up, my blood pressure drops severely. I am being rushed to ICU. I can't see what's happening to the baby or Jonathan.

The next 24 hours pass without my being aware of very much. I do remember seeing my baby, and I remember thinking that I need to take a close look to find some distinguishing marks so that when I see her again, I'll know that she hasn't accidentally been switched with some other woman's baby. Since I don't get that chance, I decide to rely on the hospital staff to keep things in order.

A plasma transfusion and close surveillance leave me well enough to return to a regular room. I stay in the hospital five days. I am put in a semi-private room with another mother who has had a cesarean. She cries the entire time. She constantly complains, pushing the call button. After a couple days of this, the nurses start to ignore her calls. She is starting to get on my nerves as well. She sometimes asks me to push my button so that the nurse will come. I refuse. I wasn't trying to get on their nerves, too. Besides, I have my own problems.

Jonathan hasn't called nor come to see me the entire three days I've been in the hospital. I keep calling the house but get no answer. I thought about calling his mom but decided against it. To make matters worse, Jonita won't nurse. No matter how I try to get her to suckle, she won't latch on and spits my nipple out. After two days, the nurses suggest that I bottle feed. Maybe this is another omen or sign, but I just don't know what the warning is supposed to mean.

The baby and I are scheduled to go home today. I am about to call Ma when the phone rings.

"Hello."

"Hey, you get out today?"

"Yes, are you coming to pick me up?"

"You don't have a ride?"

"No. You know I don't."

"I guess so."

"Jonathan, can you please bring the baby's new clothes I laid out on the bed?"

"I guess. I can't come till I get off work, so it'll be late."

"How late?"

"I don't know. I'll get there when I get there."

"Jonathan, I need to let the nurses know when I'll be leaving." He doesn't reply. I just hear the dial tone.

It's five o'clock when Jonathan gets to my room. He has brought the baby's things in a paper sack. When I open the bag, I am shocked to see that he has brought a bunch of mismatched, dingy hand-me-downs that his mother had given me and I had not had a chance to throw away. None of the new clothes were in the bag. There is no blanket and no hat to go on the baby's head. He waits outside in the hall while the nurse dresses the baby. As she picks through the crazy collage of clothes, again I am so embarrassed. I try to hold back the tears, but it's no use. I hear my oversized tears plunk down on the bed next to the baby. The nurse turns to me and says sympathetically, "Don't cry, Mother. Men do this all the time. They never get these kinds of things right. I'll find something to go on the baby's head and a blanket. She'll be fine."

We ride home in silence. Perhaps things won't be what they should be, but it at least looks like he's going to stay. Jonathan parks the car, takes the baby from my arms, and without a word or glance backwards, he goes inside the house and shuts the door. I sit alone in the car crying. That's when I remember that I haven't bought bottles, milk, diapers, or anything. After the clothes fiasco at the hospital with Jonathan, I am not about to ask him to go to the store. The only thing I can do is get out of the car, pull myself together, and call Ma.

She is leaving town the next morning and wants to be sure I have everything in place. She helps my sterilize the bottles, make formula, wash the dishes in the sink, put away clothes and stack diapers. By midnight, I am finally settling down, ready to go to sleep. Jonathan and Jonita are already asleep. I still believe that everything will work itself out. I have no idea what that is based upon—faith, hope, will power, God, or insanity. Just as I begin to dose off Jonita begins to cry and cry and cry and cry.

***

I am desperate to wake up. This pain is too much. It seems that the reality I have covered up for so long cannot stay hidden. I want to wake up. All I have to do is open my eyes.

"Open your eyes!"

CHAPTER FOUR

When I finally wake up, I am sweating and shaking. I am also furious. How could he do me like this again? He still has not come home yet. I get up and look out the window again. There is no sign of him. Looking around the house also tells me that he hasn't been home. The pain I feel in my stomach helps me to know that I am totally alone. My church family is still around, and even though I love them dearly, there is no way I want any of them to know my shame. I'm going to have to face this problem alone. The only thing that makes sense to me right now is to do whatever I have to do to keep Jonathan. I know that might sound crazy under the circumstances, but I need him and the girls need him too, at least until we can do better. He owes us that much.

It's Sunday morning, around nine o'clock. My nerves are too bad to try to go to church, so I don't. Instead, I spend the morning trying again to come up with a plan—not a plan of attack or defense, but a plan for survival. I know that I am just marking time. It's just a matter of time before there is to be no more us. I know this in my head; all the signs are pointing to that fact. Yet, my emotions, my commitment to God, and my vow to him have me bound. They somehow refuse to listen to reason; I know that they are prone to betray me at any moment if I try to leave Jonathan, especially since I have nowhere to go. Therefore, I need to clearly map things out in my head so that I know what to do next. Even the most complex segments of my subconscious are subject to a good plan.

Again I get paper and pencil and try making a list of possibilities. This time when I start, I hear Jonathan pulling into the driveway. It is about 2 p.m., so I figure they checked out at 11a.m.; then they went to breakfast. I'm sure he dropped her off at home, where it isn't safe, or by one of her sisters' houses with whom she couldn't talk because they wouldn't understand. Yeah, right! He thinks I'm stupid, and maybe I am, but those days are almost over.

As I hear him coming up the steps, I wonder what sorry story he's going to give me. I try to remember all the details from the night before so that I can catch him in a lie if he says anything different. Boy, I really am stupid. Why do I need to catch him in a lie—I just caught him with another woman in a motel. *Wake up, girl!* I can hear him putting his key in the door. Now my hands are sweating. What do I have to worry about? I'm the one who has been wronged. Should I jump up and run to the back and pretend I'm asleep? It's too late for that. I can at least smooth down my hair. Oh man, the door is opening. I feel myself jump.

"Hey."

That's all he says as he comes through the door, closes it, and heads toward the girls' bedroom. What was that? I am all ready for a fight. Well, almost ready. He doesn't intend to discuss this at all. If he thinks this is just going to wash over, boy is he in for a surprise. Who am I fooling? I'm just happy she didn't win, and he didn't just decide to stay gone. Better yet, he could have decided to bring her with him and build me a room in the basement. Then what would I do? What I'm doing right now, trying to come up with a plan.

I stay on the couch and wait, mainly because I can't think of anything else to do. He has on the same clothes he had on the day before. He apparently decided not to go to work today. I smell stale cigarette smoke as he passes me, but I also smell the faint aroma of his cologne. I have to prepare a plan. Focus! Then, it hits me. I get the bright idea that Jonathan needs to see what it feels like to be abandoned. If he thinks somebody else needs him and I don't, let's see how he likes trading places with me. I make up my mind that I'm leaving tonight. Let me show him how that feels. That's my plan. I've heard women talk about running away, now I'm ready to do it myself.

46

I wait what seems like forever for him to come out of the girls' room so that we can talk about the night before. After waiting so long, I ease off the couch and go up the stairs and down the hall so that I can peek into the room. Jonathan is laying across the bed with his head in Jonita's lap, the oldest girl, while she brushes and twists his hair. The other two girls are leaning against him watching television. He is sound asleep. When the girls see me at the door, they all looked up at me and smile. They are completely content having their daddy all to themselves on a Sunday afternoon. I feel sorry for them, but his attempt to dismiss me only makes me angrier. I don't lose my nerve; in fact, I'm more determined than ever to show him. Again, I believe that God will take care of my babies. He hasn't failed me before. I don't waver from my plans. It is his turn to see how it feels; I'm out of here.

I get on the phone and put my plan in motion. I call a family friend, Patricia, who went to school with my mother years ago. She moved away a couple of years earlier and I tell her I am on vacation, and I want to come see her tonight. She sounds confused but welcomes the company. I take a quick shower and feel a sudden urgency about getting out. I make one more phone call. I call my best friend, Kathy.

To know Kathy is to love her. But first you have to get past the fact that she is a five foot seven inches, one hundred twenty-five pound beauty. If that were not intimidating enough, she has plenty of money and she's a genius. She and I went back to school at the same time. We met in the college cafeteria. We both have husbands who didn't expect the school thing to last, and we are both raising small children. We must have had a break in our classes at the same time because we would see each other sitting in the lunchroom all the time. One thing led to another and before I knew it I had told a total stranger my whole life story.

Kathy's story is docile next to mine, but it is not without its ups and downs. Her husband is in top management for a major home improvement company. She can vacation monthly if she wants, pretty much any place she wants, just from his leftover frequent flyer miles. I remember thinking, what is a woman like this doing at a junior college? She has a house to die for in the Spaulding Heights subdivision just in the outskirts of Kalamazoo, Michigan. Their three-car garage houses her Lexus, his

BMW, and a small pickup truck that he uses for work. Entering from the garage, there is a hallway that leads to an oversized family room, complete with a plasma, flat screen, high definition television. The carpet nap is so thick that it can catch you off guard and snag your heel in it. The furniture is all white leather. There is a fully stocked wet bar in front of a window at the far end of the room. Off the same hallway there are two guest bedrooms and a full bath. A winding staircase leads upstairs to the main floor where there is a state of the art kitchen, another full bath, the living room, another family room, complete with a baby grand piano, and a dining room that can seat twenty to twenty-five people. Another staircase leads to the upper level where the master bedroom boasts a full size Jacuzzi, a round bed in the middle of the floor, and closets the length of two walls. The two kids' bedrooms are also on that level. They are decorated like the displays you see at children's furniture stores. Everything matches from the carpet to the ceiling.

Kathy explains that she met her husband, Clark, when he was just finishing college and she had just finished high school a year earlier. Clark came into a small inheritance and invested it well. His strong engineering background landed him a middle management position with a fairly new company, and he moved up very quickly. When Clark was introduced to Kathy by a mutual friend, he was so taken by her beauty and warm nature that he scooped her up and married her within a year of their meeting. She had always intended to go to college. But, after she married Clark, there were always too many functions to attend, affairs to sponsor, and other work-related events in which the upper management's wives were expected to participate. Kathy falls right in line with that corporate image. Everyone loves her, so she is called on constantly. Two kids and 10 years later, she still hadn't been able to realize her own dream. For some strange reason, Kathy wants to be a kindergarten teacher. As different as our lives are, we found we have a common goal in finding our own destiny. In that lunchroom, we began a bond that not even Jonathan has been able to sever.

I admire Kathy because she is the type who can read something once and know it. I, on the other hand, have to study until my brain actually hurts to retain anything. To get through school, many nights Kathy and I got together, turned on the coffee, and we stayed up all night, dozing off every now and then. The naps allowed our stomachs time to recuperate from the countless cups of coffee and gave our brains time to refuel. One and a half years later, all our hard work paid off; we conquered junior college. Of course, Kathy graduated with honors. I'm just happy to have made it, although I do have a B average.

Jonathan thinks I'm wasting time, so he doesn't bother to come to my graduation. I guess he never realized when he was pushing me out there to go, that there would be two more years of school to follow. When he does, that's when things really get tough.

He says, "You're the one who wants to get your education. That's fine. Do it on your time and without my help. And take those kids with you."

It's hard to believe he can be so callous. He's home some of my school days, doing nothing, but he refuses to watch the girls while I go to class.

As I begin working on the last two years of my bachelor's degree, I have to take Jonita, who is only 10 and a half, to school, and take Jolisa, who is three, and Jovida who's one, to daycare, and get all my books and myself to class. When there is no school or I can't pay a sitter, I get to class early and move to a corner at the back of the room. I push two chairs together and create a sort of play area for the two younger girls. I lay out crayons and coloring books and tell the girls that they have to be quiet. I have Jonita do her homework. Amazingly, they sit quietly, working on homework and entertain themselves with the coloring books. At break time, Kathy, who is finished for the day, meets me in the cafeteria and takes the girls home with her. I pick them up later after class.

Jonathan tries everything to stop me, including cutting off my money. That forces me to apply for assistance from the school. They allow me to do work-study. That, along with the federal grant I receive, are enough to pay my school expenses. Fortunately, one of the benefits of working for the university is free childcare.

Somehow I'm not bitter about Jonathan's decision not to help me. In fact, I would have been surprised if he had. Jonathan says school is my choice, and I'm beginning to realize that it is this choice that will help lead me to my freedom.

***

"Kathy, it's me." I whisper. "I need your help. I'm on my way over."
"OK. Bye"

As I pass by the girls' room this time, they don't look up. He is still asleep. I don't take anything with me. I just get my purse and my keys and leave.

The drive to Kathy's is one of uncertainty, confusion, hope, and despair. It doesn't take much thought to get there. Everything in this town and nearby towns can be reached by traveling in one direction or another on either Hwy 43 or I94, both of which I know very well. So, I don't think much about the drive. I do think, however, about how I don't know if I am doing the right thing. I know one thing for sure; I need to do something. This is the something that is going to show Jonathan that he can no longer play with me like some little toy that he's grown tired of. It is time for me to show him that I, during the past thirteen years, have done some growing, too. There can be no more of his calling the shots while I cower down and whimper like some sad, sick puppy. I'm a woman. I'm intelligent. I'm strong. And, I'm running away from home.

It is about a 10-minute drive to Kathy's. As I drive, my mind continues to drift back, reminding me how things led up to today. I cry through the memories.

***

Right after Kathy and I graduate from junior college, Jonathan gets sick at work. This illness affects his digestive system, and he is unable to digest his food properly. No one knows if it's something he has handled at the post office, but this strange virus has attacked his intestinal system, too. This causes food to backup in his stomach. This back up creates other problems and vomiting is the end result. Jonathan goes days at a time without eating food. Naturally, he's lost quite a bit of weight. To make matters worse, our limited health insurance prevents Jonathan from seeing a specialist. The doctor's response is that some viruses have to run its course. This happens to be one of those viruses.

My mother sees his sickness as an opportunity to witness to Jonathan about the healing power of God. I believe this is what she must have been waiting for, planning for. While I'm at school, Ma comes over and prays with Jonathan. Ma doesn't try to have lessons with me. She comes to work with Jonathan. That often puzzles me. Because her way is so easy and her manner so tempered, she has no trouble getting Jonathan to believe that God is a real possibility. Before a month goes by, Jonathan has given his life to Christ.

Ma is a member of a Pentecostal church. This is an experience all in itself. I've been there a few times but prefer my Baptist denomination. That essentially means to me that you confess Christ on Sunday, and do whatever won't kill you until you return the next Sunday. I am faithful to that end and satisfied. Don't get me wrong. I don't do anything that's going to rouse the interest of Satan.

Jonathan, however, has always been an extremist; it's all or nothing with him. When he serves the devil, he drinks, smokes, uses weed, lies, and cheats. You name it, he does it. Well, now he commits to giving God his all, too. A magical transformation is taking place right before my eyes. He stops drinking alcohol, and he is working hard to quit smoking cigarettes. He starts attending church at 5 a.m. for prayer, and most nights he goes back to prayer at 6 p.m. He goes to Bible study midweek, and he has Bible sessions with Ma almost daily. Now Jonathan has graduated to rolling in the floor and speaking in tongues just like the rest of them. I am no stranger to these activities, but it just isn't for me, and it certainly looks strange on Jonathan. He begins to live for Sunday morning service, Sunday evening service, Monday night choir rehearsal, midweek Bible study, and Friday night Deliverance Service. While I am pleased to see the change in him, he doesn't spend his time with me or the kids; he spends all his time with God. *Ironic, huh?*

I like my noncommittal Baptist life. I love God and pray whenever it is needed, but four nights a week is what I consider a little fanatical. He drags me in with him, kicking and screaming albeit silently. It is very difficult at first. People come up to us saying, "I love you." Then they begin to hug us and smile at us. They don't know me. How can they say they love me? Why do they have to hug all the time? I'm not comfortable with this at all. The only thing that makes it easier is that Ma and a few other people I know are members here.

In time I start to enjoy the services, although, secretly I am annoyed with having to give up television time or having to stop whatever activity we're doing to get ready for church. I try not to let Jonathan detect my attitude. He never says anything, but I know in my heart that I'm not as supportive as I should be.

Jonathan becomes so involved that his transformation carries over at home. He begins helping out around the house: taking out the trash without me asking, making the beds, picking up his clothes, dressing the girls, and, most surprisingly, I convince Jonathan that the washing machine and dryer have no respect of person. If he twists the dials and pushes the buttons, it will work for him just as well as it does for me. He even begins to watch the girls while I go to school. He is finally the Prince Charming I thought I married. All those days of secret discontent and frustration are beginning to melt away. I find myself falling in love with him all over again because he is really showing that he loves us. Now it isn't just in word; it is also in deed.

One Friday night while we are preparing for Deliverance service, Jonathan says, "Tonight's my night. I'm going to receive my deliverance from this disease." I'm totally confused about the meaning of his statement. I keep preparing for church but have no idea what to expect. We arrive at church early, because Jonathan wants to sit on the front row. Once I get the girls settled down in children's church, I come upstairs and sit on the row behind him. The organist comes in and begins playing softly. At 7:30 sharp, the praise and worship leader stands. She is a hippy, pleasant looking woman with a strong alto voice. She begins with prayer. We all stand and bow our heads, as she prays long and hard. With every pause in her voice, Jonathan says loudly, "Yes, Lord." It is in such perfect sync that he begins to rock as though he is being magically pulled along with her. This seems to encourage her to go on and systematically, like hypnosis, she begins to take other members with her. As I look around, people are crying out to God, waving their arms, lifting their hands, clapping, stomping, and some are even screaming unintelligible words. It is like a scene out of some old movie where aliens are taking over the minds of poor, defenseless human weaklings. As strange as it is, I keep my eyes on Jonathan; I want to see him be delivered.

When the praise leader finishes, the pastor asks that anyone who wants to be delivered come to the altar. Jonathan runs the few feet and falls to his knees. The pastor seems a little startled at first, and then he reaches down and lays some liquid substance that looks like oil on Jonathan's forehead. Then he begins to speak in words I do not understand. As he speaks, he kneels down next to Jonathan and rubs this substance on Jonathan's throat and stomach.

He tells the congregation, "Call Jesus till he comes."

The church voices rise up with, "Jesus, Jesus. Jesus…"

I don't take my eyes off Jonathan, but I do call for Jesus. I want to see; I want to believe. I want the vomiting and the pain to stop for him.

I have no idea how long we call on Jesus, but I never change my stare, and I see nothing happen. Yet he suddenly jumps to his feet and begins yelling,

"I'm healed! I'm healed!"

I stand amazed, with a stupid look on my face. People begin clapping and voices of praise to God go up all over the sanctuary. People are shaking his hand and congratulating him on his faith. Ladies make their way to me to tell me how wonderful this miracle is. I do not open my mouth; it is as though I can't or maybe shouldn't speak. All the way home, Jonathan continues thanking God. When we got home, I undress the girls and we all go to bed.

The next morning, instead of waking to the usual vomiting, Jonathan has made us breakfast and is sitting at the table eating his second helping.

I asked, "What on earth are you doing?"

He replies, "Enjoying my Deliverance."

CHAPTER FIVE

When I reach Kathy's house, she is standing at her door, waiting. She knows something is wrong. I tell Kathy all the events that happened at the hotel the night before. We talk about how Jonathan has changed back to what he was before he was delivered. She is really frustrated and hurt for me. We reminisce about the impact Jonathan's salvation has had on both of us. It was he who caused us to want to change for the better.

After Jonathan's Deliverance, Kathy and I marvel at Jonathan's transformation during the next few months. His health improves rapidly, and within a few weeks of his healing, the puzzled doctors release him to go back to work. We decide that the next first Sunday will be our day of conversion. When the invitation is extended, we plan to go up hand in hand, not fearing what God might do. After all, if He hadn't struck Jonathan dead, we have a pretty good chance. Plus, Ma, Jonathan, and a host of other friends will be there praying and encouraging us on. Nothing can go wrong. We'll be on our way to everlasting life and a miraculous transformation.

We both remember the pastor's words. "At this time, I'd like to open the doors of the church. If there is anyone here who'd like to give their life to Christ, make your way to the front." Those are the words Kathy and I have been waiting for. The church is crowded and everyone is standing. Kathy looks at me and me at her. It's time. We hold hands and start to pass through the people in the pew excusing ourselves as we press toward the outside aisle. Kathy is right behind me, but suddenly I feel this urgency. I let go of her hand and begin to push my way through to the front to get to the altar. I desperately want this thing Jonathan has. I know in my heart that my noncommittal Baptist thing really hadn't been enough. Don't get me wrong, there is nothing wrong with being Baptist. The problem is me. I need Deliverance, not in my body like Jonathan, but in my mind, my heart, and my spirit. Something! I need to feel something! I need to know that there is hope that exists beyond things that we try to control. I want to be healed on the inside. I want to be free of the resentment of Jonathan's relationship with Christ and my lack of it. I'm ashamed, and I want God's love too.

When I get to the front, I seem to no longer be in control. I don't look back for Kathy. I just throw up both my hands like I have seen so many do before me. My eyes are blurred from the flood of tears. I want to believe God will touch me like he has touched Jonathan. I want the pain, hurt, fear, and insecurity to leave me.

The pastor comes over to me and softly lays his hand on my head and I fall to the floor. My mouth is moving and words are coming out. I try to make myself stop. I try to make my mouth listen to me, as a rush goes through my entire body. I hear myself speaking praises to God as I roll in the floor, looking totally undignified. Somehow I don't feel ashamed or embarrassed, instead I feel a sort of calm like the relief a child feels when she thinks she's been left alone in a department store and suddenly her mother comes around the corner. I lose all track of time. I speak all my concerns to God in this strange, different language, and He speaks back to me.

Finally, He releases me to my own faculties, and I get up from the floor; as I try to pull myself together, I look over toward the organ and see Kathy. She, too, is regaining her natural senses looking most unsophisticated. We smooth down our hair and smile at each other because we finally understand about the transformation. All the way home we sing, pray, and rejoice. We are exhausted! We are sweaty! We are saved!

As Kathy and I reminisce, I believe this was the best time of my life. Everything was finally right in my life. We spend hours talking. We also talk about how wrong things went with Jonathan's conversion. It seems perfectly clear, and we pinpoint when it started to go wrong.

***

After my conversion, Ma and I become closer, and we all enjoy church services together. She holds Bible lessons with both Jonathan and me now. Twice a week, Ma, Kathy, and I attend a Christian aerobics class. This week, it's Ma's turn to bring a healthy snack to class, but she doesn't show up. I go to her house and find her curled up in bed. Sometime during the fall months, Ma started to develop a cough. She has also been complaining about stiffness in her neck and shoulders, and now her cough is much worse.

I take Ma to the doctor, he prescribes a cough suppressant, and he sends her home. Two months later on medication she still isn't getting any better. After many trips to the doctor, it's clear that his intentions are not to go any further than he already has. We decide to leave the HMO doctor at the first of the year and to return to the high-option insurance that allows her to go to her old family doctor or anyone else she chooses.

During those months of coughing, she develops a couple of small lumps on her collarbone, so a biopsy is the family doctor's first plan of action. Afterwards, there is a series of x-rays and an MRI. After all the results are back, her doctor asks me to call a family meeting. Ma, Jonathan, my brothers, my aunts, and I are present at the meeting. First we are told that the biopsy came back malignant. He also tells us that the x-rays confirm lung cancer. The doctor continues by saying, "It's inoperable."

His words hang in the air, dangling like a hangman's noose. *Why? How? What? NO!* I have a sinking feeling inside, and from then on I am consumed with the feeling of impending doom. This is way too much for me to hear at one time. I can see the doctor's mouth moving, and I comprehend what is being said, but allowing it to penetrate is literally impossible. The doctor says that the only treatment he can recommend is chemotherapy and, even with that, Ma only has a 40 percent chance of recovering. The doctor leaves us all in the room alone to consider what he has just said. I feel my finger tips go numb, then cold. I use all my strength to keep my knees from buckling. We all look across the room at each other, trying desperately not to make eye contact. Right here in this conference room, all our hopes slowly, silently slip away, all except Ma. Her faith in God never wavers. None of us speak; we can't.

The family lingers, trying not to speak as though the sound of their voices will make matters worse. As if acting out parts in a play, each family member gives Ma these sad, pitying smiles, eventually saying their polite goodbyes to Ma and then to me. And, one by one, they leave the hospital. I wheel Ma back to her room, but because of the diagnosis, she has been moved to a different floor. The nurse says she's on the "Oncology" floor now. It sounds like a dirty word when she says it. I wheel her up to that floor, and it's different than anything I've ever seen. People are coughing all over the place. This is the only place in the hospital where there are designated smoking areas. We pass by a man with a hole in his throat. He places a cigarette in the hole and smokes. It scares me to know that some people don't change, even in the face of death.

Once I get her settled into her new room, I don't know the right words either. What do I say? *It's going to be alright. You'll beat this, Ma.* I don't really believe that; I know how cancer works. I don't know anyone who is a survivor. I want to say something encouraging to her. I want to be her tower of strength for a change. But no matter how hard I try to think of something, words fail me. I can see for myself how she has deteriorated in just the few months she has been coughing. I know the pain she's in. I can think of nothing appropriate to say, so I say nothing. I just continue to fight back the tears. The least I can do is be strong for her.

Ma acts as though she has not heard the doctor. I wait until I can compose myself and collect my thoughts before I speak.

"Ma, what do you want to do?" I ask.

She replies calmly, "First, I'm going to pray. I'll see what God has to say. He's still the head of my life, and I know He can heal me. If He doesn't, it's not because he can't."

I sit still, again not knowing the right words to say.

We sit in silence the rest of the day. Ma dozes off now and then, and

I sit in a chair looking out through the window watching the sun go down and the night creeping in on us. I want to hug her and tell her everything will be fine, but we have never had a hugging and kissing type of relationship. I think it will feel phony, so I just sit quietly. It is as though someone has just sucked my essence from me. Maybe I'm in shock. I never thought about life without Ma. She's young, successful, and beautiful. This is not fair! This is a nightmare! How can God do this to her? Why doesn't He stop this? How could God do this to me? I lose my battle with bravery and the tears will no longer obey me. I release deep sobs that wrench my body, causing all my strength to pass from me, and I find myself on my knees. Everything hurts. I suddenly become aware of the sounds that are escaping from my twisted lips, and I look over at Ma. She is asleep, so I let the tears flow. My faith is not nearly as strong as hers. It is in this selfish moment that I face the truth in accepting the fact that I know it is her strength that really holds my family together. I try to clear my mind of my personal sorrow and pray for Ma. I pray softly out loud because I need to hear the words to help convince myself that I believe she can be healed. She has to recover. She just has to.

***

The hospital has done its job now that the news has been broken to the family, so this morning they release Ma from the hospital, even though she continues to cough. There are no special instructions sheets for us to follow like those that most patients receive when they are discharged. They give her a death sentence and send us home to wait for it. Whether or not there will be any chemo now depends on Ma. No one knows yet what her prayers will bring.

When she gets home, I can see some of her resolve escaping from her tired, cancer-invaded body. She doesn't bother using a spoon anymore for the cough suppressant. She just takes swigs directly from the bottle. After a few days, Ma makes her decision; she has prayed and feels God has released her to begin chemo. I am relieved. Maybe there is hope.

Starting chemo is an interesting process. I learn later that apparently she is part of a group study headed by a large research hospital with a satellite located near our local hospital. Each member of the group is given different doses of varying strengths of medicine ranging from the most severe without being lethal to a placebo. Not even the doctors know which patients have received what. They will only find out when the appointed numbers of injections are over and the patient either gets better or dies. Before taking her to her first session, I talk with different people and hear a number of horror stories. But there weren't enough stories to prepare me for cancer close up, eradicating the physical and mental well-being of my mother.

On our first visit, I sit nervously in the waiting room while the nurse wheels Ma into an examining room. They give her a series of injections that only take a half hour and then she is finished. They warn me before we leave that she may get nauseous. We make it home and all is well. This is great. For the first time since getting the news I am a little bit encouraged. Things are finally going better.

However, she has lost a lot of weight and a great deal of her strength, so I help her undress and get into bed. She appears sleepy, so I leave her alone in her room to rest, and I call home to check on Jonathan and the girls. I give him a complete account of what has happened all day and how Ma is doing. This conversation suggests the first signs of a change in his deliverance. He listens to me impatiently, interrupting me several times by shouting something to the girls. Finally, I ask what has been going on there at home. I find out from him that the girls are still in their pajamas and he is still in bed. Jonita made cereal for herself and the other girls and they have been happy spending the day watching cartoons, but now they are hungry again. Before I can respond to what he just said, I can hear Ma gagging; it has started.

She has gotten up and gone into the bathroom. I hang up the phone and run to the bathroom. I find her down on her hands and knees with her face in the toilet, vomiting. I stand in the doorway, helpless, again not knowing what to do. After there is nothing left in her stomach, she begins to have dry heaves. Her face is twisted and sort of a gray color. Her arms look like they are barely able to support her weight, to prevent her from falling in the toilet. I fear one more violent episode and she will lose her grip and fall in. I should do something, but I am frozen in the doorway, mummified. Finally, I ask if she is all right. She doesn't answer right away, so I just wait.

"Baby, help me up," she requests with a soft, weak voice.

Fear finally releases me, and I let loose of the doorframe; I get her to her feet and help her back to bed. Still not knowing what to do, I call the pastor.

"Pastor Johnny, I need your help. Ma has started vomiting and I don't know what to do." I say. It all comes out quick and garbled.

"Slow down, honey. What did the doctor say do?"

"He gave her some nausea medicine, but I just got back from the clinic and haven't had time to get to the pharmacy yet. I can't leave her alone and Jonathan's at home with the girls," I ramble.

"Alright, calm down. I'll send Sister Blue over to help," she replies.

"Thanks Pastor."

I hang up the phone and return to Ma's room. She has dozed off. I tiptoe out of the room and decide to wait outside for Sister Blue so that the doorbell won't wake Ma.

***

After a week or so, the vomiting stops and Mom is back to her normal self except she had no appetite (a chemo side effect). In the beginning she forces herself to eat, but that only lasts until the second chemo session. This time we don't make it home before the vomiting starts. I can tell Ma is getting weaker, but we never speak about it. I just continue making adjustments and alterations when necessary.

I go to school in her neighborhood, so I make all her meals at my house and bring them over the next day. I visit her daily on my break. While there, I dress her, straighten up, comb her hair, and do whatever else needs to be done. This isn't the ideal set-up, but it seems like everything can work out if I just stay on schedule and take care of Ma. I put everything and everyone that I can on hold, and I stay in a constant state of terror of losing her. I know something else is coming. I will it back, pray it back, and imagine it back, but I know things cannot continue the way they are going.

A few weeks after the second chemo session, Ma sees a magazine ad about how natural foods can heal cancer. She decides to find out more about it. She has me take her to the health food store. There they have books about the miracle diet called macrobiotics. The main course or foods in the diet are tofu and seaweed. We spend about $200 that day buying all these strange foods. This tofu seaweed soup becomes her main nourishment. The soup, barley, and brown rice are all she will eat in false hopes it will cure her. Yet, she loses an alarming thirty pounds in three weeks from her already slim frame. Her steps become even slower. She has very little energy. Her clothes have to be altered constantly, and her shoes flop off the backs of her heels when she walks. Because most of her skin has darkened to a deep black, the strange yellowish pink color that her palms take on cause her to look almost alien. I am beginning to have to look harder and more intently to recognize Ma behind the devitalizing effects of the chemo. Jonathan and I bring the girls over as often as possible for Ma, but Jonathan isn't coming to the house as often to continue his Bible lessons with her. When he does come, she insists he read to her. If she dozes off in-between, he must wait until she wakes. Again, I begin to see him become less faithful to God, to her, to me.

***

I spend every moment I can at Ma's. One of our favorite pastimes has been for me to style her hair. She has shoulder length, thick, all-black hair. I get out all the supplies and get her ready to be styled beautifully. I stand behind her while she sits in one of the dining room chairs. I pick up the wide-tooth comb and start a few smooth strokes from the crown of her head down past her shoulders. As I begin to comb her hair, the comb fills with hair. At first, I'm not surprised because she has been lying down a lot and has not combed her hair. But as I start again to pull the comb through her hair from the top to the back, clumps of her hair begin to slide off her scalp. I am stunned. I have never seen hair do this before, and I don't really understand what I'm seeing. When I lift the comb from her head, her scalp is exposed everywhere I moved the comb. That's when it hits me what is happening. I try to stay composed; I try not to let this affect me, but my face tells the story. I begin to step back from her. She turns and looks at my face. Apparently, she has been expecting it. I, however, am in no way prepared. She sees the terror in my face. She bends down from the chair and picks the hair up from the floor and places it back on her head. Everything changes for me. I drop the comb. I try to hide my terror, and I don't want her to see my reaction. But, it's too late for that because she keeps saying, "It's alright, baby." I can't hold it this time; the tears, the terror, the strain of another moment of facing all this faithlessness is simply too much. I rush to the door, stumbling down the few steps leading to the foyer. My mouth is quivering, my brain racing, and my vision blurry as I reach the front door. I leave her with Sister Blue, who has been coming to sit with Ma since that first chemo session.

As I open the door, a quivering voice yells back, "I have to go, Ma. I'll call you later."

I rush out of the house, run to my car, get in, slump over to one side, and weep. How can I make it without her? I need her. I want her to stay here and help me through my drama. Being aware of my own selfish, self-centered thoughts only add further turmoil to my already deteriorating state of mind. But, I can't stop myself.

She's too young, God. She serves you, God. She loves you, God. What are you doing? Why the suffering? Why is she dying?

No answer comes.

***

Kathy and I finally stop reminiscing about how Ma's was responsible for leading Jonathan to Christ and how when Ma gets sick, Jonathan starts moving away from Christ. We get back to the problem at hand. I tell Kathy of my plans to meet with Patricia and spend a few days at her house while I try to figure out what to do next. She promises me she will be praying and that everything is going to turn out all right. I promise to call when I get to Patricia's.

CHAPTER SIX

I drive out of town on Sunday night to Patricia's house, just outside of Detroit. It takes me several hours to get there. Patricia is happy to see me, but she seems a little confused when she sees I don't have the girls or Jonathan with me. Most people would start in with all kinds of questions, but that isn't Patricia's style. She invites me into her comfortable, little, two-bedroom townhouse and shows me upstairs to the guest bedroom. She sees I have nothing with me, luggage or any type of bag, but, still she asks no questions. I go to the neatly decorated restroom, wash my tear-stained face, and head back downstairs to the kitchen. Patricia is making coffee. I ask to use the phone so that I can call Kathy.

"Kathy, I made it."

"Are you alright?

"As alright as I can be."

"Are you sure you know what you're doing?"

"Kathy, at this point, I'm not sure about anything except I have to do something. Let him see how it feels to be abandoned. I've got to go, Kathy. I'll call you tomorrow. Take care. Bye."

By the time I hang up, Patricia has the coffee cups on the round, butcher-block kitchen table. I'm not sure if she overheard my conversation with Kathy or not, but she's the type who will not intrude unless she is invited in. We sit at the table and I take a sip of the hot, black coffee. I try to hold myself together; I try to be strong. Unfortunately,

I am out of steam, out of self-control and confidence, out of my home. Without warning, the tears begin to drop into my coffee. It is a silent weeping as though someone has died. There is a deafening silence in the house. I can hear time clicking and ticking away and the plunking of my tears and nothing else. Patricia sits across from me as still as a corpse. Suddenly I begin to feel foolish. A grown woman runs away from home, with no place to go, no money, no clothes, no plan, not even a toothbrush, and now she's sitting here crying like the fool she is. She leaves her home and her children in the name of self-respect.

Patricia is patient. She finally moves when she puts her cup up to her lips and sips some coffee. I want to talk. I want to tell her everything that this man and this marriage have done to me, yet I can't speak. Patricia gets up and stands behind my chair. She places her hands gently on my shoulders and softly begins to massage my neck and shoulders. At the same time, she begins singing very softly. It is so soft that I don't notice it at first; it's low and sweet, like a mother singing comfort to her restless child. She continues singing, humming, moaning, and massaging. I feel myself relaxing. My shoulders droop and the tension reluctantly releases the muscles in my neck. I feel very tired. Sleep begins to force its way in. Patricia must sense it. She stands me up like a child who has fallen asleep at the table after a hard day of play. She leads me back upstairs to the guest bedroom; all the time she never stops humming. She sits me down on the side of the bed. She stoops down and slides off my shoes and swings my legs up into the bed. As though in tune with the actions of my feet, my torso glides downward toward the mattress and my head settles on the pillow. I don't feel my eyes shut, but I feel the warm blanket being pulled over me.

When I awake, it is morning. Patricia is downstairs making breakfast. She has been a close friend of the family ever since I can remember. I start downstairs feeling pretty stupid. I also feel a sort of peace that I haven't felt in a long time. I feel safe and, in some strange way, I feel at home. This place feels familiar. I feel like a little girl who has been lost and finally finds her way home. I want to forget about everything and everybody and just stay and let Patricia take care of me. She seems to need someone to care of, and I need someone to take care of me for a change. I try not to think; I just want to be someone's little girl. It is this desire that forces me to deal with reality, because my little girls need me the same way I need Patricia.

I try to figure out what I need to do first. What about school, my house, my friends, my church, my girls, my marriage? How will I deal with all this? Patricia must have heard me bumping around upstairs because when I come around the corner into the kitchen, she has my plate ready on the table.

"Good morning. How'd you sleep?" are her first words.

"I slept like a log. Something smells great, but I don't have much of an appetite."

"Sit down and drink your coffee and eat what you can."

I sit down and start picking at the food with my fork. Slowly I begin eating forks of scrambled eggs and grits. Before I know it, I finish everything on my plate. That's when I remember that I haven't eaten since Saturday afternoon, and today is Monday. Patricia sits quietly across from me at the table like she had the night before. I finally speak. I tell her the whole story. I start from the phone call, then the changes in appearance, the parties, the motel, the coming home, and me leaving. Patricia sits expressionless long enough to let my words soak in and make me feel like I had made a foolish mistake by leaving. She finally speaks.

"Are you finished with Jonathan?"

That question is too direct and unexpected. I liked it better when she didn't say anything. If I say yes, then I will be forced to act. If I say no, then I might as well go back. I don't like this question. I feel myself getting angry. I try not to direct it toward Patricia. I try to focus, but I am not ready to answer this difficult question, but I know I have to say something.

"I don't know," is all I can say.

"Have you thought out what you'll do next?"

Darn it, another hard question, one for which I have no answer.

"Patricia, I don't know what to do or where to go. I just know I had to leave."

"Ok, you've done that, so what's next?"

"I need to get my girls."

"All right, how will you do that?" she asks.

"Why do I need to answer all the hard questions? I don't know anything. I'm almost 35 years old and I don't know anything but how to be stepped on."

"That's not true. You know you've had enough. You know enough to get away from it. You know that things must change. You know that you need to get your girls. You know how to ask for help. I'd say you know quite a bit."

"The problem is that I don't know where to go from here. Can you help me, Pat?"

"Yes, I can help, but you're not going to like what I have to say."

"Go ahead. I'm listening" I say with some reservation.

"First, you have to fight fire with fire. You can't let him run you off. You've done nothing wrong. You must pull yourself together and go back."

"Go home? I just left!"

"Baby, if Jonathan is what he appears to be, he's going to say you abandoned him and your girls. This can make it difficult for you to get them. You must go back! You cannot fight him from here."

I don't want to hear what Patricia is saying. I feel like I am surrendering before anyone knows that there is a war. I know I will have to cower down, swallow my precious self-respect, and return home. I don't want to listen, but I know she is right.

She continues, "Don't go back the way you left. Don't go without a plan. Be prepared for the fight and this time you need to have some ammunition." I sit and listen to Patricia tell me how to toughen up and how to remove my emotions from the situation. She tells me how to avoid internalizing anything negative that he says to me. She tells me to see him and not see him. She says for me to focus my heart and pain into the weapon that will free me of Jonathan forever. She tells me to never let him see me cry and to laugh when I feel like crying. She says I should keep him from really knowing this sweet, young woman that he has spent years abusing. I set my face like flint and resign myself to go back. This time I have a plan; I am not going back to be the victim.

I take a long bath, trying to relax and prepare myself for what is ahead. I continue to flip over in my mind the night at the motel. When I close my eyes, I see the skinny, cross-eyed lady standing behind a window looking out at me. I remember Jonathan's indifference towards me. This memory only adds to my determination to get out of this situation once and for all. I take my time drying off and dressing for the long drive back home.

By two o'clock I am ready to leave for home. Patricia and I have a word of prayer before I leave. I get in my car and turn it toward home. My mind drifts. I fight to focus on the things Patricia has rehearsed with me. The drive takes me longer than it should have. I stop at several rest stops trying to strengthen my resolve.

I pull up in front of my house around 6:30 p.m. The house looks deserted. It is dark outside, but there are no lights shining through any windows on the front of the house. I park across the street slightly up from the house. I take a few minutes to collect myself before getting out of the car. I reach over to the passenger side, grab my purse, and step out of the car. The street is empty, too. There isn't a person or moving vehicle in sight. The feeling is kind of eerie. As I cross the street, I can swear the entire block is peering from their windows, hiding behind their curtains, laughing at my cowardly retreat back to where I started. The feeling is so strong that I spin around quickly in the middle of the street straining my eyes, looking into windows in an attempt to confront my accusers; but, I am alone. *Calm down! Pull yourself together!* I keep telling myself it is time to face whatever awaits me.

Slowly, I move across the street and walk toward the house. Jonathan's car is nowhere in sight. I go to the back door and begin digging through my purse for my keys. It is bitterly cold and my hands tremble while fumbling with the ring of keys, trying to get the right one into the lock. The key slides into the knob, and I turn it to the right, then to the left, but the door won't open. I feel a rush swelling up inside me. I begin moving the key, violently pushing, pulling, and jerking at the knob. This unexpected betrayal sends me running to the front door, letting my purse fall to the ground behind me. Shaking fiercely after my first few attempts to put the key in the lock, I lose my grip and drop the key ring on the ground. This puts me on my hands and knees scrambling around on the ground trying to retrieve my keys. As I stand between the storm door and the front door forcing my conscious mind to comprehend what has just happened; again, I feel the neighbors' eyes on my back, penetrating me like the ghosts they are. Where are they when I need help, when I'm being abused? Where are their kind words? I know they are there, but they remain invisible, watching. I finally find the right key and slide it into the lock. It too refuses to turn. It is finally clear that he has changed the locks on the doors.

Twenty-four hours I've been gone, twenty-four hours; and he has changed the locks. My shaking hands are no longer due to the weather; it is from the gall that he has to lock me out.

"Think girl! Think! You will not be out done." I remembered! The kids' upstairs window is never locked. I have seen Jonathan climb through that window before. I run around back. The fence that covers the back and sides of the house will keep the neighbors' eyes away. I climb up on the railing that surrounds the basement stairs. It allows me to reach a trellis that hangs on the back of the house down to where the railing meets it. Once I start up the trellis, it takes careful placement of my feet to keep from falling. I have to hold on tight with one hand in order to free myself from my jacket with the other. It is getting tangled and holding me back. After climbing a few feet, I am able to pull myself up to a low roof ledge and stand up to reach the window. Looking through the window, I can see no one is home. Somehow things look different, but I don't know why at the moment.

I brace myself, grab the edge of the sliding window, and begin yanking at it. That yields me no success. My left hand loses its hold and my feet begin to slip on the damp roof top. I stop and steady myself. This time I pull smoothly and evenly without jerking the window from its tracks, and it obeys. The small window slides easily to one side, leaving enough room for me to shimmy through it. I silently close the window behind me.

Once inside, I find things pretty much the way I left them. But again, I sense something is different. As I creep through the girls' room toward the upstairs hallway, I figure out what is wrong; there are too many toys. Toys are everywhere. They are toys that I have not purchased nor seen

68

before. From the upstairs hall, the entire living room area can be seen littered with toys. As I look down into the living room, I notice lots of suitcases, two very small ones like for children and two large ones. A sick feeling comes over me, and again I have to brace myself. I ease my way down the hallway toward the master bedroom, feeling the same way I had a few months before. The hall seems to move, making itself longer as I journey down it. When I reach the master bedroom doorway, I freeze. I stand terrified of what I will find inside. I grip the knob. My hands are sweaty and unsteady on the knob, making turning it even more difficult. I have to keep my nerve. Turning the knob, I push the door open slowly, inch by painful inch. It is as though I'm afraid I'll let the family pet escape into the street if I open the door too quickly.

I don't need to turn on the light. An outside street light shines through the bedroom window into the room allowing me to see every part of the room in the dark. The bed is neatly made and everything is in its place, neater than it usually is. There is something lying on the bed. I need to move from the doorway to determine what it is. I strain my eyes to make sense of the object, but only a closer look will tell. I move to the edge of the bed and bend over to pick the thing up. When I lift it, small things fall from it. It is a black negligee. I examine everything and find that the small things on the bed are rose petals. The tag is still on the gown, and I know it does not belong to me. It is safe to assume that it isn't a gift for me since Jonathan has locked me out of my house and has no idea if or when I will return. He obviously has other plans.

At that realization, I perch myself on the edge of the bed. I begin thinking about how quickly he plans to replace me. I jump up suddenly and begin opening my dresser drawers. They are all empty. I run full speed toward the stairs, crashing into the bedroom door on my way out of the room. The door draws blood from my forehead, but I don't feel it and I don't stop. I charge down the stairs and grab one of the large suitcases. I flip it on its side and unzip it. There jumbled and balled up are all my things. Upon opening the second large case, I find more of my things thrown inside without care.

My pulse is racing; and my thoughts are flashing by too fast for me to grasp what I'm thinking.

I say out loud, "If you can move this quickly, so can I."

I drag both cases up the stairs. Quickly their contents are emptied back into my drawers. I gather up all the strange toys and pack them into the two large suitcases. I set both of them outside around the back of the house. I don't have time to investigate the smaller two bags. I simply throw them into a closet.

I need to move fast if I am to catch Jonathan and his new interest off guard. I know Jonathan has very little mechanical ability; replacing the locks is not even close to his specialty. These kinds of things are my job, so he probably didn't think to throw the old locks away. A quick look around the kitchen rewards me with the jackpot. I find the old locks in a bag under the kitchen sink, next to a couple of Jonathan's work thermoses. It is getting late and I have to hurry. I get my keys and find out which one is for the backdoor. The screwdriver has been left under the sink too. Grabbing it and turning the screws as quickly as my hands allow me, I unscrew the knob. There isn't time to redo everything, so I only replace the tumbler. I always have difficulty with lining up the holes to reinstall the knobs, but this time it fits like clockwork. It only takes 15 minutes; I consider doing the front door too, but decide the ghosts will see me because the fence doesn't cover the front of the house.

I think it is sweat running down into my eyes, but when I reach up to wipe it away, I discover that its blood coming from the cut that the bedroom door delivered to me. I go back to the kitchen, wet a paper towel, and pat at the injury. I don't feel any pain; yet it must have been pretty bad because it takes me a while to stop the bleeding. My mind is not on the cut. I am looking ahead to the return of Jonathan, my children and, I suppose, Miss Cross-eyed Plain Jane. I can't help but wonder what crazy lies he must have told her about where I am. Even with a lie, what kind of woman just moves in with another woman's husband? I chuckle to myself thinking how surprised they will both be to see me when they return. Surprise is just what I need.

I grab my keys and head out the back door, circle around to the front, get in my car, lock my door, and start it. I know the kids will be tired and whining when they come back, so no one will think to look in the backyard for my car. I come up through the alley that separates the residents on the street from the train tracks. It comes to me to turn off the car lights before turning into the yard. I enter through a gate in the back wall of the fence and park away from the back door under a large weeping willow tree that stands guard in the yard. The hanging limbs nearly cover the entire car, causing it to be almost invisible to a probing eye. I close the car door softly so as not to alarm any ghosts who may not have yet abandoned their posts at the windows. Gloveless and coatless, I glide away from the car and I glance back. It reminds me of some sort of burial shroud.

I disposed of the lock into someone else's trashcan along with all evidence associated with it. I know Jonathan is the type of man who will take the time to go through every piece of our trash looking for evidence that doesn't exist. He only had a day, so he had to work fast. Maybe he'll think he changed it or maybe he won't. Either way he'll be confused and never know what went wrong until it's too late. I'll keep playing the good wife while I wait for my chance to escape.

You see, men who are unfaithful, cruel, rotten liars expect the same things back. They think women think like them. Because Jonathan knows that what goes around comes around, he expects betrayal; in fact, he's almost paranoid about it, and that's just what he's going to get. Who knows what he's told this woman about me or us? Without knowing what he said, one thing is for sure—it has to be a lie. Now it's time for the lies to catch up with him. I ease inside through the back door without being noticed. I need everything to seem normal when they return. This is my house and I'm staying right here.

I put the kettle on the stove and run upstairs to find a gown. I open the drawers I had just refilled with my balled up gowns and start sifting through my things looking for something to put on that looks decent. That's when my eye catches the black negligee. I throw the clothes back into the drawer and lift the gown from the bed. Holding it up in front of me in the mirror reveals the fact that it will fit. It also shows that Jonathan has good taste, assuming that he bought it. Anyway, there is no time to ponder that question. I remove my clothes and put the gown on. I lotion my arms and legs and spray on some cologne. The negligee is clingy and brings out my best features. I find myself slowing down. I take the time to tend further to the cut on my forehead. I pin up my hair and head back downstairs without my robe. I want to be ready when they return. Everything needs to look normal.

The whistle from the kettle startles me. This tells me how unprepared I really am for their eventual return, but that doesn't stop me. I find the instant coffee and make myself a cup. Finally, I sit down with it at the kitchen table and inhale. The warm steam gives me time to relax. I keep the portable phone next to me within reach, just in case things don't go well.

Barely five minutes go by when I hear them coming. The car pulls into the driveway. The kids are making sleepy noises as they get out of the car. I hear her voice saying something that I cannot distinguish. I do not move; there is no impulse to run this time. Only the light over the stove burns in the house. Jonathan does what I suspected he'd do. He takes everyone to the front door. I sit in the kitchen, clearly visible from the front door. She comes in first, followed by the kids and Jonathan bringing up the rear. When she sees me, she stands stark still. Jonathan has to push her to get inside. He turns on the light as he starts to ask her what is wrong with her, and then he sees me. I give him back what he gave me the day before.

"Hey."

CHAPTER SEVEN

We all stand around watching Ma in her final hour. The last time she regained consciousness and opened her eyes; she seemed so tired and ready to go. Her face is a slate, gray color. As she breathes, I can hear gurgling in her throat. She is in so much pain that the doctors keep her sedated, even though her wish is to be awake. But every time she is awake more than a few moments, she begins that bone chilling cough that wrenches her entire body.

Ma died on a Friday. The funeral arrangements have to be made, and all my brothers seem mummified. It all becomes my responsibility to find the funeral home, select a burial site, pick the casket, write the program, hire a printer, order the flowers, and secure the church. I'm making arrangements as quickly as possible so that the funeral can be held on the upcoming Sunday. The hospital asks me which funeral home I want the body to go to. I know absolutely nothing about funeral homes, but one of Ma's friends here at the hospital suggests a funeral home nearby, and I agree to that place. The funeral home is willing to take care of the body, the program, and the family car. I select a cemetery close to home because it feels right. A local florist is taking care of all the floral arrangements. Our church agrees to hold the funeral services even though they plan to have the regular Sunday church services in the morning. All four princes and Jonathan do their parts and show up on Sunday for the service.

After Ma's death, my walls begin to crumble. Each task is laborious for me. I'm suffering, but I am unable to share that with anyone. No one knows how close we really were. I start developing breathing difficulties immediately after her death. I inhale suddenly, unable to catch my breath, similar to the way a child gasps at air after a hard cry. No one seems to notice my trauma. It doesn't stop me though.

This crazy, old fashioned, holy roller who was my mother had somehow moved into the position of my closest friend. She was the one who listened without judgment. She had a quiet unassuming nature that could ease its way into my earth-shattering situations, makes a strategic move or impression, and then quietly back away. She loved me unconditionally, and I know it now.

The Home Going Service is fantastic. The church is over- flowing. I didn't know Ma had affected so many people's lives. The service takes so long that we simply have to cut it off. Everyone wants to say something, so it is hard to end it. As long as it lasts, it seems I am still connected to Ma.

The burial is Monday morning. We all sit around the grave site in nice white chairs, waiting for the last words to be read and the prayer to be prayed. None of it actually seems real. But seeing them lower the casket into the ground makes it all too real for me.

***

Once the funeral is over, according to Ma's will, her house has to be sold; her personal belongings have to be disbursed. Decisions have to be made concerning her estate. We are, surprisingly, all in agreement as to how we decide to handle things. My brothers and I inventory the whole house and determine who gets what based on need. After everyone gets what they want, I have a garage sale. When there is still a half house full of things after I've had the sale and given things away, I find myself throwing away all Ma's good junk. It bothers me that I am throwing her life away. I try to keep as much of the things she loved as I can. I have to go to Ma's house and get it ready for the sale; those are the terms of the will. One prince insists on staying at the house until it is sold.

Eventually everything is settled, and I get my share of the estate. It is just in time because ever since Ma's death, nothing is important to

Jonathan. Jonathan has been calling in sick from work. Most days he never gets out of bed. He stays off work for so long that he has to take a medical leave so that he won't get fired.

I have my practicum and one more semester of nursing classes before graduation, and all the responsibilities of our lives fall on me. Jonathan insists that we use my inheritance to support our household while he tries to find himself. We can probably manage without Jonathan's income for the next six months, yet I wonder if he cares about what I'm going through. He probably doesn't even notice.

"Jonathan, why won't you go to work?"

"I can't."

"Why not?"

"It's too much."

"What's too much?"

"Losing Ma."

"Losing Ma? What do you mean? She was my mother."

"I can't explain it to you. Just leave me alone."

I have to put my grieving on hold, for Jonathan is doing enough for both of us. The girls still need to be dressed and taken to school and day care. All the problems with Ma and her estate keep me from finishing all my classes in the spring. The classes I need to retake are only offered once a year and I won't be able to take them until January. I am, however, able to get special permission to take the practicum. It is scheduled to be at the local trauma hospital. I have them schedule me for the night shift because of the girls, and it's usually the busiest and the most stressful time at the hospital. I am on my feet all night. Regardless, I have to keep going because Jonathan is spending his nights and days mourning Ma's death.

Surprisingly, my practicum at the hospital has become a blessing. It gives me an opportunity to escape all the troubles that are fast trying to smother me. They start me in pediatrics. There are babies, toddlers, and adolescents who reach out to me and appreciate my help. It makes me feel like I have some importance. In pediatrics, using small butterfly needles, finding tiny veins, and dispensing drugs, become second nature to me. Oftentimes, most of the things that can go wrong do during my shift. The few quiet moments I have there are spent studying for finals. It is imperative that I memorize the chemistry elements. Taking these snatches of time to distinguish between the different drugs and the effects each one has as well as the ill effects of an improper mixture of chemicals are my main focus.

Jonathan is too distraught to save us money by caring for his children while I work the night shift. He needs his nights to be free, so I have to take the girls to a night-time sitter. I realize that this is just another attempt to make me quit school, the school he insisted that I attend. When I started school three years ago and came to realize how good it could be for me, I made up my mind that I would not quit. If I have to walk barefooted across glass with all three kids strapped to my back, I vowed not to quit. It's time for me to take care of myself for a change. My entire married life has been about Jonathan. This education is for me. Of course, though, everyone will benefit in the end.

Jonathan sleeps during the day, but he still expects me to do laundry, clean the house, cook meals, and get the girls after school. Since school is now my choice, I don't complain. I catch a nap whenever I can, mostly on the weekends. I say nothing to Jonathan. I need to focus on graduating and tending to my girls. Everything else is up to God to work out.

After two months of grieving, Jonathan starts to disappear. My first break at the hospital is about midnight. Since Jonathan sleeps all day, surely I won't be waking him calling at midnight. At first, I get him and we talk a few minutes; then he rushes me off the phone. Eventually there is no answer when I call. I try to convince myself that Jonathan is asleep, or maybe he is sitting outside and can't hear the phone. Maybe he is having a difficult, depressing night and he just doesn't feel like answering. There is also the possibility that the phone was not working properly. I choose to accept one or the other of these excuses and convince myself that everything is fine.

Jonathan has never been all the things I dreamt about, but, to date, he has never failed to love me and the girls. I know everyone has problems, but we always seem to find our way through ours. I try to let that thought console me, but finally I feel I have to ask Jonathan where he is when I call. He says some of his coworkers who are on the 3 – 11 shift need to unwind after work at a club downtown. I guess Jonathan is still recovering from Ma's untimely death, and spending time with his buddies will help him recover more quickly. There are so many other things for me to worry about that I don't spend time trying to borrow trouble. If unwinding is what he needs to do, then that will be all there is to it. Although prayer and surrounding himself with the people of God seems like a more reasonable solution for him, but I do know that every man has to mourn his own way.

After four or five weeks of night time relaxing, Jonathan decides he's ready to return to work. I'm more than excited to learn Jonathan is back to normal. The winter holidays are coming and we need to have a good Christmas because this will be our first one ever without Ma.

Jonathan's transition back to work is a smooth one. His family doctor writes an excuse for him to return to work based on a type of depression. The postal service is thrilled that Jonathan is back and as good as ever. Somehow, he is just as charming to them as he had been to me the day we met. After a few weeks, things fall back into a regular routine. Slowly our relationship returns to normal, except the girls and I are the only ones going to the church meetings now. I stay on the night shift at the hospital and prepare to finish the last of my practicum.

Fortunately for me, I have an uncanny knack for being able to block out whatever else is going on and focus on the task at hand. My experiences with the babies enable me to make injections or drawing blood look like one single, fluid motion. I soon begin to pride myself in my ability to be a top-notch nurse.

I have several weeks left of my practicum when I'm moved from pediatrics to emergency. That is an experience in and of itself. Once there, I witness the aftermath of how enemies punish each other. However, that brutality is nothing compared to how family members treat each other. The night shift exposes me to brothers attacking brothers, aunts against uncles, but worst of all are the attacks husbands and wives make against each other. My short time there invited me into the world of women who are beaten half to death by the men who they believe love them most. Everything from broken bones to stabbings to gunshot wounds are results of those trusted relationships. The men who claim they really love their wives come in with hats in hands and tails between their legs declaring their sorrow and undying love for their spouses. This always disgusts me. I think what I have at home is so much better. He loves me; he just has some major issues that the two of us need to work through. I vow never to be like them.

Just before the Christmas holidays my hospital work is complete, and I only have two classes left to take during the winter semester. Jonathan seems to be back to normal and really jazzed by the upcoming holidays. It is always a special time for us and the kids, but this one is not as festive as the ones before. We do go to church Christmas morning as a family. The pastor acknowledges all the members we've lost during the year. Most of us have a good cry, but the pastor allows a few people to come up and say something special about a deceased member. Jonathan raised his hand to speak about Ma. The things he says are beautiful. He talks about her laughter and about the games she used to play with the girls. He talks about her being in heaven. He talks about her commitment to God all the way to the end. He says it took him awhile to realize it, but she's not gone, she's still here with all of us. At that moment I am so proud of him. Our Christmas is beautiful.

But the beauty doesn't last in the New Year. It isn't until I start my last semester at school and accidentally overhear Jonathan's phone conversation that I realize our relationship is in serious trouble. Even then I don't do anything about it, and it takes me even longer to understand what I need to do.

CHAPTER EIGHT

S itting at the kitchen table, I take another sip of my coffee and smile. Strangely enough, I find this to be kind of funny. It feels great to be the hunter and not the hunted. I'm the one in control. He doesn't know it yet, but he's going to play my game. He'll discover that he doesn't know me at all. All the tricks he used to hold me down are what I'll use to strengthen myself. He'll never see it coming.

Not very long into my master strategy, things start to go wrong. Jonathan steps around the cross-eyed lady, and I can see the shock in his face. While he is trying to figure out what to say, I say, "What's going on? Where have you all been? You didn't leave me a note or anything. Come here girls; give Mommy a kiss." I get up from the table and open my arms out to my girls. He looks confused. I guess he is wondering how I got in. He finally finds his voice.

"The question is where have you been? I thought you were out of here."

He says this trying to look hurt. He puts on a good show for her, but it's nothing compared to what I have planned.

I look up at him as I continued to squeeze, coddle, and caress my babies and say, "Honey, don't be ridiculous. You know I would never leave you and the girls. I just went for a drive to clear my head and I ended up out at Patricia's house. Once I stopped, we talked into the wee hours of the morning. I kept trying to call home, but there was no answer. Finally, I fell asleep. When I woke up this afternoon, I tried calling again and again and got no answer. You can imagine my panic! I jumped in my car and raced home as fast as possible. Anyway, thanks for the gown. It was thoughtful, along with the beautiful rose petals. Is your friend here still hiding from her husband? I think I'll go put the kids to bed."

I don't wait for an answer. I know he can't figure out what to say, so I continue.

As I turn to walk away, I stop, look back and say, "I suggest," speaking to the cross-eyed lady, "that you go home and do the same."

With that, I swoop up Jovida and usher Jonita and Jolisa up the stairs to their bedroom. I leave the two of them and her children standing at the door. I pretend not to be concerned about them at all, but all my nerve endings are alert once I realize her children are present too. I think for a moment about all the times I have joked with the girls about having eyes in the back of my head. Right now, I find myself wishing that that were true. When I reach the girls' room upstairs at the end of the hall, I take a final quick glance around the room to ensure that my method of entry will not be discovered. I encourage the girls to be quiet by holding them close and rocking Jovida as I pull off coats, shoes, pants, and socks. I am doing all this while keeping my ears in tune with what is being said downstairs. I make a mental note to question Jonita tomorrow about the events of today and yesterday. I can't hear what is being said below us, but I can hear her voice elevating and becoming excited. That brings a smile to my face, trouble in paradise?

The girls are on their way to dreamland, but I stay in the room pressing my body against the wall behind the bedroom door where they cannot see me, yet I can see them clearly. I hear Jonathan tell her to send her kids into the kitchen so that they can talk. Now she's waving her arms and Jonathan is trying to calm her down. At this point, I decide to fuel the fire. I slide one negligee strap down off my shoulder allowing part of my breast to be exposed. I turn off the light in the girls' room and begin making my entrance into the hall. They both stop arguing and look up at me. I place myself directly in her field of vision. I fold my arms across the wrought iron railing and lean down just enough for her to see that I have nothing on underneath.

80

"It is really nice seeing you again." I say as sleepily and sexy as those women on those 900 numbers.

"Jonathan, don't forget to turn out the lights when you come to bed. Goodnight."

I rise up from the railing and start for our bedroom. Jonathan is facing the front door and she is facing him, but still looking past him and up at me. When I am sure that only she can see me, I begin to slip the already fallen strap of the negligee all the way off, exposing the upper part of my body. She sees and she knows what it means. I enter my bedroom closing the door behind me. I remember Patricia's words, "Fight fire with fire."

Their voices carry up through the bedroom door. Whatever she is saying equates to the discovery of some of Jonathan's true character. He keeps shushing her, but she keeps getting louder. Eventually the front door opens, and it sounds like she's leaving. Jonathan follows her out. I peek out the bedroom window that faces the front of the house. I look across the street to see if the ghosts are watching. I'm sure they glued themselves to their windows once they heard Jonathan pull up. Now they are waiting for the show to begin. This will give my faceless critics plenty to discuss for the next few months. I can't see them, but I know they're there. I guess seeing them would be even more humiliating. I try to believe that their discretion is a courtesy to me. I pull my eyes away from my unseen distractions to look down at the two fools still arguing in the driveway. I watch her ducklings file into her car, one behind the other. Right then a wave of sorrow for them sweeps over me. Her babies and mine are both headed for a childhood void of their fathers. We both know how important that is because we're both scrambling for the same man to take the job. She has lost her husband to gambling, drugs, and abuse, and I have lost mine to lies, infidelity, and abuse. We have so much in common.

It's funny, in a sad sort of way, that both of us want this certifiable liar. Jonathan has told me so many lies in our short 15-year marriage that he has begun to believe them himself. I wonder if he still believes in God. I wonder if he even thinks to pray or thank God for the things he has done for us both. I have to shake myself free of this wondering. I

81

need to be ready for when he comes back in because I know he is not going to be happy. I leave the window and find some clothes to step into. I get my robe off the closet door and wrap it over myself. I tuck the cordless telephone into my robe pocket with 911 already programmed in it. If he doesn't leave with her, I know when he returns there will be trouble.

I slip into my house shoes, thinking to myself about all those women in the movies who run upstairs when danger comes, trapping themselves in a bathroom or behind a weak bedroom door. I spent years ridiculing them, so I don't want to make the same mistake by staying in the bedroom. I take one more look out the window, and the lady is getting her kids strapped into the car. Jonathan is busy talking while she keeps belting all those kids in. How many are there? One, two, three, four, five! Oh my God! She drags around five kids to the home of a stranger and sets up housekeeping. She's unbelievably desperate, but so am I. *"I can't help wonder what Jonathan told the girls. "Hey girls, here's your new mom, sisters, and brothers. I have to snap out of this, I'm not doing the girls any good by allowing them to watch me be demoralized by their father."*

The thought of breaking up the family haunts me. Daddy, leaving me as a child, has had a devastating effect on me. In fact, I spent my adolescence looking for someone to care about me, not knowing why I always had that knot in my stomach or that ever-lurking feeling of emptiness and loneliness. It was at my wedding that I really understood what was wrong with the way I constantly felt. Mom was busy making a living for us, and dad, was just gone. No one was there to stroke my ego. This lacking in a teenage girl can cause her to marry young to the first man who shows her any attention, attaching herself totally to someone else's dream. First, she gives up her power to someone who doesn't deserve it. Then, he takes her power and abuses her with it.

I leave the window when she slams her car door. I rifle through my purse, removing my car keys and wallet which holds my identification and what little cash I have, and I slip those items into the back pocket of my pants underneath my robe. I open the bedroom door and peek down into the living room seeing that it is still deserted. Moving slowly down the hall, I look into the girls' room. Standing in the doorway, I watch their angelic faces as they sleep. I think about their innocence. Jonita is the oldest, and she's like a sponge. She soaks up and analyzes everything that is said or done. I can tell she has figured things out. She is asking questions about the changes in her dad. I believe she is awake sometimes when Jonathan and I have some of those loud discussions concerning his frequent absences from home. As I stand in the doorway watching them, Jonita opens her eyes.

"Are you leaving us again, Ma?"

I walk into the room and sit down on the side of her bed. I lean down and embrace Jonita in an attempt to comfort her.

"Jonita, you're a big girl, so I'll try to tell you as much of the truth as I can."

I try to remain calm and convey some type of real understanding to her, but my mind keeps returning to the reality of Jonathan coming through the door at any moment. I do not want Jonita to see me have to deal with Jonathan's temper.

"Baby, mommy didn't leave you. I needed a few hours to think about what to do."

"About daddy and that lady?" she asks.

"About all of us. Listen, Ma's not going anywhere, so you go back to sleep, stop worrying, and we'll talk tomorrow. OK?"

"Ma, your head is bleeding!"

"I'll be all right, honey. Go to sleep now. We'll talk in the morning."

I cover her up, give her a peck on the cheek, and leave the room, closing the door behind me. I head straight down the stairs, fearing my delay may cost me. Just as I get to the bottom step, Jonathan comes through the front door. He closes it behind him while never taking his stare from me. I know that stone-faced stare. I also know the rage that hides behind it. I can hear tires screeching out of my driveway. I mentally gauge the distance between him and me and the backdoor and me. There will be no beating tonight or any other night ever again. Standing here looking at him repulses me—how could I have ever lived and loved him for so many years? This feeling is new. For the first time, I want to lash out at him with everything in me. I want him dead. I think for a moment that I might be able to grab a knife on my flight through the kitchen to the back door and turn and defend myself for the first time and the last.

In the middle of this insanity, I remember Patricia's words, "Plan your work, and work your plan. Don't allow yourself to be subject to your emotions."

I know not to take my eyes off Jonathan because clearly he does not operate according to any code of honor. Worst of all, he has forgotten everything God has done, especially how it feels to be delivered. He is now only subject to the whims of his flesh, and at this moment, I stand between him and his newest conquest. It isn't he who stopped this little night of romance. She is the one who sees me as an obstacle and decides to leave rather than to stand around and watch him try to make me leave. Plus, I have confused her with my actions. I must have put a little doubt in her mind about her knight in tarnished armor.

Suddenly, Jonathan starts moving toward me, yelling.

"What the hell do you think you're doing? You walked your sorry ass out on us. That left me free to handle my life and the girls any way I see fit."

I say nothing, concentrating on keeping distance between the two of us.

"I've got news for you, bitch, you will not come back here and mess up my good thing."

Still, I will not speak. I just hope that Jonita isn't listening, but I know she is. As he rants, I continue moving through the kitchen toward the back door, keeping him at more than arm's length. He has not physically "corrected" me since he got saved a year ago. Somehow with Mom's death all that has changed. I see that look on his face that is waiting to catch me off guard so that he can "sucker slap" me. That's the kind of man he is. He will try to catch the side of my face with his hand and knock me silly. Then he'll go for the hair, wrapping his fist in my hair and snatching his arm in which ever direction he chooses, and the rest of me will follow without a struggle. *Well, not today, buddy!*

He continues to swear and degrade me, but I turn a deaf ear. I keep my eyes on his body movements and tune out his voice. Today it will be different. If there is a beating, this time, I will not be the only one hurt.

I will also know that it isn't my fault. I did not have it coming, deserve it, cause it, make him do it, or any of the other excuses I have listened to for years. Finally, I can see him for the animal that he really is.

I get the back door open and I'm halfway out when he says, "Stop, Baby, I'm sorry. Come back in. Let's talk." I stand outside in sub-zero weather in house shoes and a robe with my right hand still holding on to the screen door handle. The outside light shone back into his face making him appear to be two people. The light illuminates the face of the man who took me to California and showed me true love and tenderness that I had never known but always wanted. But then he shifts and that part of his face is hidden from the light and the point of my focus. Only the visage of a dark and sinister man is in the light. There is an evil, lying, sneakiness that outlines his features.

While I indulge myself in the stare, searching for his features, looking for my husband, Jonathan steps out of the door and catches hold of my hand that is still holding the latch. At first he holds it gently and continues trying to coax me back into the house, speaking in his smooth lover tone that I have fallen for so many times before. But I resolve myself to a plan of action, and this time, all of me is able to see through him and resist the monster that lives beneath the words. I begin pulling away, trying to get him to release my wrist. That's when his tone changes. He begins ranting again. He holds my wrist with both hands and is literally dragging me back into the house. This time I will not go silently.

I begin screaming, "STOP! LET ME GO!"

My screams are ignored. I pull back in the other direction with all my strength, risking dislocating my arm at the shoulder. This resistance is unexpected and yields me a few feet backwards, away from the door and dead center into the driveway. More ground could have been gained had it not been for my slippery house shoes on the frozen pavement.

Jonathan first looks stunned, then angrier than ever. After recovering from my unexpected resistance, he comes at me, now holding my wrist with only one hand. His intention is to pick me up and carry me back into our home, his torture chamber, where no one will hear my cries, my objections, my pleading, or my surrender. He stoops down trying to wrap his arms around my knees, forcing me to fall forward onto his shoulders. If he's successful, I know I will be helpless. I have to stop this. I look around desperately for something with which to defend myself. I remember the telephone. As I scuffle and wiggle, struggling to get free from him, I slip my left hand in my robe pocket and retrieve the cordless phone. It fills my entire hand. He is still bent down and does not notice my weapon. I know I'll only have one shot at him; then it will be his turn.

Continuously flailing my legs buys me enough time to keep him from disabling me. I'm straining every part of my fingers and hand turning the phone around in my hand pointing the sharpest part of the phone downward toward his face, aiming at his temple. He is making growling noises under his breath. His heavy breathing lets me know I am giving him a little trouble. I continue screaming and wondering where my ghosts are. Finally, I'm ready and I know I only get one shot. I raise my arm as high as it will go and then bring it and phone down as hard as I can, striking the side of his face as near to him temple as possible. That's my "sucker punch."

The impact is so powerful that the phone breaks into pieces and drops to the ground. It also breaks his hold on me causing him to fall backwards, but directly into my path. Realizing I am free, I close my eyes and jump over him, landing crazily, like a beginning ice skater. Without stopping or looking back, I slip and slide across the driveway, fleeing toward the street. As I reach the sidewalk, I see the police cruiser with its lights flashing, but there is no siren screaming through the night, no sense of urgency. Why are they here? I had not called them. But that doesn't matter. I am free and I fought back. I am standing at the edge of my driveway breathing hard, looking frantic, but feeling strong. Some impulse prompts me to look up and around. I spin around and look again. This time I see them. They are there now, in the windows and spilling out onto the street. One of the ghosts goes over to the officer, who is now standing in front of my driveway, and he speaks quietly to him pointing past me toward Jonathan.

Jonathan gets to his feet and stumbles the few feet it takes to reach the officer. He has composed himself and begins telling the officer in his wounded voice how I assaulted him for no reason. He says that I just took the phone and broke it on his face. He picks up the pieces of the phone, ignoring my presence, showing the officer how his injury occurred. As he speaks to them, he steps in a direction away from me; instinctively, the officers follow. I watch quietly, beginning to feel defenseless as Jonathan tries to portray me to the officer as violent and disturbed endangering him and the lives of our girls. When the officer returns to me, my first impulse is to assume the position, spread eagle and surrender. Instead, he asks me in a compassionate voice, "Were you defending yourself?"

I stand trembling almost unable to speak.

"Yes."

He says he's calling an ambulance and that Jonathan is going to jail. I'm totally confused. I don't realize during the struggle that my cut has reopened and is bleeding down my face onto my clothes. I don't feel a thing, but I apparently look a bloody mess, which does not line up with Jonathan's story. The officer cuffs him and puts him in the back of a squad car. He stares that stare at me through the window. But, the stare doesn't work if I'm not looking, so I turn my head and ignore him. I have finally had enough, and apparently so have my ghosts.

The paramedics wrap a blanket around me, clean up my face, and place a few butterfly bandages tightly across the cut on my forehead. They say the cut looks a lot worse than it is and that the scar should be minimal. They suggest I visit my personal physician in a few days. I get to my feet and stand at the head of my driveway. The squad car with Jonathan in the back pulls off, the paramedics leave, and one by one the ghosts leave. As I look up at the windows they smile and sort of nod and vacate their windows. They let me know that I am not alone. I turn around and head up the driveway to the back door. When I open the screen door, I find Jonita curled up on the floor, cowering down, with her eyes closed, and her ears covered, sobbing as though someone has died.

CHAPTER NINE

This night has been a victory—the first victory I've had in more than fifteen years. However, even victory is not without its casualties. My baby is terrified and will probably be scarred for life. Unfortunately, I am no more equipped to repair her young, damaged life than I am to rebuild my own. All I know to do is hold her. I help her upstairs and take her to my bedroom. I release her long enough to take both my hands and, in one swooping motion, flinging all those insulting rose petals from my bed to the floor. I put Jonita to bed with me. I hold her like a baby and rock her and sing to her until she quiets down and falls asleep. Then I ease her over onto a pillow and push another one up against her and slip out of the bed.

I go into the girls' room to check on the other two. They are still sleeping. As I make my way downstairs to the kitchen, my mind is again flooded with questions. *What do I do now? At this point I've gotten Jonathan out of the house, but is this what I want? It doesn't feel as good as I thought it would. I thought I would feel happy. All I feel is sadness and impending doom. Do I even know what I want? Keep your nerve, girl! Don't go back without a plan! I know what I must do. My girls are depending on me. I'm depending on me.*

I start the kettle for coffee and pick up the phone to call Patricia.

"Hey, baby, I've been praying for you. Is everything all right?"

I start from the beginning and tell Patricia everything that happened tonight. I am surprisingly calm. There are no tears, no emotion, just a recounting of the events. Pat says that I'm halfway there. Controlling my emotions is the hardest part of all. As Pat talks, things become clearer to me. I am not so afraid of tomorrow. There are things I must do, and I am ready to begin.

I hang up with Pat and sit quietly sipping my coffee. It's funny; at 2 a.m., I'm sipping coffee. It has never had an insomnia affect on me, which is why I can drink it anytime. In fact, it relaxes me. I finish, leave my cup on the table, and go into the living room to lie down on the couch. Finally, I sleep.

***

I don't know what the ghosts told the police officers yesterday, but apparently Jonathan's silver tongue did not work this time. Ironically, I get a call from Jonathan's former girlfriend, Gabrielle. She introduces herself and speaks a little hesitantly. Gabby says she read Jonathan's paperwork that came across her desk at the county courthouse. She says she is immediately reminded of why they had broken up some years ago. She recalls having spent many nights recovering from his choke holds when he could not get from her what he wanted. She thought I might want to know what's been going on with his case. She doesn't wait for my response; she goes on to give me a blow-by-blow account of Jonathan's encounters at the jail.

Once the officers refused to listen to Jonathan's version of the truth, she says he tried his verbal abuse tactics on them. Our police department has long been known for its lack of tolerance for abusive men. When cursing and yelling didn't work, he began pushing his handcuffed body up against the smaller officer, trying to bully him into listening to his story. I guess it really wasn't Jonathan's lucky night. It turns out, according to Gabby, that the short officer he pushed and his mother had been terrorized by an abusive man most of his young life. Dealing with Jonathan brought back horrifying memories of his dad. Jonathan butting up against the officer sent the officer into action. The officer responded with a head-butt that knocked Jonathan to the ground. The cop placed his knee in the middle of his back and let go of a few choice words

89

before pulling Jonathan up to his feet. The swift and sudden retaliation of the officer won Jonathan's cooperation and his silence. Assaulting an officer was added to his charges.

Jonathan managed to bring out the worst in the officers and everything, including a deep cavity search, was justifiably implemented. Gabby implies that his paperwork may disappear for few days due to someone's error, which will ensure him a longer stay. I think she is trying to tell me I have a few days before I have to worry about seeing Jonathan. Gabby's call is strange but appreciated. This knowledge frees me somewhat and gives me time to decide what to do next and to straighten things out at home without worrying about Jonathan showing up unexpectedly.

The first thing I have to do is deal with the phone calls. The phone rings all day and all night. Each time I answer, the person on the other end hangs up. I refuse to allow that to distract or frustrate me. I find an old answering machine and hook it up to the phone.

The message says, "Hello, if you are calling for Jonathan, he's not here. I don't think he'll be returning. However, if you're calling for his wife, leave a message, and she'll call you back as soon as possible."

The machine is doing its job and gives me peace of mind. My next order of business is to return the girls to their regular schedules. I have finished all but two classes, which I have been given incompletes. I need to contact those teachers to take the finals. I am able to focus and do those things during the next few days. I also have an interview at a temporary agency that employs nurses.

Despite all that is going wrong in my life, these past few days have also yielded me a measure of success. I pass the finals and all my information has been submitted to receive my diploma. I do not have a need to participate in the graduation ceremony, so I get the temporary job and start working the next day at the county hospital as an RN in the infectious disease unit.

***

A week has gone by since the ghosts came to my rescue, and I haven't heard a word from Jonathan. The hang-up calls have stopped, so

I figure the cross-eyed lady knows where to find him. Lucky her! It is just a matter of time before she will really know who he is. Jovida and Jolisa both make inquiries about their daddy, but Jonita remains silent on the subject. Wanting to be left alone, she's almost 13 years old now, and I can see her pulling away from the younger girls. She's a beautiful young girl, the spitting image of her dad, but already I see a lack of confidence creeping in like a poisonous vapor determined to destroy all that lies in its path. She thinks her daddy left her for his other family. I know this is going to take real work; unfortunately, I'll have to take care of my problems first.

Three weeks have passed. Jonathan has not called nor has he tried to see the girls. I get my first full paycheck from the temporary service today. Because I haven't spoken to Jonathan, I don't know if our bills are paid or not. He didn't leave me any money, but I learned long ago that stealing from the grocery money for a rainy day is a good idea. The lights, gas, and telephone are still on and the mail is piling up. I have never paid any bills in the past. Even when my inheritance was paying the bills, Jonathan just told me how much he needed and I went to the bank and got the money. I decide to leave the bills where Jonathan usually stacks them for now.

Fear about how we are going to survive on my temporary job and the few dollars I have left from my inheritance is starting to worry me. I know that some plan has to be put into action about my marriage, but I still choose to do nothing. None of his family members have called either. It is as though we have disappeared from the face of the earth as far as they are all concerned. I try not to let these hurtful thoughts penetrate me. I do what I know to do to survive for the moment.

CHAPTER TEN

Day by day, I realize that fear is starting to become my constant companion. I fear what people think of me losing my man to the cross-eyed lady. I fear the lights going out. I fear not having the money when the lights do go out. I fear making a mistake at work and getting fired. I fear the shutdown and deterioration of childhood that I see in Jonita. I fear telling anyone about my fears. Most of all, I fear Jonathan's return.

Kathy calls today to encourage me to take the kids and go with her on a weekend retreat with the church. It's free, with lots of activities for the kids, and an opportunity for all moms to get a break from their children and meditate on God. After much pleading on her part, I agree.

I get off early Friday afternoon, pick up the girls, and we are ready to go by 5 p.m. Kathy has rented a van so that we can all ride together. Before she picks us up, I check all the windows and lock all doors. We load up and start to the retreat campground. Kathy is busy chattering about one thing or another, but I'm not really listening. Something is nagging at me. I have forgotten to do something, and for the life of me I cannot remember what. Eventually, I dismiss it and I try hard to enjoy myself.

After a while the hum of the engine, the passing of the never-ending white lines in the road, and the giggling sounds coming from the backseat begin to ease my tension. I almost feel happy. The trip only takes an hour and a half, and we pull up to a quaint, little church that sits on the side of some long, winding road. This small place is not representative of the grounds as a whole. Someone meets us at the small building and gives us directions to the campgrounds, which are several yards further down a dirt road. Finally, we reach a nest of single cabins neatly hidden behind a grove of trees. In the very center of this complex, there stands a beautiful chapel. The stain-glassed windows are glowing from inside, sending out rays of light that look warm and inviting. It makes me think of images I'd read about as a child. My spirits are lifted because I know many of my church friends are here too, some of whom I have not seen much of since Ma died.

After about an hour, the girls settle in with their sitter, and Kathy and I head off to fellowship together. Everyone is very polite, and no one asks me any embarrassing questions. You know news travels fast in a church, and juicy news can move faster than the speed of light. Most of these women were present when Jonathan rushed up front and claimed his deliverance, and those same witnesses know how he has fallen. They look at me with eyes so full of empathy, and with holes burning in their tongues. Their knots of pity are chunked in my throat choking me. They make me sorry that I agreed to come on the retreat. They continue talking and laughing, trying to include me. I smile and nod, but I'm not listening. I am busy summoning up all the courage I have trying not to flee from the room like the wounded animal I feel I have become. I stay and read the scriptures that are posted on the walls. I examine the images and words on the chapel windows, and somehow, the atmosphere of the place forces me to look at my own relationship with Christ.

"I can do all things through Christ…."

"No weapon formed against me shall prosper …"

"They that wait on the Lord …"

I realize I have become so caught up in my own drama that I too have fallen away, not from God, but from regular prayer and devotion, causing me to lose my strength, peace, and joy. I have spent the past few months just trying to keep putting one foot in front of the other attempting to propel myself forward, but now it's clear to me that I have to stand still. Meditation, consecration, and devotion are what I need.

One of the church teenagers comes by for the girls early Saturday morning to engage them in a full day of activities. I am ready as soon as they leave. I go to the picturesque temple on the church grounds. Several women have already come and have started without me, each pulling on God for whatever deliverance they seek. I fall prostrate before God, releasing everything from within that is threatening to snuff me out by breaking my bond with Christ. Soon, my noises are in tune with the other women who were there before me. No one intrudes on my time with God. We are each separate but somehow united as one. I stay all day, denying myself food and water for the day, knowing that some things only come through fasting and prayer. I don't know what to do next in my life, and God's direction is what I'm seeking.

The day flies by, and the small chapel goes from shadowy figures on the wall to total darkness. I like the darkness; it allows me to hide from the world. Only God's eyes can find me, see my hurts, and heal my broken heart. Before getting too comfortable, someone turns on some subdued lights, designed, I suppose, to keep us from falling or crashing into each other. By midnight, I am totally drained. I drag my body back to my cabin. The girls are asleep, still attended by the teen girl who had picked them up that morning. She has been assigned to me for the weekend as my sitter and handmaiden. She has a snack prepared for me and asks if I want her to prepare a bath for me. I tell her that she has already done way more than I can ever repay, and I release her for the night.

As I shower and prepare for bed, I feel a sense of relief. Maybe everything is going to be all right after all. Things are beginning to feel better already. Maybe it is time to see a lawyer. It is time for me to make the first steps to independence. It is time for me to stand up and be a woman. I fall asleep thinking I'm going to make it. Look how far I've already come. It feels good.

Sunday morning arrives bringing with it a whole new sense of purpose and resolve. The first order of business Monday morning is to find an attorney to represent me. I need help financially, and I don't like things being left up in the air the way that they are. I need some closure and some solid rules to follow. I need to know where I stand and how to survive as a divorced, single mom.

By midmorning, Kathy and I load up the kids and start for home. We all sing songs and talk silly talk until we reach my house. Kathy turns into the driveway, and it is at this moment that I remember what I had forgotten to do.

I can't believe it. Kathy has not noticed it, so I don't tell her. The kids file out the van and head for the back door. We wave good-bye to Kathy and go inside. I take a deep breath before entering. It's Jonathan's car that I saw when we pulled up. I meant to get around to changing the lock on the front door, but I didn't. When we come through the kitchen, we see Jonathan sitting on the sofa in the living room. Jovida and Jolisa run straight to him and jump into his lap. Jonita stands stock still at my side. Somehow, I am not surprised to see him. I knew he'd come back sooner or later. That I expected. But, what I didn't count on was him bringing his lady friend. She, too, is sitting in my living room in my favorite chair with her legs crossed, looking as smug as she is ugly. I don't shorten my gaze this time. I look her squarely in the face. I want to take in everything about her. It isn't beauty. Shoot, she isn't even appealing. As I continue my scrutinizing stare, I do notice one thing. My stone face causes her to look away. She begins to fidget and look toward Jonathan who completely ignores us both, busying himself with the two girls. I continue my stare, wondering if she has completely lost her mind coming to my house, this time knowing that I live here. Apparently she has learned nothing. I speak to Jonita without changing my stare.

"Jonita, get your sisters and the three of you go up to your room and close the door behind you. You may turn on the television. I'll be up soon."

When they hear my tone they immediately jump down from their daddy's lap and start up the stairs. I continue staring at the cross-eyed, lady waiting to hear the girls' bedroom door close. When I do, I walk over to the lady and stand directly over her.

"The first time you came here you may not have known this is where I live. Today, you have no excuse and no business here in my home. You are openly disrespecting me, my house, and my children"

The lady continues to sit in my chair, staring back at me as though I were speaking a foreign language. I feel the rage coming. It is surging upward from my feet. I can feel the warmth traveling up through my torso as she continues sitting in my chair, saying nothing. I suddenly remember her face protected behind the motel glass. I remember promising her a beating to match that of her husband's. The heat has risen to my head and my entire face is on fire. She has been given two chances to escape me, but her luck has just run out. Without resisting the temptation, I reach down and grab a hand full of her skinny braids. I twist my hand around in her braids to get a good grip on her head and move from in front of her to behind her before she has a chance to react. This woman will think twice before she parks herself in another woman's house again. When I snatch her head backwards, she really looks surprised. I am determined to snatch her crossed-eyes straight.

At first Jonathan does not move. He just yells for me to stop. He even kind of chuckles. I believe he is enjoying this. When he does get up from the couch, I pull her up from my chair and get her body between him and me. I know he'll continue to betray me, just as he has betrayed her by bringing her to our home. She tried to reach me with her arms, digging in with her nails. I yell commands at her to move this way and that, twisting harder if she does not respond. I'm careful to stay behind her, so she is not able to reach me, and I twist her head every time she gets close. I got this maneuver from Jonathan. Still, I can see Jonathan clearly, and he is definitely enjoying this. Well, one thing is for sure, he is not going to be disappointed. In an attempt to keep her between Jonathan and myself, some of her clawing is working its way through to my hands. I can feel the welts coming. This infuriates me, and I yank her head down and sling her to the floor. Her braids begin to yield to the pressure I put on them, and they come out in patches in my hand. Jonathan is finally able to grab me from behind and pulls me away from her. Immediately, she scrambles to her feet in an attempt to get away. When she is able to get her balance, she runs for the front door almost tearing it from its hinges. Watching her tickles me, but I have other problems. Jonathan is again angry with me, and he has me from behind, trying to take me down. I can hear the girls crying from behind the closed door of their room. The cross-eyed lady runs out leaving my front door open. I start yelling,

"Let me go. People are watching."

He turns his head quickly toward the door to see who is watching. I don't know what stops him. It could be the fear of the police, the cries of the cross-eyed lady, or maybe the cries coming from the girls upstairs. Whatever, it may have been, he releases me immediately and starts toward the door. I get up and gather the pieces of hair she has left behind, and I open the screen door and throw them out at him.

"Don't leave this crap behind; your bitch may need it."

Jonathan doesn't know what to do, so he bends down and picks up the braids and joins his lady friend in his car. Standing at the screen door, I watch them in the car trying to repair her looks. That will take a miracle. If I hadn't been so angry, I would have been on the floor laughing. Man! I have never started a fight in my entire life. The realization of what I have just done frightens me. I begin to tremble. I close the door, make my way to the sofa, and sit down before my legs give way. As shaken as I am, all I can think about is teaching her to respect my home and me. She has Jonathan and that's all she's going to get. Maybe Jonathan will learn a little something too.

Just that quickly, I had forgotten all about my fast and my prayers.

CHAPTER ELEVEN

It's been years since I've worked a full time job. Getting up and out with the girls on a daily basis is truly challenging, but rejuvenating. Our day starts at 5 a.m. with waking them up, putting on clothes, brushing teeth, eating breakfast, and out the door by 6:00. I have them at daycare by 6:15. The two older girls are shuttled to school later on by the center. Even though it's a struggle, we have our routine down pat, and working has been a Godsend. I kiss the girls goodbye and leave them to start my short drive to work. My shift starts at 7 a.m., so I usually get there by 6:35.

Most people cannot begin to imagine what goes on at the county hospital. There is never a dull moment. It is this fact that makes life bearable for me. It's full of distractions from my real life. I come into the hospital through the emergency room, which is just getting revved up to start another day of mayhem. I have no time to focus on their dilemmas because my infectious disease patients are waiting. It's extremely important that I'm alert and fully protected from my patients; and, in many cases, they need to be protected from me. The infectious disease unit is on the top floor of the hospital. I cut straight through emergency and head for the stairs. This is my opportunity to get my daily exercise. I like challenging myself in the morning, sometimes taking two steps at a time, feeling the burn but pushing on anyway. After just a few months of working for the hospital, I have allowed myself a measure of personal success through climbing the stairs. This is the one time where my body will listen to me and follow my commands. Week after week and flight after flight has helped me to feel strong and ready for anything. Maybe it is some of that same strength that made me lash out at the cross-eyed lady. Ah, who am I kidding? She was overdue for a beat down.

Before entering the floor from the stairway, I always stop to catch my breath. This is no place to enter with your mind or body out of sync. This floor is where they house all the known and unknown viruses, bacteria, and AIDS patients. I have gotten used to that, but the hardest part of the job is working with the children. The county cannot afford to have a separate infectious disease section for children, so adults and children are on the top floor together. They are young and don't understand what is happening to them nor why they have to be confined to their rooms or beds. Sometimes they have to be strapped down in order to immobilize them. That is hard for me to take because it makes me think of my own children.

The children with infections usually get visitors; moms, dads, aunts, uncles and other family members come at regular intervals, almost never leaving their precious babies alone. We dress the visitors in paper shoes, gowns, masks, and latex gloves. They shuffle in and out like stiff zombies looking for live bodies to consume. These visitors make my job easier. The children are less frightened and easier to manage. However, the real bonus is that when parents do come, they free us up to spend more time with the children for whom no one comes. We too dress up like Martians and pop in and out of each room, checking temperatures, giving medicines, changing IVs, checking monitors, and reading charts, all while trying to bring a smile to children's faces. When time permits, we pick up the little ones and play games with the older children who aren't too sick to follow along. We take the time to read to them or just watch silly cartoons with them, if we can. I remind myself to be extremely careful with needles and blood, never forgetting that for us, these children could be deadly.

I thought I would be freaked out by the AIDS patients' lesions and deteriorating bodies, but somehow I find myself drawn to them the most. Every chance I get, I spend extra time sitting and talking to those who are too sick to move on their own, many having lost their vision and use of their limbs. For most of them, no one comes. They are alone. I guess I can relate to that feeling of being totally alone and helpless. I want and need to help them, mainly because there seems to be no one to help me.

My job makes me feel useful, important, and worthwhile. People actually thank me and appreciate my help. This has done a lot for my self-esteem. At work, I am in control of my destiny. I always do my best and work hard. After only a few months here, human resources called me down asking if I was interested in a permanent position at the hospital. Of course, this is exactly what I had hoped for. Things keep looking up. Some of my goals are actually being met. Heck, who knew I even had goals? It's all a surprise to me. Fifteen years ago my highest aspiration was to be Jonathan's young wife and a good mom someday. I have hung on to the good mommy part, but I've grown out of the other.

That reminds me, I need to speak with Kathy about finding a lawyer. I know I've been avoiding what seems like an obvious decision. I admit it makes sense that my next step should be to file for legal separation and child support, yet it's a real struggle. Letting go and feeling like a failure is a hard pill to swallow. Hard or not, I know I have to stand my ground. Besides, I have to do something. Jonathan's been gone for almost two months and hasn't paid one bill. I finally decide to go through the pile of bills sitting on the desk and I've paid the light, gas, and phone bills and bought the groceries; and I spend the balance of my pay on childcare. Jonathan is living free and clear and probably paying someone else's bills while our mortgage is being ignored. He hasn't just abandoned me, but the girls too. Before long we may find ourselves out on the street. Better yet, he'll force us out and bring his new family in if I don't protect myself.

As I travel from room to room, I try hard not to get too attached to the patients. My emotions are already fragile. I can see that some of my patients will not recover, but I haven't lost one yet. Sometimes after lunch, when all the meds have been distributed and vitals have been taken and things slow down before the shift change, I visit Mr. Andrews in room 403. He's a fairly young man who's dying of AIDS. He's almost totally blind; he's lost control of his bowels; and, he has no T cells left. Yet, talking with him always encourages me. He tells me how he spent much of his life being a womanizer, and how much he now regrets it. He says it's taken all this to see what he has done to himself and his family. What encourages me about him is that somehow he has made peace with his situation. He's not angry or bitter that no one comes to visit. He doesn't complain because he realizes that things could have been different. The choices were his. His family knows where he is; they just can't deal with the way he is, so they stay away. Sometimes he has me write them notes of apology. When I finish, he always has me fold it up and put it in a drawer. When I ask why he never mails them he says, "It's too late for apologies. I write them because I am truly sorry." He does this nearly every day. I find myself praying every day that when tomorrow comes, he'll still be here for me.

Mr. Andrews's disease makes him horrible to look at, so I avoid looking directly at him. He had probably been of average stature, but he now lies before me barely weighing ninety pounds. His face is sunken in, his skin is covered with lesions, and his eyes hardly ever open. I have to be careful because sometimes his lesions bleed. The other nurses are happy that I am his favorite and send me to his room whenever he needs help. At first, I talked very little about myself, but as weeks pass and we talk more, he gets more out of me than I intend to share. Mr. Andrews has gotten quite good at seeing people without seeing them. He has a way of putting people at ease when he speaks. I eventually get over his looks and feel his heart. Soon, we talk about all my troubles. After all, who is he going to tell? He keeps encouraging me to be strong.

"Don't let him push you around like I did my wife. I wish she would have stopped me. A man will use you as long as you let him. He won't stop until you do."

***

After work, I pick up Jonita and Jolisa from after school care and Jovida from the daycare. The real work is about to start once we get home. Thank God that Jonita has become my left arm. She decided on her own to take over caring for Jolisa and Jovida. She gets them unbuckled from the car, brings them in, takes off coats and boots, gets them a snack, and helps Jolisa with homework and entertains Jovida. This gives me time to start dinner right away. The early shift allows me more time with the girls in the evening. I usually have dinner on the table by 5 p.m. That leaves time for watching cartoons with the girls, checking Jonita's homework, bathing everyone, prayers and 8:30 bedtime for the younger two. By 9:00 everyone is in bed.

For me, bedtime is the worst. There is only me. There is no one to share the day's activities with, no adult conversation. Even Kathy needs a break from my drama. I try not to bother her unless the loneliness becomes too unbearable. To busy myself until sleep arrives, I decide to use this free time to catch up on all the reading I intended to do but never had time for. My favorite types of books are murder mysteries. Looking for clues and paying attention to details make books exciting for me. My evening companion lay dog-eared, showing want of a reunion with its delinquent reader. I flip through the pages prior to my marker to try to refresh my memory. I am just settling in, remembering the villain, when the phone rings. It startles me, and I drop the book on the floor next to the bed. At first I decide to let the answering machine get it, but for some reason, maybe it's my desire for human contact, I change my mind and lift the receiver.

"Hey."

My heart skips a beat, and I hesitate before answering.

I answer "Hey."

"How are my girls?"

"They are getting along fine, thank you."

Why did I say thank you? That was dumb. Why am I so awkward? Is my heart betraying me again?

"How have you been?"

"I'm OK."

"I miss you all."

Yes, my heart is definitely trying to betray me. I feel a large knot in my throat, and I can barely breathe. I have to pull myself together quickly.

"It's getting late and I have to get up early. Maybe you can call me tomorrow. We need to talk about some things anyway."

"Can I stop by tomorrow?"

"I don't know. Call me tomorrow. I've got to go."

I hang up the phone fast without giving him a chance to break down my defenses.

Why am I so upset? Surely I knew he would call sooner or later. I wonder if the lady with the five kids got to be too much for the "daddy of the year." Stop it girl; now you're just being catty.

I pick up my book and try to read again. I read the next page three times and still have no idea what's happening. Just as I am about to give up, I hear a knock at the door. I jump up and peek out the window. It's Jonathan.

I hadn't taken any special care when I put on my night clothes, but I did take the time to untie my hair and straighten out my PJs before opening the door. I offer him a chair at the kitchen table and put on some coffee. He apparently needs to talk. It seems that his lady friend is more in love with her drug addict husband than she thought. While she runs around with my husband, her husband checks himself into a treatment program. That's where he has been for the past few months. He gets out and comes to claim his family, and Jonathan is living in his house. That leads to both of them wanting to flex their muscles and fight for the damsel in distress. Eventually, the police come and the cross-eyed lady tells Jonathan to leave.

So, I guess you know his next question. I can hear you yelling at me to wake up. I hear you yelling, but something inside is yelling louder. Besides, I'm so lonely. *This man is still my husband, and he's been my life for years. You don't want to throw all that away too quickly. Lord knows we have to be less trouble than the lady he just left. Anyway, he needs my help.*

"Do you think I could crash on the couch tonight? I'll find somewhere to go tomorrow."

"Jonathan, I'm not sure if that's such a good idea." I protest.

"Baby, I promise; it's just one night. I need your help."

I want to say no. This can only spell trouble. I know it will not turn out well, but I can't say no.

"OK, Jonathan. I need to get to bed. I have to get up early. I'll get you a pillow and blanket for the couch."

I get the linens from upstairs and give it to Jonathan. I say good night and go back to bed.

I toss and turn for at least an hour before falling asleep. Suddenly, I am awakened feeling my breath being cut off. When I open my eyes, Jonathan is lying on top of me. The dim light shining through the window exposes his naked body to me. He is talking to me.

"Babe, I miss you. I need you so much. You remember how it used to be, don't you?" I start trying to push him off me.

He says, "Keep your voice down, the girls will hear and be frightened."

I demand repeatedly, "Jonathan, stop! Get off me."

He ignores me and begins shifting his weight from side to side in order to remove my panties. At one point, he puts his hand over my mouth, telling me to be quiet and listen.

"I have always loved you. I know you love me too. I need this and you want me too. Besides, you have this coming; you owe me this. You caused me a lot of trouble, so this is nothing. I'm a man. You know what I need. You let me in. You know this is what you wanted. You found out how hard it is to find a good man. That's why you don't have one here to replace me already. You ain't goin' to have one either. No man will be over my girls. You and them are going to have me, like it or not. Now stop moving before I really hurt you, and Jonita will know all about that too."

His last words strike me just as though he had slapped me, and I stop resisting. It's difficult for me to breathe.

As he penetrates me he says, "Be glad! This is for you."

He goes to work with his body. There is nothing beautiful about him. Our bodies are not in sync. There is no ecstasy for me, only horror. I stop fighting and I stop feeling. Something dies. I accept my fate and lie still until he finishes. I feel ill, but I don't move. I brought this on myself. I had him out of the house and my life, but I let him back in. He's right. I had this coming.

Jonathan finally releases me, gets up, and goes back downstairs to the sofa I had prepared for him. I don't say a word, nor does he look back. He's right; I asked for it. I roll over and face the wall. At 5 o'clock I get up, take a shower, dress the kids, and we all leave the house. Of course they see Jonathan on the couch. No one is allowed to wake him; we leave him in my house sleeping.

***

I drop everyone off and hurry to work. I change quickly and head for Mr. Andrews' room. He is not in his bed. I look for his chart. It, too, is gone. The head nurse calls me to the side and tells me that Mr. Andrews died during the night. His body has already been sent to the morgue. I know I should have been prepared for his death, but I'm not; I'm shocked by the news. I need to talk to him and he's gone. He could help me through my episode, but he's gone. I have to face the facts. I made this mistake, and it's up to me to figure things out, not Mr. Andrews, not Pat, not Ma, but me. For a moment, I have to wonder if I think for myself at all. I've spent my whole adult life looking for someone else to make me happy. I have to make some steps toward taking my life back. Mr. Andrews told me, and Patricia told me. Today has to be different; I have to stop feeling sorry for poor me and open my eyes to see what I can do for myself.

I volunteer to take care of Mr. Andrew's personal effects. The light in his room is off. It should feel cold and lonely, but it doesn't. Since he couldn't see anymore, he often had me sit with him in the dimly lit room. It feels like he is still here. I smile to myself remembering how he liked to laugh. I'd share some of the girls' antics with him, and he'd give me his best laugh. He always felt better, he said, after a good laugh.

I'm careful to protect myself from the body fluids Mr. Andrews has left behind. I wrap the remaining sheets from the bed into a small bundle. His clothes and shoes are already in a neat pile on the small closet floor. They, too, are laid on the bed. Then I open up the nightstand drawers. As I collect all his letters from the night table and find an envelope in which to store them, I find myself weeping silently. This is my first patient death.

I drag through my daily duties almost unaware of anyone's presence. No one knows the pain I feel right now, and I keep silent. Mr. Andrews would have known what to say. I miss him already. It surprises me that I'm not feeling sad for myself anymore. In fact, it is good that Mr. Andrews' suffering is finally over. I just wish I had had a chance to say goodbye.

Earlier, I had left everything belonging to Mr. Andrews in the room, while waiting for all the final paperwork to come up to our floor. Later in the day when I'm ready to send his personal effects to his family, I come across the large envelope with the letters. I give it considerable thought before I address the envelope to mail all the letters of apology I had written for him to his wife and children. I kind of think that's what he wanted me to do. If it wasn't too late then, it's surely too late now. But I send the letters anyway. I include a short note:

Dear Mrs. Andrews,

I never met you but Mr. Andrews told me how much he loved you and your family. He didn't realize the mistakes he was making until it was too late. He had me write these letters as a form of punishment to himself. He's gone now, but please read the letters and know once and for all that he did love you all. Then free yourself by forgiving him.

The rest of the day simply slips away. I know my mind is not on the job. I try continuously to evaluate what happened to me the night before. I have done a good job of pushing past the episode to keep moving forward. I have to open one of those drawers in the dresser of my subconscious and stuff every bit of this violent violation inside and quickly close it so that none will spill out and corrupt me. His words keep repeating in my head.

"Be glad! This is for you. Jonita will know this too."

Was that what I really wanted? Maybe? Was that how I wanted it? No! Do I get to choose? What about Jonita? Let it go, girl. Remember, no emotion. You have a job to do. What about your plan?

CHAPTER TWELVE

The shift has changed, and it's time to go home. Yet, I linger around to do some paperwork. I know it's time to go, but I don't want to leave. Work has become my refuge. Now, however, even my refuge has changed. Mr. Andrews is gone.

Returning home this night will be more than difficult. I left Jonathan sleeping, not knowing his schedule or his plans. I do know one thing for sure. He feels he has made a conquest and his position at home has been re-established. We are even now. Rape is my punishment for having him arrested and putting him out of his home. Everything should return to business as usual. That's how he thinks.

Finally, I leave the hospital. I've stayed as long as I dare; I have to leave to pick up the girls. I decide to take the stairs. I can be alone and not share my grief with anyone. Avoiding people means avoiding the awkward questions that concerned co-workers, family, and friends tend to ask. I can feel depression trying to creep in on me, but there is no time for depression. I have to pick up the girls, cook dinner, help with homework, clean house, do at least one load of laundry, and expect to get raped again.

There is no place to go, nowhere to run. I can only go home. I get to the daycare center and after school care later than usual. The two younger girls are excited about going home. They ask a million questions about their daddy as we travel the short distance toward home. They want to know if daddy will be home. I don't answer them because they ask questions to which I have no answers.

I get a glimpse of Jonita's face in the rearview mirror. It catches me off guard. There is coldness in her eyes. They are not the eyes of a child, but that of a woman scorned. I cannot break my stare. Her look has become the manifestation of all my pain and heartache. I recognize all my agony in her face. This scares me even more. An attack of sirens breaks my stare, returning my attention to the road and finding that I need to jerk the wheel hard to avoid being in harm's way.

I don't know why, but it just begins to occur to me that I have not planned things well enough to foresee all the events that are tugging at me simultaneously. I need to deal with Jonita immediately, before things (whatever they are) change her forever. She has barely spoken at all since the incident with the police.

I try to ignore the other two girls who are still chuckling and screaming with delight from when I swerved the car. I keep my eyes straight ahead until I can no longer resist looking back again at Jonita. There is no smile, no laughter, just terror. It is covering her entire face. Somehow it seems that she knows the terror I'm feeling right now in my own heart. Maybe she had been awake last night. Maybe she'd heard the things he said to me. Maybe she'd heard me beg him to stop. Maybe she knows what rape sounds like. I can feel the tears swelling up in my eyes, but I have to hold them back. I have to have courage. Running away is not an option. There is no place to go but home. If Jonathan is there, I have to face him.

The 10-minute ride from the day care takes me twenty minutes because I slow-poke around, going the long way looking to tie myself up in traffic. Had it not been for the younger girls beginning the "I'm hungry" whine, I would have gone further out of the way, circling a few more blocks. I work on convincing myself that things can't get any worse. Things have to go up from here because I'm already on the bottom. I just have to pull myself together and go on with my plan to escape.

We finally reach our street. A sense of pure terror envelops me. I don't realize I'm not breathing. As I pull up slowly to the driveway, the fence that separates my property from that of my ghosts on the left prevents me from seeing into the driveway until I am turning in.

Originally, I thought Jonathan had insisted on buying the high privacy fence to protect our girls from intruders or wanderers who might seek to harm our unsuspecting children. However, it is now clear to me that it is meant to be just what it has been, our prison. Its true purpose is to keep the eyes out and us captive inside.

Prior to my starting nursing school, my sole objective was to serve Jonathan and the girls. It had been enough for me, and I wore my badge proudly: Domestic Engineer, Stay-at-Home Mom. I even endured the label Chief Cook and Bottle Washer. In fact, in retrospect, I realize that going to school wasn't just for my benefit. He got the pleasure of many hours of free time with me being preoccupied with classes and the children. His refusal to watch the girls while I was gone all day gave him time to do God knows what.

I drive past the fence and pull into the driveway. It's there. I knew it would be. I hoped it would not be, but I knew it would. Just for a brief moment, I marveled at how much I really did know about him. As I park the car and begin to unbuckle the girls, I have no trouble turning my face to stone. My heart has already made the journey. Heaviness comes over me and makes every movement a painstaking one. The two younger girls are almost screaming to get out of the car. The garage door is up, and they can see their daddy's car parked inside. I notice that I'm sweating while I find my door keys to enter the house. I must return to my torture chamber, shackles, and lead boots. I tell myself to put on the mask. I kiss my babies as they exit the car. I look back into Jonita's face. She does not share the excitement of the other two girls. Her expression is solemn, and she does not say anything.

Once I get the door open, Jovida and Jolisa tear though the house looking and yelling for their father. Jonita and I just stand in the kitchen doorway, not sure what to do. I know she's not quite 13 years old, but she has an old soul. She does her best to help with the girls, and I appreciate that. But, there is something unnatural about her overly serious behavior. She doesn't smile anymore. I am worried about her. All the pressure I'm under is trying to drain me of what it takes for me to go on. I'm determined to continue regardless of the struggle. I pray that I can rescue Jonita from this downward spiral of emotions that has invaded my child. I stop Jonita after we get inside. I wrap my arms around her and hold her close.

"I love you, baby."

"I know, Ma."

"I promise, everything will be all right. Just hold on. Trust me."

"I do."

Jolisa and Jovida find Jonathan upstairs. Of course he's in my bed. I don't think he's been to work today. A closer look into the room from the doorway reveals to me that he has moved all of his things back in. Jonathan looks up from the girls and says the infamous, "Hey."

You rape me the night before and all I get is a "Hey." You cheat on me with a girl from work and stay out all night, change the locks on my house, move your girlfriend and her five kids into my house, and all I get is "Hey?"

Without saying a word, I turn from the doorway and go downstairs into the kitchen to begin preparing dinner. That's when I catch the smell and realize someone has been cooking. I fight back the tears of despair. I don't want to frighten the girls, but I feel like I'm being held hostage. I'm stuck with no way out. Right now I know it's important that I pretend that everything is all right, especially for Jonita.

Jonathan is no cook. It didn't matter anyway. Before I can get my boots and coat off, he is downstairs, making like everything is great.

"Hey, baby, let me help you with that. I know you had a long day. I expected you to be home before now."

I do not reply. I allow him to help with my boots. All three of the girls are watching. Jonathan is putting on a great show. I know that my refusal will require me to speak and I hate him too much to speak.

"What took you so long? I thought maybe you may have gotten the idea to run away again and take the girls with you." Again, I don't answer. I'm careful not to make eye contact.

"Oh, I see, you want to give me the silent treatment."

Before I can say anything, Jolisa and Jovida come flying over to their dad grabbing one arm a piece begging him to come off with them to eat.

"Daddy, we smell food," yells Jolisa. "Did you cook for us? What did you make? Let's eat!"

Their interruption is enough for Jonathan to release his attention from me. I jump up and offer to fix the girls' plates. They insist that their daddy do it. They are not taking no for an answer as they both begin pushing him into the kitchen, one on each side tugging and prodding him to attend to them alone. Apparently, he has made hamburgers for dinner. Once Jonathan and the girls are in the kitchen, I look up and see Jonita at the top of the stairs.

"Jonita, go into the kitchen with your dad and sisters so that you can eat dinner."

"I'm not hungry, Ma."

"Jonita, please try to eat. I'm worried about you."

"Ma, if I go into the kitchen with Dad, will you go too?"

"Nita, you don't need me in there to eat. Come on down."

"Ma, if you don't come in too, I'm not going either."

"Girl, what is wrong with you? You don't tell me what you will or won't do."

My voice is elevated. Though I know I'm not mad with Jonita, I feel the anger in my voice. This is the most she has spoken in weeks, but I don't like what she is saying, regardless of what her problem is. At this moment, I have enough problems without dealing with her disobedience too.

Apparently, Jonathan hears her too and comes into the living room. As he enters the doorway far enough for Jonita to see him, she turns and runs into her room and slams the door. Her behavior surprises me, but I remain seated trying to figure out what has just happened. But before I can decide my next move, Jonathan starts up the stairs, yelling Jonita's name.

"Jonathan, leave her alone for awhile."

I know Jonathan doesn't like being told what to do. I make sure that my response sounds like a request. Jonathan, to my knowledge, has never been rough with the girls as far as discipline is concerned; that's my job. But, as he turns to go up the stairs, I see something in his eyes. It's a look I've seen directed toward me before. He needs to be stopped.

"Come on. I'll come in the kitchen with you and the girls. They are probably making a mess over your hard work. Come on."

The last two words are spoken with a sound of invitation. I muster the sweet voice of an angel to catch his attention with the promise of more. It makes my stomach turn. He stops at the top step and turns to face me. I walk past him into the kitchen, praying my cooing has worked. I glance back over my shoulder to see him coming down the steps. Quickly, without him noticing, I release my breath.

I'm mad at myself for having to play seductress with Jonathan, but I subconsciously considered how ugly it could get if he turns his anger on Jonita. I can't risk that happening. I can't be held responsible for what might happen to him or me if he hurts my child. I pray that he has other things on his mind and does not try to capitalize on what he supposed was an invitation. Once in the kitchen, the girls provide a new distraction. They are making such a mess that even Jonathan has to notice and make an effort to clean it up and put a stop to the horseplay. They have him so wrapped up that he completely ignores me. He gets their hands wiped, gets them down from the table, and exits the kitchen, and quickly goes back to the bedroom as though he were afraid that I'd ask him to clean up the mess.

After they finish eating, I hang around the kitchen. I just pick over my food until I finally decide to give it up and clean the kitchen. The girls go up to their room to play. As I begin cleaning the kitchen, my tears drop freely into the dishwater and create a kind of wave in the water that causes a plunking sound that vibrates the water and sends tiny splashes of water back up toward me. *Pull yourself together, girl. Think! Think! How are you going to handle this? You are not beaten!*

Jonita comes downstairs and breaks up my unproductive planning process. I try to hide my red eyes from her, but I know she sees them. She knows, but she doesn't say anything. She just starts helping me with the kitchen.

Before long, it's bedtime. This has been my secret dread. Nothing is going to make me get into the bed with Jonathan. The girls know our routine and are in the tub by the time I get upstairs. I finish them up, put them in pajamas, and I'm ready to tuck them into bed. First, the girls have to say their prayer. We all get on our knees and Jolisa starts the prayer. "Lord, thank you for my mommy. Thank you for bringing my daddy home forever. Thank you... Amen." I know their dad will not be staying. That is not part of my plan. Nevertheless, I do not discourage them. The girls deserve to be happy as long as it lasts.

After getting the girls to bed and lights out, I go downstairs to the couch. All the bedding I had given Jonathan the night before is laying half on the couch and half on the floor. I decide that this is going to be my new home, so I might as well make it comfortable. As I spread the blanket out and prepare for bed, I continue looking upstairs, not wanting Jonathan catching me unaware of his presence. I undress quickly, jump into my gown, then between the sheets, and I settle myself for the night. If he got up, I don't know it. He does not bother me tonight, and I sleep deeply.

CHAPTER THIRTEEN

The weeks have gone by very slowly since Jonathan's violent return. I've managed to make myself comfortable on the couch. Jonathan makes little or no attempts to be civil to me. I guess he has decided that I am not worth the effort, so he does his own thing, He comes and goes at whatever times he chooses, trying if possible to say nothing at all to me. Financially, he pays the mortgage, but I'm still responsible for everything else. Again, he throws this month's house note on the sofa, for me to mail, as he goes out the door. He thinks we're even. He thinks everything is square with us, but he's dead wrong.

The younger girls are still happy to have their daddy here. They don't ask me questions about me sleeping on the sofa or why Daddy locks his door. It seems that they instinctively do not want to rock the boat. He spends a little time with them when he's home. He doesn't take them anywhere, or read with them, or do anything that requires anything physical. He basically tickles them and lies in the bed with them watching television. They climb all over him and play with his hair and usually fall asleep, if he stays long enough.

However, Jonita's behavior is another story. She doesn't lie in the bed with them anymore to watch television or to get tickled like she used to. She has created a wide gulf between her and her father. When he comes home, I have seen the way she stiffens up. She used to be just as excited as the other two girls, but not anymore. When he comes into the girls' room, she leaves the room and goes to the basement. At first I thought she was being rude to him because of the trouble between Jonathan and me, but now I'm not so sure. There seems to be something else that's bothering her. She seems to be so angry. To tell the truth, I'm afraid to know what's really wrong. I don't feel like I can deal with one more thing.

***

I guess I reached my limit too soon because today I get a call from Jonita's teacher. She informs me that Jonita has been acting out in class. She is angry all the time. She has verbal outbursts directed mostly to the other students, particularly the boys, but sometimes it's directed toward the teacher, too. I asked how long this has been going on. She tells me that Jonita's behavior has been changing during the last few months, but it got really bad within the last few weeks. Furthermore, she isn't doing her work in class, nor is she turning in her homework. At this point, she is in danger of not passing to eighth grade.

This is definitely an unexpected blow. I realized awhile back that Jonita was having problems, but I hoped that the problems would just straighten themselves out. My preoccupation with the Jonathan drama has clouded my vision as far as my children are concerned. I have been convincing myself that if I just hope and pray hard enough, everything will work itself out. It is now clear that that's not going to happen. This is going to be work.

I immediately call Jonita after speaking with her teacher. Jonita gets very defensive, telling me that I don't understand what's going on. I confess to her that I don't know what's going on, but I want to know. She then begins to cry—not the little girl, I've done something wrong cry. She's crying like someone has tormented her. I am upset about the school report, but I become more upset about Jonita's reactions to my questions. There is something else going on. I intend to get to the bottom of it. It's clear however, that it's going to take time for me to find out what's really wrong. I'm almost afraid to know the true problem, but this is my baby. I refuse to rest until I know.

***

This is one of those restless nights, when tossing and turning all night seems to be my fate. I find myself half in and half out of sleep all night long. That's when I hear it. The sound is so familiar that it causes me to doubt whether or not I am awake. I shake off the remnants of the lingering twilight and sit up on the couch and listen. I am not mistaken. It is what I think it is. Slowly, I throw off the covers and make my way up the stairs and head toward the bathroom. That's where I find him on his hands and knees with his face inside the toilet. I just stand and watch in disbelief. I have been here before. This time, there is no pity in my heart; I would have loved to simply push him all the way in and let down the lid. Instead, I do what any human being would do for another human being. I open the linen closet door, take out a hand towel, and drop it down on the floor where he can reach it. His reply is continued gagging.

It's early Saturday morning, and Jonathan is off this particular weekend. I believe the girls are still asleep. I crack their bedroom door and peek in. I have to look a little more closely at Jonita because she's learned how to play possum. I'm convinced that they are all still out cold, so I quietly pull the door shut. I marvel at my lack of emotion. I am not moved by the gagging sounds, his red face, or any other disgusting sights and sounds that he emits. I have no idea of how drunk he may have gotten the night before.

***

We live in the same house, but Jonathan does as he pleases. We make no attempt to communicate with each other, so the way I see it, he's getting whatever he deserves. In fact, he walks around with his jaws tight as though I have wronged him in some way instead of the other way around. He did, however, speak to me briefly about a month after his abrupt return. He informed me that he'll pay the house note because it's his house. And since I have a job now, I can pay the rest of the bills. Ever since then, he throws the money for the house note onto the couch where I sleep.

Back when Jonathan first moved back in, he left the house to go to work, and I moved all my belongings from the bedroom down to the basement. Even though there is another bedroom upstairs that I can make mine, I choose to sleep on the main level. Being upstairs will make me feel too vulnerable. The couch suits me better. I feel safer here. My plan was to use the downstairs bathroom. There is an exterior door down here, and I can exit in a hurry if I need to. I will never be caught off guard again. I purchased a few cans of mace the day after the rape. I have them hidden in different places throughout the house. I'm ready for his next attack, and there will be one, but it will not be successful.

The day I was down there getting things together in the bathroom, I notice Jonita has left a few pairs of her panties balled up in a few places down here. I have to get on to her about that. This makes no sense; she has a hamper in her room. I also have to talk to her about changing her panties everyday because there is some type of white crusty stuff on the backs of them.

Jonathan has installed a lock on his bedroom door. I suppose it is designed to keep me out. He wasted those efforts; I haven't stepped foot in that room since the week he came back. Apparently, Jonathan is really using his cell phone now. I have noticed how thick his cell phone bill envelopes have been lately. I guess I should be upset, but I'm not. This actually works better for me. I consider him using his cell phone more respectful to me than when he had his women calling whenever they pleased on the house phone and hanging up when I answered the phone or filling up my answering machine with silly messages.

His cell phone rings all night. I've asked him to turn down the ringer so that it doesn't resound throughout the house. Of course, he refuses. That's his way of letting me know that he is still the man. It's also a way of letting me know that he's still out there chasing women because whoever it is that calls during the night, will not hang up. The phone may ring a few times, then stop, and start again. I know that sign of desperation. It tells me that Jonathan is headed for trouble. I just hope that trouble doesn't end up at my door. I know Jonathan believes he's getting back at me, but now I can sleep through the ringing phone. After all, it's not for me.

***

As I stand here in the doorway looking down on him, vomiting, it almost makes me smile. I heard him come in last night. He made no attempt to make his entry or his stumble up the stairs a quiet one. I think he's still foolish enough to think he can make me jealous. He just does not understand that you have to care first. Jonathan has wrung all the care for him out of me. He thinks I'm still the same little "can't breathe without you" girl he met some 15 years ago. Even I marvel at how much I've changed. I thought he was all I needed in life, and I was willing to put everything and everybody on hold so that I could live and love Jonathan. It sounds so stupid now.

Before leaving the bathroom doorway, I take another look down at him to make sure he's not drowning, something I'd surely be accused of if he did. Then I decide to go downstairs and make myself a pot of coffee and wait.

After about 30 minutes, Jonathan comes downstairs. I can hear the difficulty he is having maneuvering the stairs. When he enters the kitchen, I can smell the stale odor of liquor. As he passes me to get some coffee, he doesn't speak and neither do I. He looks bad, but I've seen him look like this before. It is sickening. Jonathan turns around and steadies himself against the sink, careful not to look me in the face. His voice is weak and slurred when he asks me, "Do you know where a thermos is?" I don't look at him either. He doesn't want to look at me or speak to me, but he wants me to find one of his stupid thermoses so that he can have some coffee.

"I guess it's where ever you left it." I snap back at him. Let him find it himself. He turns back toward the sink and fumbles with the coffee cups in the cabinet before knocking one off the shelf. The cup bounces off the sink and falls clumsily into his hands. I remain in my seat, indifferent, waiting to see what happens next. He looks ready to hurl again, but instead he stumbles over to the counter and splashes out some coffee. He tries to manipulate the cream and sugar, but mostly misses. He leaves the mess he makes on the counter as well as in the upstairs bathroom where he didn't quite make it into the toilet, and he creates a new trail as he attempts to mount the stairs, sloshing coffee every which way while returning to his bed.

As soon as he gets through the bedroom door, the phone in his room begins to ring. The sun is not up yet and someone is calling. I don't move from my chair in the kitchen, but I can clearly hear him talking.

"Hey baby…Yeah, I'm awake...I had a great time too...Girl, what did you do to me? I can barely stand up. What was in that drink? Your secret, huh?...Did your man get back?...Then he don't know?...That's good…Hey, baby, I'm gonna try to get another few hours of sleep. I'll call you when I get up. Then we'll get together...I love you too. Bye!"

Jonathan is talking loudly. It isn't just the alcohol. He wanted me to hear. He thinks he's being slick. What he doesn't realize is that this is just fuel for the fire I plan to set. He is helping me make my case. One thing I have learned too well in nursing school is to take good notes. I have begun to document everything. I have written down every detail since I returned from Patricia's house. I have gotten copies of the police reports, the license plate number of the lady with the children, phone numbers I've found, and anything else that I find and think will help me. Poor Jonathan—he thinks I'm still 19 and mesmerized by him.

CHAPTER FOURTEEN

Jonathan's vomiting begins to be more frequent. After the first time, I have not again come to his rescue with a hand towel or anything else. I have left him to fend for himself. However, I must confess that this did not stop me from being concerned about him. He has started missing work again, but he's still not too sick to stay out all night. It really doesn't matter because I have made a conscious decision to work on changing my focus. My plan is to continue my routine with work and the girls. I am going to start enjoying life. Church, work, and the girls are the most important things to me.

I have enrolled the girls in Kiwanis; it is very similar to Christian Girl Scouts. They meet every Monday night. I volunteer as the arts and crafts helper. This has us all out on Monday night. We don't come home first; we go straight to some hamburger place to eat and talk about our day. We leave there and head to the meetings. Wednesday nights feature Bible class. The routine is similar except we do go home first. Because it meets later in the evening, I have time to cook dinner, usually leftovers, and then we leave for church. This keeps my girls engaged in Christian activities, and it also allows them time to make lifelong friends.

Jonita isn't exactly thrilled with our evening activities, and I believe she's actually feigned sickness a few times, causing me to have to leave her at home with Jonathan. But she seems to be adjusting, and I guess, like me, she makes the best of things. I do notice, however, that her mood changes back and forth. Sometimes when we come home, I can see her begin to stiffen up and other times she seems happy to be there.

I have checked with my insurance coordinator at work, only to find out that I declined the family coverage. Then I remember that I chose to decline because the girls are already covered by Jonathan's employer, and it is pointless to spend the extra money by insuring them through mine too. Besides, Jonathan is the primary carrier anyway. I have to make myself a note to remember to call his company from work tomorrow to find out what type of family counseling services they offer. Of course, I will need to do all of this without Jonathan's knowledge. Surely, he won't want his precious family to be known as dysfunctional or crazy. But, more than likely, his real problem will be the fear of someone finding out how abusive he is.

While I have committed myself to holding my kids together, I find that the fulfillment of my job at the hospital helps me to manage life's little disappointments. Things at work are busier than ever. We are coming into spring, and that seems to be the time that diseases start to wake up. My supervisor allows me to choose which section of the infectious unit I want to work, and I choose the AIDS patients, mostly working with the children. I have been continuously cautioned about becoming too attached to the patients, which reminds me of Mr. Andrews. But, I decide that someone has to love these children left in our care, and, as long as I'm doing this job, it might as well be me who loves them. Giving to these children helps me focus on someone other than myself. My prayers can be filled with words other than "me, myself, and I", or "my four and no more." Also, it makes the day fly by and creates a sense of self-worth, which I desperately still need.

***

A few weeks into Jonathan's illness, I get a phone call at work. It is from one of Jonathan's cousins, Debra.

"Hey girl," she says. I don't catch the voice right away.

"Hey girl! What's up?'

"Well, girl, we've got a little situation here."

"A situation? What do you mean?"

"Well, Jonathan is here at my house, and he's not doing too well."

"What does that mean?"

"That means he's vomiting all over my house, and he's too weak to drive himself home."

"So why are you calling me?"

"You're his wife. You need to come get him before he stinks up my house permanently."

"I tell you what, I'm at work right now and I can't have this conversation. I'll call you back during my lunch and tell you what I'm going to do."

"But…"

"Bye," and I hang up the phone.

Jonathan's entire family knows what's gone on between the two of us. Yet, not one of them has said a kind or encouraging word to me or our children. But now, when Jonathan needs somebody, they know my number. And, they don't call me at home—no, they call my work number.

The longer I think about the situation, the angrier I get. Yet I keep watching the clock. It's getting close to my lunch break. Jonathan didn't come home last night. The phone hadn't been ringing either, so I assumed he was with whomever it is that calls all the time. It never occurred to me that he may have spent the night with his cousin Debra. Perhaps I've been jumping to conclusions about where he's been going every night. As much as I hate to go get him, I know what it feels like to watch Jonathan's body wrenching with convulsions. I know I'm not responsible, but who is? How can I just leave their dad there?

Debra is one of those women who get off by causing trouble. She finds out about your most embarrassing moment and never lets you live it down. She creates little jokes directed towards you then rehashes your personal incident for the people who are present that don't get the joke. Once everyone is in on it, and the laughing dies down, she may start singing a little jingle about you that she makes up to keep the jokes going. Or, she'll take whatever situation that may come up and rhyme words or create puns that draw everyone back in to humiliate you.

I know Debra knows all about our situation because she's one of the first people Jonathan would tell. It's the kind of stuff that makes her mouth water with juicy gossip. She would like nothing better than to rub it in my face. I don't know why she's like that. She has never worked a day in her life; she sits at home playing Susie homemaker and local gossip while her husband brings home the money. I'm not mad at her for having an easy situation, but the way she hates on everyone else is sickening. I don't really want to deal with her. I should leave the two of them there together. They are two of a kind, two users—or should I say losers. They both have a chance to see each others' true colors. Well, it's lunch time. I had better make that phone call.

"Hey, Debra."

"Hey, girl, you on the way?"

"No. I told you I'm at work. Unlike you, I have to work."

"Yeah, girl. I know it's rough. Well, what are you goin' to do?"

"I have to make arrangements for the kids after I get off and then I'll be by to collect Jonathan. Maybe you and your husband can bring his car home later."

"Well, girl, I hate to have to wait till you get all that done before you come."

"Hey, girl, that's the best I can do. Take it or leave it."

"All right, I guess I can wait till you get here."

"Yeah right. Later."

I hang up again, mad and disgusted. That's her blood, and she's acting like he's a stranger to her. It's not like she has anything better to do. Now she's getting a taste of what I have dealt with through the years. One sure thing about Debra is she will let every family member who will listen to her know how much trouble Jonathan has caused her.

I barely get a chance to finish my lunch and my break is over. The afternoon is busy. I need to bathe and change the gowns of several of the young children on my ward. I never rush through it. Most times, the nurses' aides give the kids sponge baths in their beds, but once a week, if they are well enough, we must give them a bath. I always try to make it fun. Although, I must be very careful with their IVs and sometimes body fluids. I have all types of toys in the water, and we always splash everything up, so I am usually as wet as they are.

Today is Wednesday and Bible class night. I need to make some arrangements for the girls. While talking to Debra, I figure I can pick the girls up as usual and take them over to Kathy's house. She can take them to Bible class with her and I'll meet them all there. When my next break comes, I'll dry off and call Kathy.

"Hey, Kath."

"Hey girl. What's up?"

"Listen, I just have a minute and I need you to do me a favor."

"Sure, girl."

"Can I drop the girls off over there after work today? I have some errands to run."

"Sure. No problem. You want to have dinner here?"

"Oh, girl that would be great, but I'm not sure if I'll be back before dinner. I was hoping you could bring the girls to church with you tonight and I'll meet you all there."

"Sure. Is everything ok?"

"Yeah, girl. Everything is fine. I've got to go. My break is over. Bye."

"Bye."

Man, I hated not telling Kathy the whole story. I'm just not in the mood for any more negative criticism or advice on what someone else would or wouldn't do. I know Kathy isn't like that, but I just feel stupid enough without having to say anything out loud.

The rest of the afternoon flies by with loads of laughs and water. I get through all my baths and leave everyone happy, as happy as one can be when dying of AIDS. When it is time to go, I find myself rushing to leave to get to the girls. I guess I just want to get this over with. Worse yet, I don't want anyone to know what I'm doing.

I get to the daycare early and the girls pile into the car. They are all excited when I tell them that we're going to Kathy's. Even Jonita smiles. She likes Kathy. Kathy always treats her like a big girl --she doesn't baby her like the other girls. She always has some special thing or treat just for Jonita. It makes Jonita feel like a real young woman. We haven't visited with Kathy and her family since the retreat.

It isn't until I pull into Kathy's driveway that I tell them I have

124

somewhere else to go. The other two girls say bye and run to the door. Jonita turns to look at me and stops dead in her tracks. She walks around to my side of the car, and I let down my window.

"Ma, where are you going?"

"I have some business to take care of."

"Ma, is something wrong?"

"No, Nita. Nothing is wrong."

"Then let me go with you."

"Nita, go on and take your sisters inside. Kathy has prepared dinner for you girls. I'll meet you all at church tonight."

"Are you sure you're coming?"

"Of course I'm sure. Now give Ma a kiss so that I can hurry back."

Nita reaches into my window and gives me a big hug. This is the first time I have taken a good look at her in a long time. I hadn't realized how she has grown up. This is also the first time I've noticed that she needs a bra. How did I miss that? Her chest has really begun to fill out. It also dawns on me that she'll be starting her period soon, and I haven't even had our mother/daughter "birds and the bees" talk yet. We really need to have that talk, and I need to take her to the doctor for a physical, soon.

Before I release her from my hug I whisper, "Take care of your sisters. Don't let them mess up Kathy's house."

"OK, Ma."

"Love you."

"Love you too."

By the time Nita leaves the car, the other two girls have already rung the doorbell and gone inside. Nita turns around at the door and waves, I watch her enter before I pull off.

***

Debra doesn't live far; she is in the next town over, up Hwy 43 toward Benton Harbor, just outside of Kalamazoo. I'll have to take the freeway to get there. On the drive over, I begin to wonder what I will do when I get there. How am I going to take this sick man, whom I hate, back to my house? It is no longer my job to nurse him back to health.

Yet, old habits die hard, and I'm still on my way, once again, to rescue him. I'm not sure what is wrong with me. I must be suffering from some sort of mental illness.

Debra lives in a very nice subdivision; the sign above the huge lions that guard the subdivision says 'Lincoln Estates.' You have to come through a fenced entrance, just like ours, but that's where the similarities end. The road winds and is lined with lots of trees and foliage before reaching the first house. Each home sits on at least an acre lot. Even though it's early in the spring, and winter hasn't finished leaving her mark, each yard still reflects the outline of well manicured lawns cascading around beautiful, all-brick homes. Debra and her husband live near the rear of the subdivision, backing up to a wooded area. It is very quiet and very private.

I pull into the cul-de-sac and onto their driveway right at 5:30 p.m. There are a few cars parked in the driveway, one of which belongs to Jonathan. That must have been some party. Debra's husband travels a lot. I wondered if he knows how many social gatherings are held at his place in his absence. I remember the time and know I've got to get moving if I'm going to make it to Bible class. On top of that, there is no telling what kind of shape Jonathan will be in.

I ring the doorbell and after just a few moments, Debra opens the door. She has this stupid grin on her face. She looks just like the cat that swallowed the canary. No doubt she has something up her sleeve.

"Debra, is Jonathan ready?"

"Yeah, Come on in."

With hesitation, I enter the house, close the door behind me, and follow Debra. She goes down a short hallway that leads to the family room just at the end of the hall and to the right. As soon as I round that corner, I know what the stupid grin is all about. There in the middle of the room is an oversized loveseat and a bucket on the floor. Jonathan is stretched out across the short sofa with his head lying in the cross-eyed lady's lap. I must admit that this did catch me totally by surprise. Though, I don't know why it surprised me. At this point in the game, I should have learned to expect the unexpected.

I look over at Debra and see she is about to leap out of her skin with excitement. I'm really sorry to disappoint her. Today, there will be no Thriller in Manila. I walk over to Jonathan, bend down, and whisper as if talking to a child.

"Are you ready to go?" I think even he is caught off guard by my composure.

"I wanna finish watching this movie," is his reply.

"Perhaps you can see it another time. I'm in a hurry."

"Why didn't you just come later? I don't know why Debra called you anyway." At this point I can feel myself starting to simmer. I'm standing, looking directly at the cross-eyed girl, who is looking back at me.

"You're the one who told me to call her, Jonathan," shouts Debra. This remark causes the cross-eyed lady to look away.

It's clear that this is another one of his games he's playing. I take a deep breath and say,

"John, I'm going to my car. I will wait exactly five minutes. If you do not come out, I'm leaving." I turn to face Debra.

"I can find my way out."

I finish my turn and head out of the room toward the front door. When I get outside, I need to take several cold, deep breaths to get myself together. As I walk to my car, I now recognize one other car in the driveway. I fight the urge to key the cross-eyed lady's car. I do realize for the first time that she's a fool, just like me. I get in my car and start it. I don't wait five minutes. I don't even wait five seconds. I put the car in gear, back out the driveway, and drive to church. The lesson tonight is about how God will take your enemies and make them your foot stool.

I can't wait.

CHAPTER FIFTEEN

Jonathan didn't come home that night. In fact, I haven't seen him for a week. When he shows up Saturday morning, he can hardly walk. His skin is pale and his hands are shaking. He fumbles with his keys once he gets inside and starts the short journey to the steps. He's noticeably out of breath. He takes the stairs one at time, resting between each step. I try to pretend like I'm not paying him any attention. The television is on and I try to make that my focal point, but my eyes can't help but drift over to him, examining how ill he looks. He doesn't say anything to me, so I don't say anything to him. Besides, I decided a week ago that I wouldn't speak a word to him unless it's absolutely necessary. I try hard to keep that promise to myself, but I just can't. After watching the painstaking process of his climb, I wait a few minutes and follow him up and stand in the open doorway of his room.

"Jonathan, you need to see a doctor. Let me take you to the hospital."

"Leave me alone, and close my door."

"Please, Jonathan; let me take you to find out what's wrong with you."

"I already know what's wrong with me. This has happened before. Remember? This will pass too."

"Yes, Jonathan I remember, but you have never looked this bad. Besides that was a long time ago. They may have some medicine now that will help you."

"Please, just leave me alone. Anyway, if I needed taking care of, I wouldn't have a woman like you do it." His words enter my ears with a sting, and I hear all the compassion leave my voice.

"Well, if you have someone else who can look after you, why does she keep sending your sorry butt back here?"

I don't wait for a response. I meant to sting him back, and I close the door. I don't know where he's been or what he's been doing for the past week. All I know is that he looks like death. I want to call an ambulance, but knowing Jonathan, he'll refuse their help just to spite me; and no one can make him get help. Reluctantly, I go downstairs into the kitchen. Maybe if I fix him some soup, he'll eat it. As I prepare the food, I tell myself that he doesn't deserve my sympathy or my service. I rationalize my actions by knowing that I'd help a bum on the street that I don't know. How can I not help the father of my children, and the man I have loved a good deal of my life, just because he hurt my feelings? I know I'll have to put the soup in his special thermos. Everyone who knows Jonathan knows he drinks almost everything out of one of his special thermoses. This time when I look for one of them, I can't find one. Jonathan must have at least five or six of them somewhere.

I decide to go out to his car to look for a thermos. I see two lying on the back seat. I resist the urge to snoop and grab the two thermoses and return to the kitchen. I put one thermos in the sink, and I rinse out the other one before pouring in the soup. It had what I think is coffee in it, but it's strange because the color seems off. Well, who knows, he's changed so much, he might drink it black now for all I know. It doesn't smell funny; it could just been my imagination. There's no telling what Jonathan has had mixed up in this thing. I take the thermos of soup upstairs and knock on the door.

"Jonathan, I made you some soup. Please try to drink it."

"Just leave it by the bed. I'll get it." I place the thermos down beside the bed and turn to leave. Looking back over my shoulder into the dark room, I leave a reminder,

"Jonathan, don't forget about the soup." I leave and close the door behind me.

I go back downstairs and make my bed. That means folding up my linen. I have become used to Jonathan's maltreatment of me, so I go on with my daily activities without giving him much thought. The girls and I are going to the mall to buy Easter dresses. We have all been looking forward to it. Easter falls late this year, and we may get away with wearing shoes and not boots. I take my shower and wake up the girls. While they're getting ready, I make breakfast. We eat quickly, and I wash up the dishes, including the other dirty thermos I got from Jonathan's car. Jonita drags around upstairs. I have to call for her twice after the girls and I have already gone to the car.

When we get to the mall, it becomes a great adventure. We haven't been so relaxed in a long time. We travel from store to store, looking for just the right dresses for Jolisa and Jovida. We have to have the matching socks and shoes, too. The girls are having the time of their lives. I find myself being very patient with them. I'm listening to what they say they like, and I'm trying to consider their request within the confines of my budget. Finally the two younger girls are done and it's time to look for Nita.

Before we can look for a dress for Nita, I have to find her a bra. It wasn't until a few weeks ago that I noticed how her nipples are bulging through all her t-shirts. I need to remember to go through her drawers when we get home and pull out all the shirts that have gotten too tight for her. I ask Nita when her breasts started to grow like that and why she hadn't said anything to me. At first it seems as though she has an answer for me, then, she just lowers her head in embarrassment like I've asked a question that's too personal to answer.

I disregard my unanswered questions, remembering that I had recently discussed Nita with my doctor friend at the hospital, wanting to know how to talk with Nita about the changes in her body. I decide to start our shopping at a little boutique because they have a wide variety of bras in all sizes and styles. The saleslady helps us to determine the right size for Nita. She seems a little embarrassed until I tell her she can pick out three bras in any color she wants. The other girls snicker at first, and then they start saying they want bras too. We finally settle things and are off to find the perfect dress.

I can't buy the same old ruffled dresses that I've bought in the past for Nita. She's changed; she's almost a teenager. That means that she needs a teen appropriate dress, whatever that is. We travel the entire mall before finding that perfect dress. To my surprise, Jonita wears a size 0. Her Easter dress fits her just right. It's a little disturbing to me seeing her look so grownup. I need to think about moving her into her own room soon.

We finish just in time to get home and fix a late lunch, avoiding my having to spend more money by buying food at the mall. We all leave the mall in a good mood singing to the songs on the radio all the way home. By the time we get home, everyone is starving. I come in and head right to the kitchen, sending the girls upstairs with their clothes. The girls don't know their dad is home, and I forgot all about him until just now. I decide to go upstairs and check on him before fixing lunch. I knock on the door and there's no answer. I turn the knob and open the door. Jonathan is on the floor. He doesn't appear to be breathing. I grab the telephone and dial 911. I turn him on his back and begin CPR. I call Jonita and tell her to put the girls in their bedroom, tell them to stay in there, and close the door. Then go outside and wait for the ambulance. I don't waste anymore time talking. I go back to performing CPR and massaging the heart muscle trying to get Jonathan to breathe.

My blood is rushing to my head and my pulse is racing. Everything is flashing before me like I'm in a dream. I have done these things so many times before at work. This time it's different. One part of me hates this man, and the other part of me remembers the love. It's like I can see myself going through the motions, but I'm unattached to the actions. I can feel my hands tremble as each minute of life slips away from Jonathan. I fight to steady my trembling hands. I can hear the ambulance coming. I keep pressing down on his chest, breathing and counting until the EMTs show up. Nita brings them straight to the room. They take over the process while transferring him from the floor to a stretcher. I tell them how I found Jonathan and I give a little background information. One paramedic kicks over the open thermos of soup as he is trying to maneuver the stretcher. The elevated gurney is waiting down in my living room/bedroom. Two men carry Jonathan down on the stretcher, lifting him over the stairs' wrought iron railing. I can see how much weight he has lost. They get Jonathan strapped into the gurney downstairs and wheel him out to the ambulance.

I follow them out and stand with Jonita at the ambulance door. They are working desperately to get Jonathan breathing. One of the attendants prepares the defibrillator in an attempt to restart Jonathan's heart. The one man says, "Clear" while the other man moves his hands from Jonathan's body. The shock goes through Jonathan's body. His entire body shakes. He looks like a rag doll. He shouts, "Clear" again; and again, Jonathan's body jumps up. This time they get a pulse. While he closes the back doors to the ambulance, I ask the attendant where they're taking Jonathan. He tells me which hospital and says for me to come quickly. I barely get my reply out when I hear the other attendant telling the driver to go. I yell out that I'm coming as soon as I get a sitter. They pull off, leaving Jonita and I standing here.

Quickly, I come inside the house and call Jonathan's parents. I tell them how I found him earlier and what hospital he went to. Then I go next door and ask my neighbor to come over and watch the children while I go to the hospital. Of course, all the ghosts saw, so they know something serious has happened. She comes right over and I prepare to leave. Before I leave, I have a short conference with Jonita; I want to make sure she understands the seriousness of the situation. I want to be sure that she knows what to do if I'm gone for a while, and she knows how to handle the girls. I tell the neighbor that the girls haven't eaten and there is plenty of food in the refrigerator.

Once I leave, I find myself speeding down the narrow streets to the nearby hospital where Jonathan was taken. I park my car near the emergency room entrance. Once inside, I speak to the lady at the nurses' station.

"Where can I find Jonathan Liberty? An ambulance brought him in 30 to 45 minutes ago."

"Are you a family member?" she asks suspiciously.

"Yes, ma'am, I'm his wife." My reply sounds like a lie, even to me.

"Please have a seat in the waiting room. The doctor will be out in a few moments to speak with you."

The nurse points in the direction in which I should go. I go over to the area she pointed out. I cannot be still. The wait for the doctor is about to kill me, so with nothing else to do, I begin pacing the floor.

After about 15 or 20 minutes, two police officers enter the waiting room. They are with the nurse who had pointed me to this room. The officers walk directly to me.

"Are you Mrs. Liberty?" The larger officer asks.

"Yes, what's wrong?" I respond with growing fear in my voice.

"We need to ask you a few questions," replies one of the officers.

"Questions about what? I'm here to see about my husband. I'll have to talk with you later." I know my voice is elevated. I can hear it, and they hear it too. I'm trying to stay calm, but something is definitely wrong and I don't like the look of these two officers.

Suddenly one of the officers says, "Maybe you should come with me."

He reaches out to grab my arm. Keeping my cool has now become only a faint memory. My voice has now escalated to screaming.

"Look, I can't go anywhere right now. My husband was just brought here a few minutes ago and I need to check on his condition. I don't know what you want, but right now I'm not going anywhere with you or anyone else."

I snatch my arm back, avoiding his grasp, and move away from both officers, heading around them and back to the nurses' station. Amazingly, it becomes so quiet in the room that I can hear my own heart beating. When they come toward me again, I brush against one officer, trying to get clear of both of them. I don't get very far before the two officers position themselves one on each side of me, each grabbing one of my arms. When I know anything, I am face down on that nasty waiting room floor with both my hands behind my back. I feel myself falling, but they have my arms and there is no way to break my fall except to use my face. My face slams into the floor hard. The cops cuff me and swing me up from the floor onto my feet. I'm in shock and have no idea what is going on. Why are these officers attacking me? Where is Jonathan? What is going on?

It is becoming difficult to breathe. I now feel pain throughout my face. Blood is dripping from my nose down the front of me. The officers seem to be angry. I glance around the room and all the people who had been waiting have moved back against the walls.

Someone yells, "Police brutality, leave her alone."

Their calls go unheeded. They swoop me out the emergency entrance through which I had come earlier and throw me in the back of a waiting police car. Now my lips have begun to swell and they are sticking together due to the drying blood that has seeped down from my injured nose.

I'm sitting in the back of the squad car trying to calm myself down. It's a little difficult to breathe; my breaths are short and raspy. I can feel the dried blood on my face and the clots that move around in my nose when I breathe in and out through my nose. Breathing through the cracks at the corners of my mouth makes it easier for me. As I look out the window, my head is pounding. Everything is confused. I can see the two officers who assaulted me standing nearby talking to a man who looks like a doctor. One officer turns around and opens the car door nearest to where I'm seated.

He says, "The doctor here is going to look at your face before we leave."

I start to say something to the officer and decide against it. The doctor bends down and leans into the back seat. He has on gloves. He moves my face from side to side and touches my nose.

"It's not broken," he says, not really talking to me.

I decide to try to communicate with him. I attempt to open my mouth to speak. Nothing happens. My lips are stuck together with the dried blood from my nose. I know I don't have much time. I have to try to generate enough spit in my dry mouth to wet my tongue and slowly move that wetness across the inside cracks of my lips, forcing my tongue through to break the seal that has locked my lips shut. The doctor seems finished and there is no more time. I break my silence, feeling the tear of skin on both lips as I open my mouth to speak.

"Do you know what's going on? I don't know why I'm in this police car, and do you know if my husband is all right?" I rattled all this out in one breath and probably almost unintelligibly.

I think he hears the pleading in my voice.

134

He says, "You don't have to worry about Mr. Liberty. He passed away. You really need to worry about yourself."

Then he backs out the car and begins speaking again with the officers. He leaves me speechless. *Dead?*

Waves of emotions hit me as I replay the doctor's words in my head. I thought I would cry or be sadder than I am to hear about Jonathan. I don't want to go dancing or anything, but I'm not devastated. In fact, I'm relieved. The doctor's words have freed me. But that doesn't explain why I'm in this police car. That's what's troubling me. I feel the pain from my lips. I lick the blood from them and try to assuage them.

When I look out the window again, the officers are still standing outside talking, and just up the street I see Jonathan's parents rush up and go in through the emergency room doors. They don't notice me sitting in the squad car. The doctor continues talking with the officers. One policeman has out a note pad and is writing things down. After some time, I look back to the emergency room doors and see Jonathan's parents coming back out with that same nurse who must be the hospital's public relations coordinator (of bad news), pointing them in the direction of the doctor and the officers. The Libertys rush over to the doctor. He starts talking to them. I can't hear what he's saying, but the expressions on their faces tell the whole story. I watch the distortion of Mother Liberty's face and the flow of tears that begin to pour down her face. Daddy Liberty holds his composure and helps Mother Liberty as she begins to stagger. I'm wondering how long it will take them to notice me. I start to move around a bit trying to get their attention. I'm desperate, hoping they will see me and help me, even though I know Ma Liberty never really liked me.

The officers wait until Ma Liberty is able to compose herself and then he begins to talk to her. That's when he turns around and points to me. I can only imagine what he's saying about me. I just don't know why I'm in the backseat of this police car. A large tear rolls down my face when Ma Liberty looks in the car at my bloody face. All of this is just too much. She begins crying and she is visibly trembling. One of the officers opens the door.

I blurt out, "Ma Liberty, I'm sorry about Jonathan. I don't know what happened or why I'm in this police car. Please go to my house and see about the girls."

It came out as one big garble too, but I don't know how much time I will have, and I need her help. Mother Liberty leans in and says,

"Did you do it?"

"Do what?" is my response. That's when the officer tells Ma Liberty to move and he closes the door.

"Do it?"

Finally it all starts to make sense. They think I killed Jonathan. Just before we pull off, I glance back at the emergency room door and see a familiar face coming out through the doors.

Oh my God! It's the cross-eyed lady. What's she doing here?

CHAPTER SIXTEEN

I am taken directly to the local police station. The officers don't say anything to me during the short ride. It makes me think about how Jonathan looked earlier this year when he was riding off with the police. I want to ask them questions. I want to know why they think I killed Jonathan. I found him on the floor barely breathing. I don't know what happened to him. I told him to go to the doctor. I tried to take him. He might still be alive had he listened to me. I want to scream at these stupid officers, but my nose still hurts from my last objection. What about the girls? What am I going to tell them about their father?

The car stops and both officers get out. The larger one opens my door.

"Move this way, Mrs. Liberty, and exit the car."

I manage to slide myself across the hard seat, trying not to lose my balance as I get out the car with my hands cuffed behind me. I put one leg out, then the other, and I stand up. The officers grab me by each arm and escort me inside. Once inside, I am taken through an inside door and into an interrogation room. I guess that's what it is. One officer takes off the cuffs and tells me to have a seat. My arms are shaking from the strain of having them behind my back for so long, and my head is pounding. Only one officer comes into the room with me. After he tells me where to sit, he pauses a few minutes and then he leaves, closing the door behind him. I sit down at the table and begin looking around the room trying to get my bearings. It's a small room with only a table and two chairs, one on each side of the table, and a large mirror on the wall directly in front of where I was instructed to sit. Almost instinctively, I get up and move toward the mirror to assess the damage to my face which is throbbing fiercely.

Now I've always been a murder mystery nut, so I've seen every episode of *Perry Mason, Law and Order, NYPD Blue*, all the *CSI's* and every other law program on television. That's how I know that the mirror is two-way. That fact, however, does not stop me from examining the damage. Furthermore, I want them to get a good look at my face. My hands tremble as I move them across my swollen visage. My nose is tight to the touch, and my lips are almost swollen shut. They took my purse when I was handcuffed, so I have nothing to help me clean away the blood from my face. I'm upset, but I decide that my face is the least of my problems. Here I am standing in the police station facing possible murder charges for the death of a man that I both loved and hated for more than 15 years.

I decide that once the officers return, I will not speak. They have not read me my Miranda rights, so I am not under arrest, I think. I turn from the mirror and walk back over to the table and sit down. My mind wants to race in all different directions at one time. I have to focus and devise a plan, or list, or something. First, I decide to pray. I pull my mind in and try to focus on God. Once I close my eyes, the room begins to spin and my thoughts become jumbled. I open my eyes and pray anyway. I begin to ask the Lord for mercy. I tell Him that I don't want to go to jail. I ask Him to be my lawyer and protect me. I remember how many times I've heard the preachers say, "He'll be a lawyer in a courtroom… "I work hard to push out of my mind the knowledge that people who are innocent sometimes go to jail. My prayer is that this won't happen to me. As I pray, my girls flash into my mind. I pray for them too. I already asked Ma Liberty to go get them, but she has spent so little time with them, that I'm not sure if she even knows all their names. I'm afraid of what they're being told and what's happening to them right now.

Before I can get lost in despair, the door opens and two officers enter. One officer is the large one from the squad car, and the other is a female. The female asks me to stand up. She tells me I'm under arrest for the murder of Jonathan Liberty and for resisting arrest. Then she reads me my rights. She takes me over to the wall and tells me to put my hands on the wall. She pats me down, checking for weapons, I suppose. I turn my face to stone and keep my swollen lips shut.

The female cop takes me by the arm and leads me from that room. She takes me down a short hallway into the restroom. She tells me to get a paper towel and clean my face. Once I'm finished, she takes me to another room where there is a camera and finger-printing materials. I'm thinking that things are moving along rather swiftly. Jonathan has not been dead five hours and I'm being charged with his death—correction, murder. None of this makes sense to me. They haven't even asked me any questions. Apparently, they think I did it, and that's it: an open and shut case.

I'm fighting back the panic and terror. I know that won't get me anywhere—although this cool and calm, show-no-emotion approach just makes me look like a maniacal, cold-blooded killer. I can't let this get to me, so I have to take the chance of looking guilty and remain emotionless.

"Hang this plate around your neck, place both feet on that X, and face the camera."

These instructions spill from a small, mole-like man sitting behind the desk with the camera. The female officer has found her a spot leaning against the wall. I follow the officer's instructions.

"Now, turn to your right, and keep your feet on the line."

I move as though I were being mechanically turned. There are a few more shots, and then he's finished. The female officer reanimates herself, disconnecting herself from the wall, and guides me by the arm over a few feet to the fingerprinting desk. The shrunken camera man leaves his post and comes over to the desk and fumbles with some papers and ink pads.

"Give me your right hand first," he commands.

I do as I'm told. He takes my hand and sticks each finger on the ink pad then onto this card. I offer him no assistance, and his tight grip on my wrist and fingers indicate to me that he doesn't want my help. One finger is placed firmly in each square box that decorates the face of the 5" by 7" cards. He moves from my right hand to my left. As he does his job, I try to remember from watching all my "whodunnits" what will come next. My hope is that it is not the strip search, but I'm sure it will be. I guess the female officer's job of leading me around from place to place is just the foreplay. I soon discover that her real job comes in when we enter another room.

"Remove all your clothing and stand on the line."

That is all she says to me. She walks over to a desk and takes out a pair of rubber gloves. I don't move. I feel like I'm frozen to the floor. The lady looks up at me from what she's doing and sees me standing motionless, staring at her. She continues, "Ma'am, you must be searched to ensure that you are not carrying any weapons or drugs before you enter our jail." Her words seem to bounce off my forehead. Still, I don't move.

"As you take off your clothes, fold them, and place them on the desk."

I stall as long as I dare do so, and begin undressing. As I place each piece of clothing on the desk, she pats it down and checks the pockets. Finally I get to my bra and panties. In my mind I try to imagine myself preparing to take a shower and disavow the knowledge that, once again, I am about to be violated. She already has on the rubber gloves before she begins checking my clothes. I'm standing in the middle of the room naked, chilled to the point of shivering. Tears begin rolling down my cheeks. She comes over and tells me that there is nothing to be afraid of. She says she won't hurt me, and it will go quickly. She explains the process of a strip search step by step. Knowing what's coming next makes it a little easier. It feels a little less of a violation until she tells me to go over to the table in the corner and lie down on my back. I move very slowly toward the table.

The table looks very much like the examination table at the gynecologists' office except this one is a relic with leather straps attached to it. There is no clean white paper sheet running down the middle of it, only the cold steel with torn padding here and there. I am repulsed by it and can feel the bile come up from my stomach, resting in my throat. My shaking is very visible. I move forward and start by placing my rear end on the table. Of course, the chill shoots through me. I use my hands to push myself all the way up on the table. Those steel stirrups are waiting to be mounted. I force my body to do what needs to be done and I settle myself, except for the shaking, and I wait.

The wait isn't long enough. The lady officer comes right over. She doesn't speak nor does she prepare me. She just walks over, pulls one of my knees to her chest and she enters me. I scoot up almost off the top of the table. Well, I guess she has done this many times before and is prepared for that because her hand comes right with me. She puts pressure on that knee she has pressed to her chest and does not allow it to move. If I don't come back down, my leg will be in danger of breaking. Her grip forces me to return to my former position. Still she does not speak, and neither do I, unless you want to count the long groan that comes up through my throat.

It is far more painful than any doctor's visit I have ever had. She appears to be digging around looking for something. She goes as deeply as she possible can. Every time I scoot, she tightens that knee. I'm holding my breath, praying that she will stop. Finally, she removes her hand and releases my knee. I let out a great sigh of relief.

"Stand yourself up and bend forward over the table," are the next words she says to me.

I am not prepared for this at all. I am moving in slow motion. I look over at her. She's at the desk changing her gloves. I also see her apply some sort of gel to a few of her fingers. Now, I am crying real tears. But fear encourages me to do as I am told, and I wait for her to start. This is probably the worst violation of all. It is a lot quicker than the first, but far more painful. She retreats, recovering nothing from either invasion. As she removes her gloves, she gives me further instructions.

"There is a stack of clothes on the corner of that desk. Take them with you through that door. Take a shower and dress yourself. I will be waiting right here."

When I look over to the desk, I see the clothes stacked on the edge of the desk. They look like hospital scrubs. I walk over to the desk, trying hard to keep my balance. I pick up the bundle and instinctively place it in front of my naked body. I then head to the door which leads to the showers. I can no longer describe my emotional state. I've done nothing wrong, yet I'm being wronged at every turn. They are attacking my physical and mental being; I feel I'm hanging by a thread. And I realize this is far from over. In fact, it's just the beginning.

I stack my makeshift robe in the corner of the room and turn on the shower. The spray of water is hard. I make it as hot as I can stand it. I stand in it, allowing it to beat upon my body. Somehow it is my hope that it can beat away all my hurt and pain, frustration and humiliation, and all the horror and betrayal. The water beats my naked body until it hurts to move, yet I take it. Before long, the lady officer yells through the door.

"Five minutes and I'm coming in."

Those words snap me back to the road of reality. I grab the soap from a mound affixed to the shower wall and quickly wash away as much of the stench of this place as I can. I use one of my last minutes to rinse away those things that are trying to trouble my spirit, shaking my faith. I turn off the water. I don't dry myself off before dressing into my scrubs. I want this sense of cleansing to linger with me as long as possible.

"Let's go, Mrs. Liberty."

The guard comes in and takes me by the arm. She leads me from the shower, through the torture chamber and out into the hallway and through other hallways and down some stairs. I have a feeling this will be my final stop. Once we're down the stairs, we take a few more turns and there they are. The jail cells are directly in front of us. The lighting is dim in the narrow hallways. However, as we enter the cell area, the walkway widens and the lights are brighter. There are about 10 cells on each side. There appear to be only women down here, except for the male guards. The female officer who brought me speaks with the officer who is already here sitting behind a desk. The seated officer rambles through some papers and then directs the female officer to the cell to which I am assigned.

Again, she takes me by the arm and begins leading me down the wide pathway. I want to shout I didn't do it. I want to make them stop. I want to break and run. Once again, I have to accept the realization; there is nowhere to run, nowhere to go.

We stop at the third cell on the left. I find myself relieved that I don't have to go down any further into the belly of the whale. The cell doesn't have automatic door locks. A key is used to open my cell. I am directed to step inside. There is great hesitation on my part. I suppose the officer's patience is waning because she gives me a little shove that sends me inside in a hurry. She hands me a piece of paper and says that it explains all the procedures and the daily schedule. The officer then closes and locks my cell door and leaves.

For a long while, I just stand staring at the door with the paper in my hand. My clothes are still wet from the shower and it is cool down in the basement of the courthouse. Yet, I don't feel anything. My mind just wants to slip away and let go of reality. I feel so tired. Still standing, I close my eyes. When I do, I see the smiles on my babies' faces. They warm my heart. Not knowing what is happening with them pulls me out of this slump. It brings me back to life. I do have something to live for. I have three somebodies who need me to pull through this.

I open my eyes and look at the piece of paper in my hand. I start by reading it. It explains that we are responsible for keeping the bed made and the cell looking presentable. I take a look around and think about what there is to do. I am however, happy to see that the toilet is not all out in the open. It is not in a separate room, but there is a half wall just on the other side of the sink that allows you to take care of your personal needs outside the view of the other cell mates or anyone who may be passing by.

I decide that I might as well follow the rules. Rule number one is to unroll your mattress and make your bed. I unroll it and find all the linen I need inside. I spread the sheet. That's when I discover there is no top sheet. So I just put the blanket down on top and tuck it in. There is a pillow covered in a plastic liner and I stuff it into the pillow case. After I finish making the bed, I notice the pad and pen lying on the small desk sitting in a corner of the room. I decide to sit down and write down everything I can remember that might help me before things get foggy.

Before I can get started, a guard comes for me. We travel back through those same narrow hallways through which I came earlier. I'm taken back to the same interrogation room I was taken to before. The

143

officer directs me to the seat facing the mirror. I sit and wait and watch. One thing I did learn from living with Jonathan is patience. I point my stone face to the mirror and show no emotion. After a few minutes a man enters and introduces himself as Mr. Jack Aaye, the district attorney. Right then it strikes me that this thing is really serious. It's always the assistant district attorney who comes in the movies. I feel intimidated, but I keep my mouth shut and listen.

The D.A. takes a seat across from me and places a folder he had been carrying down on the table. He seems to be reluctant to start. He fumbles with his tie and clears his throat like he's trying to decide where to start.

"Mrs. Liberty, there's no good place to start, so I'll just start. We believe you have been poisoning your husband for quite some time now. The emergency room doctors did a toxicology screening on your husband when the ambulance brought him in. The report shows high levels of ethylene glycol in his bloodstream. They believe it is that chemical that eventually killed him. The hospital contacted the police immediately. One of the reasons we moved with such speed is because when the police spoke with the ambulance personnel who brought your husband into the hospital, they told them that you did not ride with them in the ambulance. We were able to obtain and execute a search warrant for your home quickly, hoping that you did not dispose of all the evidence while you were there alone. So, you can imagine what we thought when we found the soup thermos turned over on the floor with traces of the same chemical that killed your husband still inside of it."

What he's saying shocks me. How could this have happened? The surprise is all over my face. I can see myself in the mirror, and even I am shocked by what I see. A few tears involuntarily escape my bloodshot eyes. Still, I don't say a word. I feel it is better to just listen, as difficult as it is to hear what they have against me.

He continues, "We know that you're a nurse at County General, so you know better than most how to poison someone."

I watch him as he fumbles through this folder that obviously holds everything except how long I am going to rot in prison. He continues talking, but this time I detect a deliberate note of compassion.

"Now I know living with Mr. Liberty has not been easy. I pulled his record. The officers here remember his visit a few months ago. Trust me when I tell you, he was a piece of work. Well, I guess you already know that. Anyway, everything points to you."

He pauses, stands up, and walks over to the mirror and straightens his tie as if he is trying to send a signal to someone on the other side. My eyes are following his every movement. He seems to want to say something. My tears have stopped and I only feel coldness. He finally finishes grooming himself. When he turns around, he seems visibly surprised to see that I have not broken my stare. He sits back down and opens his folder. He slides a picture of Jonathan toward me. He's lying on a table with his eyes closed. I look down at the picture and my fountains begin leaking again. I'm not sorry he's gone. I'm sorry that I wasted so many years of my life with him. I'm sorry that my life didn't turn out like it might have had I dreamt it. I'm sorry that I'm being accused of his murder when I didn't do it.

The D.A. allows me time to take this trip down memory lane, thinking it will help his case. He clears his throat again and begins again.

"We know Mr. Liberty abused you. For that, I'm sorry. That's why I came to see you myself. I want to offer you a lesser charge if you give us a complete confession. We're also willing to drop the assault charges."

I had heard enough. I can feel the tiredness moving through my body. I don't know the time, but I passed a window traveling down one of those hallways and discovered that it's dark outside. My mind is working double time to stay focused. Even through my exhaustion, I can see the railroad he's trying to strap me to. I look the man directly in his eyes. I can see he is expecting my confession. I too clear my throat, finally preparing to speak. I can see the excitement in the D.A.'s face. Again when I try to speak, I discover that my lips are almost glued shut. I'm able to squeeze out a soft, hoarse voice through broken skin and swollen lips.

"I want an attorney." With those few words, I close my mouth and shut my eyes.

The D.A. continues to talk, but I can't listen anymore. I just want to know when I can make my phone call and who has my children. I let the

D.A. go on until he is talked out. When he stops the theatrics, I open my eyes and ask.

"When do I get my phone call, and where are my girls?"

He returns to the folder and tells me that the Libertys were at the house when the warrant was served. The officer in charge at the scene felt it would be better if the Department of Children and Family Services were called, and the children be put in state custody rather than allow the Libertys to leave with them. I am forced to speak again because he only answers part of my question.

"When can I get my phone call?"

Still he does not respond. He just gets up, opens the door, and calls for another officer. They have a few words in the doorway. The officer leaves and returns shortly. He calls the female officer, who is again holding up the wall, to the door. When she returns, she tells me to come with her. I stand up and prepare to leave.

The D.A. stops me and says, "Consider my offer; it can change at any time."

I continue out the door with the lady officer, having more disdain for him than I did when the female officer was doing her job. She takes me into another room that looks like someone's office. She directs me to the phone sitting on the desk. She tells me I have one call and five minutes. The one person I know I can call and get results from is Kathy. Please let her be home. I dial her number very slowly, making sure that I don't misdial.

"Hello, Kathy, I'm in trouble."

"What's wrong?"

"Jonathan is dead, and they think I killed him."

"What?!"

"I don't have long. I've asked for a public defender and I won't talk to anyone. I don't know how long it's going to take for arraignment. Tomorrow is Sunday, so they may make me wait until Monday. I need you to contact our pastor to see if the church is willing to put up my bail."

"OK, no problem. If they don't, we will. What about the girls?"

"DCFS has them."

"Which jail are you in?"

"I'm at the big one downtown."

"Are you all right?"

"I feel horrible, but I'll be fine."

"It's too late for us to do anything tonight. We'll be out there first thing in the morning. Don't worry. We'll get together and do whatever we need to do to get you out."

"Aren't you going to ask me if I did it?"

"I already know. If you were going to do it, you wouldn't have waited this long."

"Kathy, I'm really worried about the girls."

"I know, but try to hold it together. We're going to get you out of there as soon as possible. Then we'll work on the girls."

"One minute, Mrs. Liberty," yells the officer standing in the doorway.

"Kathy, I have to go. Please pray for me and the girls. Call the church and have them pray for us."

"I will."

"I love you."

"Love you, too"

"Bye." I hang up the phone and turn to leave the room.

"The D.A. wants to talk more with you," says the lady officer.

"I don't want to talk anymore with him until I have a lawyer. Please take me back to my cell."

I didn't know if I have the right to say no, but I said it. Apparently I can, because the officer takes me past the interrogation room, back down the familiar hallways, and down the stairs back to my cell. She locks the door behind me. My entire body is exhausted and I need to rest. But, I can't rest yet. I need to prepare myself for the public defender. I didn't kill Jonathan, and I'm going to have to try to prove it.

CHAPTER SEVENTEEN

There's no time for sleep. I need to try to remember as many of the facts as I can. This can turn into a life or death situation for me, depending on whether or not 12 people believe me enough to try to see the truth in this whole mess, not just how it seems. The D.A. is right about one thing: I'm a prime candidate for this murder and the perfect patsy. Who had more reason to want Jonathan dead than me? That really is the question. Then I remember something I saw at the hospital. How did the cross-eyed lady know Jonathan was at the hospital? Why was she there? I called Jonathan's parents, but who called her? I get the paper and pen off the desk and try to write down all I know about the lady; I don't want to forget anything. My list reads like this:

Name: Unknown
Address: Unknown
Phone #:   At home on a scrap of paper
Job: U.S. Postal Service
Children: Five
Husband: Yes
Husband's Name: Unknown
Husband has a Record: Yes
Associates: Debra
Car Make and Model: Honda Civic, Tan, 1995?

Encounters:

1. Once in a motel with Jonathan
2. Once at my home with her children
3. Once at my home alone with Jonathan
4. Once at Debra's house
5. Leaving the hospital after Jonathan's death

I need more information. It shouldn't be hard to get the information I need. Starting with Debra is probably the best way to go. Debra loves to get in messes, and this will give her a chance to get in the middle of something. A case of beer and questions asked the right way can give me everything I need to know about this lady.

I write out another copy of my list and fold both pieces of paper and put them in my pocket. As I keep thinking about my situation, I think I'm being set up. I know this will probably sound ridiculous or melodramatic to most people, but I'm in a real jail charged with a real murder that I really didn't do. It's got to be a setup.

My head is spinning and I can't think anymore. I need to lie down. I have a plan. I can stop now. I can lie down. I sit on the bed first and take off the little slip-on type tennis shoes they issued to me. I lay my head back on the pillow at the head of the bed. The bars are behind the top of my bed and my feet are down near the toilet. I lay on top of the blanket. The musty stench from the mattress only distracts me for a short while. Before I know anything else, I am being awakened by the guard calling my name telling me to get up.

Her yelling startles me from a sound sleep. I jump up suddenly, and the small room begins spinning. I fall back down on to the bed. Initially, I am not sure where I am. My first thought is that all of this is a bad dream. After I'm able to clear my head, another look assures me that this is no dream. I know exactly where I am.

The guard says, "Your attorney is here to see you. Get ready. I'll be back in five minutes."

I'm surprised, but happy that they were able to find someone to represent me on Sunday. This is the best news I've heard since yesterday. I did, however, expect him to be brought downstairs to the cell like I've seen in so many prison movies. I don't know why I keep thinking about what I've seen on television. It just attests to the fantasy world I must live in. So far, the only things that have gone like the movies are the body slamming and the strip search.

A quick pat to my pocket assures me that my notes are still here. I take them out and jot down a few more things and return them to my pocket. I remember the guard's five minute rule and stand up, holding on to the desk to steady my wobbly legs. Once I'm on my feet, it's clear that I've been avoiding the inevitable; sooner or later I'll have to use that toilet. Since last night, I've been able to hold it. Now the moment of truth has arrived, and I must go. A quick look out through the bars reveals to me that no one is looking. The passageway is clear and all the other ladies seem to still be asleep. I walk the few steps to the short wall and get behind it. I'm able to straddle the stool without touching anything. Keeping my eyes peeled toward the bars, I relieve myself in a hurry and finish a quick wash down at my sink, without being noticed. I hear her coming, and I'm ready to go.

The guard takes me to a small room upstairs and leaves me. My public defender is already waiting for me. He introduces himself as Mr. Juan Miguel Martinez. He's a young, Latino man. He's quite tall, 6' 3" or better, slim, and carefully well-dressed. Initially, his good looks remind me of a pretty boy who doesn't belong in this job. However, once he begins to talk, I discover that he has already read my file. He appears to have as much information in his folder as the D.A. had in his folder last night. I realize right away that he's sharp. I also sense that he's trying to make a name for himself. Both things are a definite plus for me. I let him ask whatever questions he had first.

"Mrs. Liberty, what do you wish to plea before the judge?"

"Not guilty, of course."

"Are you aware of all the evidence they have against you?"

"Yes I am. The D.A. tried to get me to plead guilty to a lesser charge, saying that he can prove that I did it."

"Did you?"

"No, I didn't. But I think I know who did. I just can't prove it."

I pull out my piece of paper I had written the night before, and I show it to the attorney. I tell him about the cross-eyed lady at the hotel. I tell him how she tried to move in my house. I tell him about the fight (I mean the beating) she took from me. I tell about Debra's house. I tell him about her being at the hospital when I was arrested. I tell him how Jonathan had not been home for over a week and how he just showed up yesterday. I tell him how bad he looked and that I made the soup, got the thermos from Jonathan's car, washed it, and put the soup in it. I tell him how the girls and I had been gone all day at the mall, leaving Jonathan alone in the house. I tell him how I found him when I returned home. I tell how my face got swollen and how I ended up in this jail. I tell him everything until there is no more to tell.

I feel like I'm throwing up a bad meal that has soured on my stomach. Everything is pouring out of me at once. I am afraid Mr. Martinez won't be able to keep up with the details, but I don't stop. I tell him how I see this woman as almost as much of a victim as I am. This woman has suffered humiliation and degradation in front of both Jonathan, Debra, her children, and me. What better way to get even with both of us? I tell Mr. Martinez that Debra is our best chance for proving me innocent and finding out about the other woman.

Mr. Martinez does not miss a beat. He stays right in step with my meltdown. He tells me that most of his clients claim to be innocent with nothing to go on. I have, however, provided him with a place to start. He asks me if I can pay bail. I tell him that my church is working on it. I shift the conversation to my girls. I advise him that DCFS has my children. I tell him that I need him to help me get them somewhere safe. Mr. Martinez says he has a friend that owes him a favor. He asks where I want them to go. I write down Kathy's name, address, and phone number. He says he'll make a call about them the first thing Monday morning.

I lean back in the chair. That's it. I've said all I can think to say. Mr. Martinez has agreed to help me prove my innocence. I release a great sigh of relief. I have been holding my breath for almost 24 hours. I think maybe, just maybe, everything is going to work out. But, I have one last question for Mr. Martinez.

"Who will take care of Jonathan's funeral arrangements?"

"That one may be a little sticky. Normally, you would be the one. Only, the insurance company is not going to pay you as the beneficiary if you are also the one responsible for his death. However, the funeral home may agree to take care of the body if a lien can be attached to the policy. Who would be the beneficiary if it's not you?"

"I suppose it would be the children. There are no other names on the policy that I know of. In fact, for all I know, my name may not even be on it anymore. Jonathan worked out of spite. He could have changed the beneficiary, planning to try to torment me with it later."

"I'll make a note to contact his employer tomorrow about his insurance policy. Do you have a private policy?"

"Yes, we both do."

"Well, we'll worry about that later. Let's just prepare for the arraignment. It's this afternoon at 2 p.m. Do you have anyone who can bring you some presentable clothes to wear to court?"

"Yes, but I've already used my one phone call last night.

"I'll arrange for you to make a call."

Mr. Martinez must be a man of his word. Thirty minutes after he leaves, the guard comes for me and takes me to the same phone I used the night before. I got the same five minutes speech. That must be the standard length of time for everything. I call Kathy and ask her to bring me something to wear to court. I explain to her that all my clothes are bloody. She says she was preparing to come when I called. She'll find me something and bring it with her. I told her that I needed shoes, too. Before I hang up the phone, I ask Kathy to discuss with her husband before she comes whether he is willing to take the girls until this whole mess is over. Kathy agrees without hesitation, but I insist that she speaks with her husband. We say good-bye, and I hang up looking forward to her visit.

I get back to my cell just in time for breakfast. There is no mess hall or cook on site. Breakfast is brought in by a food service. As soon as we hit the bottom step leading to the final hallway to my cell, I smell the food. I realize that I haven't eaten since yesterday morning. All of a sudden, I'm starving. I take my portion from the cart and return to my cell to eat it. I eat everything on the tray. If it tastes bad, I don't notice.

After we finish with our trays, the rules say we are to lay the trays on a rolling cart left in the middle of the entire cell area between the two rows of cells. The cell doors are left open during this time and the women can move about freely. When I take my tray to the cart, I have to turn to the right and walk deeper into the holding area, past two more cells to reach the cart. I notice for the first time that each cell has a woman in it. Apparently, I had taken the last vacant space last night. I don't want to stare or make any eye contact, so I keep my head down. It seems to me that others are doing the same thing.

I hurry back to my cell, trying not to concern myself with the problems of the other women. I tidy up my cell, one of the rules on the sheet. That took all of two minutes. It is just about 8:30. There is nothing left to do, so I lie on my bed, try to relax, and wait for Kathy. At 10 a.m., I am awakened by the guard. I have a visitor. I slide into my sneakers and start my journey full of halls and stairs. I'm led to a big open room with about five tables and chairs. Sitting at one table waiting for me is Kathy. I find myself trying to straighten out my looks before entering the room. I'm embarrassed.

Only one person can visit at a time. Kathy stands up when she sees me enter the room. She isn't prepared to see my swollen face, but she quickly orders her expression to recover. I hug her with everything in me. I am so glad to know someone knows where I am and everyone has not just thrown me away. I finally release her and we both sit down. Before either of us can speak, we have to clean up our faces and clear our throats. A box of tissue just happens to be on the edge of our table. We both grab a few tissues. Kathy has brought the clothes I need for court. When she tells me how some large female guard had to search her and her things before she could enter, I smile, knowing it was nothing like the way she searched me. I tell Kathy all about Mr. Martinez. I also share with her the notes I have on the cross-eyed lady.

Kathy says that is sounds like we are going to need help proving my innocence. I tell her that I already have the attorney working on things. She says I can't put all my faith in this one man. She says it's my life and that I had better fight for it. She tells me that public defenders don't make any money and that they do the best they can with what they have to work with. Besides, she's never heard of an attorney with the last name of Martinez winning any major cases in our town or any town she could think of. At first I don't understand what she means. But then I remember his hungry look, and I understand it. That makes me even more confident that Mr. Martinez is the right man for the job, and I tell Kathy that.

Kathy accepts my assessment of Mr. Martinez, but she also say that I need more help. She says her husband has a friend who is a private investigator. He called the friend the moment he found out what was going on with me. His friend has agreed to help us with whatever we need. That's when I pull out the other copy of my list and show it to Kathy. She's not surprised about most of what's on it because she already knew most of the story. The thing that catches her attention that also has me baffled is the lady's appearance at the hospital. Why was she there?

Before we go any further, I tell Kathy that Mr. Martinez is working on getting the girls released to her. Someone from DCFS will be contacting her tomorrow. Mr. Martinez seems to have taken a liking to me for some reason or another. I know God is on my side. For the first time in a long time I feel like things are starting to work out for me. I know I sound crazy saying this from behind bars. It's just that for once I see an eventual end to my misery. The guard lets us know that Kathy's time is up. Before leaving, Kathy says that she and some of the deacons will be in court at 2 p.m.

The guard comes for me right after lunch. They had not allowed me to take the clothes Kathy brought me down to my cell. Once I'm topside again, I'm sent into the strip search room to change clothes. Then I'm instructed to fold the clothes I have on and place them into a paper bag that has my name on it, and leave the bag on the desk.

Usually there are only a few cases, if any, scheduled to be heard on Sunday. Today is an exception. The courtroom is full. Everyone seems to be here except my attorney. They bring me in and have me wait on one of the benches lining the wall to the right of the judge. Two o'clock comes and goes and my case is called. When I hear my name, I stand. They then call for my attorney. There is no response from Mr. Martinez. The judge tells me to sit back down and wait until I'm called again. I see

154

the judge move my folder to the bottom of her stack. I sit and listen to the cases now being called before me. As interesting as some of the cases are, I find myself watching the clock as the courtroom empties, one person after another. Now I'm starting to worry. Maybe I had put too much confidence in Mr. Martinez.

The judge moves quickly through the cases. It's like she has somewhere to be at a certain time. She cuts the attorneys off in mid-sentence and adds her own brand of cynicism when she deems it appropriate. I look around and see Kathy and a few of our church members sitting at the back of the courtroom. The tears are beginning to well up in my eyes, regardless of the good front I'm trying to put on. The judge finishes with everyone and calls my name again. Again I stand, and again the judge asks about my attorney. Before I can think of a response, my attorney comes flying through the door. He moves to the front and addresses the judge. The judge says a few strong words to Mr. Martinez about punctuality and responsibility. I just want her to get on with my case.

The judge finally finishes berating him and asks me my plea.

I say, "Not guilty, your honor."

CHAPTER EIGHTEEN

I don't know why my attorney, Mr. Martinez was late, but he comes in ready to go. The District Attorney who questioned me at the jail the night before doesn't bother to show up for the arraignment; he sends the Assistant D.A. There is some arguing between Mr. Martinez and the Assistant D.A. about me getting bail and Mr. Martinez wins. Bail is set at $50,000.

Our pastor has two deacons from our church here at court prepared to pay twice that amount. The courts require 10 percent of the set bail. The deacons turn over $5,000 to the court cashier. While they are taking care of my bail, one of the guards takes me back to the jail to collect my things. The bag I left on the desk in the strip search room at the jail is sitting on my bed inside the cell. There isn't anything for me to get from the cell. Everything belongs to the State. The guard tells me to get what I need, and she will be back in a few minutes. She doesn't lock the door.

I don't want anything, and I don't touch anything. I just sit on the bed and wait. A woman in the cell across from me asks me if I'm leaving. I tell her that I am. She says she wishes it were her. I don't respond to her comment, but I know if I were her, I'd wish the same thing.

Within the next few hours, I'm standing in the lobby of the police station with a bag containing my personal belonging I came in with, including my purse and shoes. Mr. Martinez has not waited for me. He left me a note saying that I should call him tomorrow. Kathy and the two deacons are seated on a bench near the rear of the jail lobby. They greet me warmly with faces full of compassion. After the first few moments of awkward conversation or the lack thereof, the deacons tell me they have to go, and they leave me standing in the police lobby with Kathy. I tell Kathy that I'm ready for this day to end, and all I want to do is go home and sleep in my own bed.

Kathy waits until we are inside her car before she gives me the bad news. She tells me that she knows why Mr. Martinez was late to court, and that I cannot return to my house. She explains that Mr. Martinez was at the crime scene (my house) with the police. The entire house is taped off and is not to be re-entered until further notice. This information is really disturbing. I've spent the last 24 hours in jail, and now I'm locked out of my house. This sure feels familiar. Kathy senses my distress. She tells me that she's taking me home with her. She says we'll sort everything out in the morning.

We ride to Kathy's house in silence. I know that she wants to talk, but I'm very tired, so I plaster my face to the window away from her. I don't feel like talking to anyone. When we get to her house, she takes me upstairs to the guest bedroom. It's not really late, but I lie down on the bed and close my eyes. Kathy covers me with a soft blanket, and she lets me sleep.

***

For the second morning in a row, I awaken unsure if I've just had some serious, lifelike dream. When I look around the room, at first I have no idea where I am. I sit up in the bed halfway between dreamland and consciousness, still confused about my dream. I'm fully dressed in clothes that aren't mine. I make my way to the closed bedroom door. Once I open the door, I realize I'm in Kathy's house. Things are still foggy for me, but after coming downstairs and picking up the Sunday paper lying on the kitchen table, I'm sure that this is no dream. Everything comes back to me, much clearer than I would have liked.

Kathy is in the kitchen when I enter. She doesn't say anything at first. She lets me read the article in yesterday's paper about Jonathan's death. My name is listed as the only suspect in his death. My heart drops to the floor. Everyone thinks I've done this. I can feel embarrassment and humiliation wash over me as I stare at the mug shot that's printed in the paper. I try to hide it from Kathy, but I know she knows how I feel. Kathy has seen me at my worst, and she's still my best friend.

Kathy pulls my attention away from the article when she tells me that she's already given the information about the cross-eyed woman to her husband, who is meeting with his P.I. friend for lunch. Kathy also tells me she got the call from DCFS about the girls this morning while I was still asleep. I know I need to find somewhere else to stay. The courts will not approve Kathy with me living in the same place where the girls are supposed to go. I have to do this by the book because I'm not taking any chances on losing my girls. Kathy says DCFS is coming out to inspect the house before noon today. Once Kathy tells me this, I get myself together and call a taxi. Before I go, there's something else I need to be concerned with. Jonathan needs to be buried. I assume the hospital has already spoken with the Libertys, so I have to call them to get information, and I dread making the call.

"Hello, Ma Liberty."

"Hello. I heard you were out of jail." I wonder how she heard. I guess it's that small town thing.

"Yes, ma'am. I'm calling because arrangements need to be made for Jonathan."

"The hospital has already contacted us, his next of kin. We have found a funeral home and set a date."

"That's good, Ma Liberty. When is it and where?"

"Well, Mr. Liberty and I have been talking. We think it best if you don't come to the funeral."

"Ma Liberty, I respect how you feel, but I've done nothing wrong." I'm responding in my usual defensive voice because she always tries to make me feel like everything is my fault. This time she is wrong for sure. I continue.

"I've spent almost half my life with that…with Jonathan, and I have a right and an obligation to be there, me and his children."

I struggle with my tone and with my words. I have had just about enough of this stuck up, "my son is too good for you and so are we" attitude.

"Oh yeah, speaking of the girls, when I was trying to get uhh, Jolita, I mean Jofita, uh, the girls, the police show up saying they need to take the girls. I had to let them go. What else could I do?"

"Yes, I know. I'm working on getting them placed somewhere safe. I thought about them staying with you guys until this thing gets straightened out."

"Well, how long do you think that will take?"

"My court date is not for two months."

"Two months, well, that's a long time. Do you have someone else you can consider? I mean none of this would be necessary if you …"

"If I what, Ma Liberty? I know what you've always thought of me, but you know firsthand that Jonathan was a mean, wicked man. You also know that I had to have loved him to stay with him so long. What's more, he didn't respect me and he never respected you. I can't make you like me or even care about your grandchildren. But let me tell you this, I did not kill Jonathan. Furthermore, whether we come to Jonathan's funeral or not is not your decision to make. In fact, if we were never to see you again in life, that would make all our lives better. I'll find out for myself where everything is being held. You have a good day, Mrs. Liberty."

I hang up the phone before she has an opportunity to say anything else. It feels so good to give that witch a piece of my mind. I have held my peace for years, waiting to be invited to grab a piece of that worn-out, old mattress. Ever since Daddy Liberty hit the jackpot in the lottery 10 years ago, she's been able to afford to buy the whole bed including the frame; and now she's turned into Mrs. Snob. She doesn't even know my girls' names. She has supported Jonathan in his wrongdoing all these years. She's made excuses for him and criticized me and everything I've done the entire time we were married. She knew Jonathan was sleeping around. That was my fault too, according to her. Well, I can't waste anymore time worrying about her. The hospital will give me the information I need to find Jonathan. We'll be there, right up front. I hope I become for her the nightmare she has been for me.

When the taxi comes, I tell Kathy I'll be in touch, and I leave. I give the driver my Portage address, which is only about fifteen minutes away. He finds my house without difficulty. For some reason I'm being drawn back to my house. When the cab pulls up in front of my driveway, I glance around to see if my ghosts are looking. It's still early. They may not have manned their posts yet. It's all clear. I pay the driver with the few dollars I have in my purse. I know that it makes no sense to get out since I can't go inside, but something catches my attention. My car is parked on the street, and I have no idea how it got here. I know I left it at the hospital. My keys are still with me, I think. Maybe one of the officers brought it here. This is a small town, and that would be a small town thing to do. But how did they get the keys?

My whole situation seems so surreal to me. There are so many unexplained things going on that it's like I'm looking at someone else's life through a kaleidoscope. Everything is out of sync. I walk over to the yellow tape that surrounds my house. I have to fight the impulse to tear down the tape and rescue my "hostaged" home from its captors. Luckily, the thought of spending more time in the local jail snaps me out of my plans of emancipation. So here my house stands, cold and alone.

I am afraid to cross the line, but I do walk the perimeter of the property and inspect every window. However, my scrutiny yields me nothing. The windows are cool and silent. Even the one that allowed me entry just a few short months ago will not give away any information. The fence on the sides and back does its job, too. It limits what I can see from the outside. I don't really know what I'm looking for. Maybe I hoped the house would speak to me in some way. Maybe I expected to get some sort of revelation that would explain what happened to Jonathan. Maybe I'm seeking a way out. Anyway, it doesn't matter; I'm getting nothing. I know standing here looking at my house is not going to solve my troubles, yet somehow this place makes me feel better, almost safe. I can't really explain it, but for once in my adult life, I'm free. I don't have to explain myself, cower down to anyone, look for acceptance, beg for mercy, or pretend all is well. I realize I'm on trial for murder, but as far as I'm concerned all is well.

Eventually, my focus turns to my car parked on the street. I can't figure out how it got home. If the police brought it home, why would they leave it on the street? Why didn't they put it in the driveway? This thought prompts me to look more closely at the driveway. The garage door is still open, and Jonathan's car is still in the garage. The one thing I do notice is that there is an oil puddle in the middle of the driveway. I'm sure it didn't come from either of our cars because Jonathan has an issue about that kind of mess. Just a few months ago he was out here cleaning up oil, and he was cussing about who might have brought their car into our driveway leaking oil. Anyway, someone has done it again.

Just standing in the street here in front of my car, I know I must look like a nut. I decide to look through my purse for my keys. I ramble through the usual papers and wallet. I look in the side pockets and zippers. I shake the bag and hear keys, so I decide to dump the purse on the hood of my car. Finally, on the bottom, of course, I find them. I resist the urge to look around quickly again to see who's watching. Instead, I throw my belongings back into my purse and as quickly as possible put the key in my door to unlock it. I'm aware of the eyes watching and somehow I feel a great sense of nervousness. It's probably more embarrassment than anything. They have already had to rescue me once. I'm counting on them doing it again. Even though at this point I look pretty guilty; I won't let it shake my confidence. The truth is here somewhere.

I settle myself once I'm inside my car and take a look around. Everything seems to be the way I left it. When I turn around to inspect the back seat, everything looks normal, too. As I lower my hand to put the key in the ignition, I notice something strange. The ashtray is open. I don't smoke, and it wasn't open when I went to the hospital. In fact, the ashtray is never open. Even when Jonathan used my car, he always flicked his ashes out the window. Maybe... Well, I don't know. There are lots of maybes, but I can't figure out everything today. I do know one thing; I need to keep my job. I have to go see my supervisor right now.

When I turn the key, she doesn't fail me; she starts right up and purrs like a kitten. I sit for a few minutes collecting my thoughts, still wondering about the ashtray. Finally, I pull off. I'm trying to figure out what I'm going to say to my boss. I know everyone has read the paper.

This has to be the talk of this small town. If our Sunday newspaper ran the story on the front page, the story has to be somewhere in the Kalamazoo paper too. It may have even been picked up as far as Ann Arbor or Benton Harbor. After the paper lists me as the prime suspect and displays the mug shot picture of me looking as crazy as this whole situation, it goes on to say how Jonathan was an upstanding member of this community and that the postal system has suffered a great loss. Right there on page one, they insinuate my guilt and try to state my motive for doing it. Surely, that does not nearly compare to how the local gossip mill will twist the story. They will have me tried, convicted, and sentenced all before the sun sets tonight. All the phone lines are buzzing with what they say I did, what they think I did, and what they think the courts should do to me. I can only hope and pray that everyone doesn't feel that way because I do have to be tried in this town.

I round the last corner leading to the hospital. I still have no idea what I will say. I just know that I need my job, but more than anything, I need to keep busy for the next two months. My usual parking spot is vacant, and my parking badge still works on the employee gate. That's a good sign that I haven't been fired yet. I want to sneak into the hospital quietly, so I don't go through emergency like I usually do. I enter through the door where the smokers come outside on their breaks. The mat is still wedged in place, holding the locked door open. My timing is perfect because there is no one outside smoking right now. This allows me to enter unnoticed. At the last minute, I decide to forego my floor supervisor and head for personnel. It may be better if I speak to the man who hired me for the job. His office is on the main level, in the rear of the hospital, away from most of the everyday traffic.

I take a deep breath before turning the knob. I walk up to the secretary and ask to speak with her boss. I can tell from her facial expression that she recognizes me from somewhere. She tells me to have a seat and Mr. Johnson will be right with me. Lucky for me, the office happens to be empty. I don't have to face those stares and questioning eyes that are restrained only out of courtesy, or maybe fear that I am really crazy. I'm too nervous to sit, so, at first, I stand near the window and look out at nothing. Finally, I perch myself in a chair at the far end of this small room. The secretary is gone from her desk long enough for me to notice the pleasant décor, which I remember noticing when I met him down here before. The office is in stark contrast to the hospital wards. This very office is where my hopes of being independent and self-sufficient began. I pray that this is not where my wishes will die.

The wait is giving me time to figure out what I'm going to say. Unfortunately, nothing comes to mind; everything jumps around in my head, all wanting to have its say at the same time. This, of course, will only convince Mr. Johnson that I am disturbed and should be dismissed immediately. My hands are beginning to shake, and they're already sweating. This job and my girls are all I have. They make up who I am. I wish there was more, but this is it, and I need this.

The secretary comes out of the office and interrupts my jumbled thoughts.

"Mr. Johnson will see you now." She exits his office leaving the door open, but stands in the doorway, waiting for me to pass through. "Thank you." I murmured. Ready or not, it's time to go plead my case. I try to straighten my unsteady gait as I walk through the door and across the room to his desk. The secretary leaves a safe distance for my passing, behaving as though brushing against me would cause her bodily harm. Finally, the secretary slowly closes the door and leaves the entryway.

"Have a seat, Mrs. Liberty." Mr. Johnson says this as he points to a chair directly in front of his desk. It matches the warm décor of the room. I'm counting on that warmth extending into his heart. I don't know who should speak first, so I just sit and wait. He seems preoccupied, sifting through papers in a folder, not ready to talk yet. So, I wait. After a long few minutes, he looks up and addresses me.

"You're in quite a mess, aren't you?"

I don't dare answer because I can feel the tears swelling up in my eyes and the lump forming in my throat. A complete breakdown right now would not help my situation. Mr. Johnson looks away and back down at his papers.

"You realize I can't have you working on the floor with patients while you have these accusations hanging over you."

He says these words like a dad scolding his child, but I can hear compassion in his voice. Unfortunately, I can also hear a "but" coming. I'm looking down now, afraid of what's coming next, afraid to look him in the eyes. Mr. Johnson is an older man in good physical condition. He has very pale, piercing, blue eyes. Somehow at the same time, his eyes are also warm and friendly. Mr. Johnson stands up and clears his throat; there is more to come. I feel my body tighten and so does my grip on the arm of the chair. I'm bracing myself for the worst. He walks around to my side, leans back on the desk, and continues.

"I pride myself in being a good judge of character."

He pauses, as though he needs his comment to sink in.

"When I had you down here before to offer you a permanent job, I was given glowing recommendations from everyone who has worked with you. Furthermore, I received a letter last week from a Mrs. Andrews. She says that she's never met you, but she feels she knows you because of some letters you sent her. She wanted to thank me for employing people who care about their patients, especially the sick ones that others just want to throw away."

He pauses again, looking as though he were making a decision based on what he has just said. Still, I say nothing. I do, however, look up at Mr. Johnson, still trying to brace myself for the worst and trying to figure out who Mrs. Andrews is. Then, I remember the letters. He clears his throat yet again. "The hospital board would have me fire you to rid ourselves of any possibility of suspicion or liability, but, that just didn't sit well with me. I believe we need to support our employees."

There is another long pause. Mr. Johnson's eyes now look like they're trying to see inside me to find out who I really am. His scrutiny makes me so uncomfortable that it causes me to look away, back down towards the floor, like a family pet that is being punished for wetting on the rug. This is a posture I know very well. I am not used to defending myself, and I don't feel today is the day to start. So, I sit still; I wait; and, I listen.

"I've checked you out, and I know you need your job. The board would not approve your returning to the nurses' floor. However, they will allow me to reassign you, but you cannot work as a nurse, so I have placed you in a job in the morgue. Your job will be to clean up the labs after an autopsy. That is the best I could do. Oh yeah, I did get them to allow you to maintain the same pay until this issue is resolved."

I allow myself to breathe again. They didn't fire me! As I loosen my grip on the arms of the chair, the realization that I've just been demoted from medical personnel to an orderly begins to penetrate. I suppose I should be more grateful, and maybe in time I will be. Right now, however, hiding my disappointment is easy since the relief of being fired is far more prevalent. It seems he's waiting for me to say something. It's my turn to do as he's done throughout. I clear my throat, buying myself time to think what might be the appropriate words of praise for which he obviously seems to expect.

"Mr. Johnson, I thank you for supporting me. You are right not to judge me like so many others have already done." I pause before going further. I need to collect my thoughts again.

"You are also right about me needing my job. The morgue is a place where I'll avoid the accusing stares."

He stands up straight from leaning on the desk and turns to go back to his seat. He seems pleased with himself. I wait until he is seated again before I continue.

"Mr. Johnson, I won't let you down."

That's all I can think to say. Letting me speak must have just been a courtesy. He obviously is not finished.

"Make sure you get a good lawyer. The hospital doesn't need the negative press. We've put you on the night shift so that you'll be free for court dates and such."

Again, he pauses. I'm not sure why he keeps stopping. At first I thought he was considering my feelings. Now, I think he just likes the dramatics.

"Stop by my secretary's desk on your way out. She has all the job information you'll need. Don't let me down."

He then picks up the telephone, and begins dialing a number. I suppose that's my cue to leave. Before I can say anything else, Mr. Johnson is engaged in conversation. I get to my feet and head for the door. I look back to say thank you, but he doesn't look up. I open the door and step out of his office. The secretary looks up at me as I near her desk. She hands me a folder before I can say anything. She says that all the information I need is inside. I don't open it in the office. Instead, I take it and leave the hospital the same way I came in.

When I get outside, the sun is shining. It has turned into a pleasant, spring day. I have to squint when I first come outside. This type of weather always makes me feel good. After all, I'd dodged the big bullet when I wasn't fired. Fate has intervened and saved me my job. Well, not my job, but a job. I can't be concerned about where they put me. I need to keep my job because of the girls. If cleaning up guts and blood is what I have to do, then so be it. I have bills to pay.

Inside my car, I open the file Mr. Johnson's secretary had given me. Here in bold, black print is a long list of 'Don'ts:'

- **Don't come into the hospital through the front or emergency doors.**
- **Don't come to work early.**
- **Don't remain in the hospital after your shift.**
- **Don't make public statements that include the hospital's name.**
- **Don't converse with any of the patients.**
- **Don't discuss your case with any hospital personnel.**
- **Don't eat in the hospital cafeteria.**
- **Don't use the hospital lounge.**
- **Don't leave the basement except when leaving the building.**

The letter attached to the list explains that these are the conditions to which I must agree if employment is to be continued. There is a place on the bottom of the document for me to sign. It also states,

"The discussion of any of the items on this list with anyone is grounds for termination of employment."

Reading all this makes my heart sink. Somehow, I know my civil rights are being violated. Some whispering voices deep within me tell me to fight back; they urge me to march myself back in, right through the front door, and throw this folder into Mr. Johnson's face. I feel the violation of this letter down deeply. Sadly, the insult of it all does not work its way to the surface. There are too many other issues taking precedence; this one must first battle its way up the ladder before it can be dealt with. My indignation has to be squashed and silenced for the greater good. I know how to do that well; I'm an expert at it. Quickly, I sign the paper and return it to the folder. The document also states that if I accept the terms, I don't start until this Thursday night, from 11 p.m. to 7 a.m. I am pleased about that. I'll have time to wrap up some loose ends before then. Finding someplace to live temporarily is one of those ends.

I've seen all these weekly hotels spring up lately. Maybe I can inquire at one of those places. It shouldn't take the police too long to finish with the crime scene. Maybe I can be home in a week or so. I begin driving around looking at all the roadside hotels that I had barely noticed before. I want to be near the girls, so I'm staying in Kathy's community. I intend to contact my attorney once I've decided on a location. I need him to talk with DCFS about the girls being placed in my custody, or at least I need to get visitations. *Slow down, girl! First things first.*

There it is. That's the place I've seen recently. The sign above it says $125 weekly. That's more than I want to pay, but hopefully I won't be there long. I pull into the lot and park. It's near noon and the place looks deserted. There are only four or five cars in the parking lot. Maybe that means everyone who lives here also has a job. This will have to do.

I look through my wallet for the first time since leaving jail. My checkbook is also where I left it. I have to decide how I will pay for the hotel. When I open my wallet, I see the one credit card Jonathan let me have. I've never used it. I wonder if I can use it now. Well, I'm about to find out. I go into the office lobby. A short, overweight lady stands up and comes over to the counter where I'm standing.

"Yes, ma'am, can I help you?"

"Yes, may I see your rooms? I think I want to rent one."

She gives me a long look before responding. I'm not sure if she recognizes me or not. I still look just as rough as I did in the photo in Sunday's paper.

"Sure, baby. Follow me."

She leads me out of the lobby and into a room just a few doors down. She pulls out a wad of keys from an apron pocket and unlocks the door marked 3. She steps inside first and I follow. To my surprise, the room is very nice. It has a double bed that sits back from the door, almost hidden behind a half wall. A small, plaid love seat greets us just a few steps from the door. It faces a 25" color television on a stand. A few feet past the stand, there is a table with two chairs. In the far corner, a sink is wedged between a short refrigerator and an apartment stove. The bathroom is behind the short wall and through a door, where there is a sink, a shower stall, and a toilet. On the backside of the short wall, there's a four-drawer dresser. The wall that leads to the bathroom has a closet. The double bed takes up the rest of the room, with a three-drawer nightstand on the side of the bed nearest the door. The room is bright, clean, and cozy not at all what I expected.

The lady explains that each unit has a telephone on the nightstand and that local calls are included in the room rate. I follow the lady back to the office to get the details. I'm satisfied with the terms and have her write everything up. She asks how I'm going to pay. I open my wallet and pull out that credit card. Nervously, I hand it to her. I'm almost holding my breath trying not to look too guilty.

The lady swipes the card and we wait. I want to break for the door and run before they discover this is a dead man's credit card. But, I stand my ground. After all, my name is on the card too, and I'm very much alive. So, I stand here and wait. The lady hands me back the card.

CHAPTER NINETEEN

I call Kathy to give her my new temporary phone number and address. She tells me that the meeting with DCFS went well. The girls will be brought to her tomorrow morning. That news brings a great sigh of relief and tears to my eyes. It was never my intentions to make my kids suffer, but that seems to be just what I have done. Even though I know these things have been out of my control, they have managed to throw my girls in what must be a frightening situation for them all. I ask Kathy if DCFS asked her about me. She says the caseworker warns her that I cannot be in the house with the girls. She says that my visits must be supervised by DCFS until further notice. She gives Kathy her name and the number for me to call, and I copy the information down.

After hanging up with Kathy, I call Mr. Martinez's office. The person who answers the phone says he's not in. I leave a message for him to contact me at my temporary number. I have no clothes, toothbrush, comb, or anything. I need to get some things from my house. Mr. Martinez should be able to take care of that. I also want to ask him what to say when setting up visitations with the girls. I guess there is nothing else for me to do right now, except to wait.

I sit on the bed to try to relax. Thinking about sleeping on this strange bed that has had God knows who sleeping on it starts to creep me out. Then, I remember the jail cell and it doesn't seem so bad. As I try to find a comfortable position, I feel the paper in my pocket. It's the list I wrote in jail. I forgot about it. I also forgot to call the hospital about the funeral.

I decide the hospital can wait. My time will be better spent finding out about my cross-eyed rival. I decide to call Debra. I need to prepare to loosen up her tongue.

"Hey, Debra, what's up?"

"Hey girl, you out?"

"Yeah, I'm out. You busy? I want to come hang out with you. I need a shoulder to cry on." I know this is the kind of thing Debra loves.

"Girl, you know I'm here for you. I'm not like the rest of the family with their noses stuck up in the air. I know how Jonathan really was. So, you comin' over?"

"Well, I guess so. Let me get myself together and I'll be over. You want me to bring you anything?"

"Girl, now you know I can always use some more beer."

"Alright, I'll see you later."

"Bye."

I know if I play my cards right, Debra will give me all the information I need. Like I said, she likes messes and drama. I'm going to have to go to the liquor store first. I find some money in one of the corners of my purse and buy a six-pack. I head into town toward the Kalamazoo Country Club. Debra doesn't live far from there. When I get to her house, she opens the door right away, almost as if she was looking out the window for me. I hand her the brown paper bag. This is the first time I have ever brought her beer in the 15 years I've known her. She should be suspicious, but she's already pretty juiced up and welcomes my libation. I follow her back to the family room as I did just a week or so ago. This time no one is here. I can tell by the way she's grinning and starting and stopping her sentences that she has something she wants to tell me. Or, maybe she just wants to throw the other night in my face. Either way, I've learned patience. I can wait. I don't think it will take long.

"Girl, come in and grab a seat. You want some of this beer. Oh yeah, that's right. You don't drink. Well, you'll have to excuse me cuz I do." She gives a ridiculing snicker. I dismiss it and reply,

"I'll take a Pepsi if you have one."

Debra goes into the refrigerator and brings me back a glass and a cold Pepsi while she carries a tall glass of beer for herself. She hands me the drink and glass and plops down on the sofa. She doesn't think she's an alcoholic because all she drinks is beer. Usually by noon her speech is slurred and she stumbles around her big house, maybe washing a few loads of clothes between soap operas and alcohol induced nodding.

"Girl, how are you? What happened? You didn't do it, did you? Cuz I'll tell you, if Tom treated me the way Jonathan did you, I would've killed him, too. It's a scandalous shame how Jonathan flaunted his girlfriend all around the family, knowing he's got a family at home. Girl, how did you take it?"

"Well, I don't know which question to answer first, so I'll just say that I didn't do it. It was hard dealing with him, but I didn't do it. But, I guess I am the most likely suspect. The police say I'm the one with motive."

Debra cuts me off. "Girl, please. If they're basin' it on motive, Valerie had more motive than you ever had." Without even trying, I've got the girl's name.

"Girl, what are you talking about? Valerie had it made. She had Jonathan at her beck and call. He left us to run after her and those five kids. I guess he left your house and went home with her last week." I use Valerie's name like I already knew it.

"You just don't know. It might have started out like that, but that ain't how it ended."

"Well, she wanted him, and she got him. That's why I left him here when I came to pick him up last week. I decided to let her deal with all his drama. After I left, he didn't come home for a week. When he did come home, he was a mess. I fixed him some soup, and me and girls went to the mall. When I get back, he's dead and I'm in jail."

I stop talking and take a long drink of my Pepsi, knowing that this will prompt Debra to talk.

"Girl, you weren't scared when you saw him layin' there dead?"

"He wasn't dead, and I didn't think he was going to die. I knew he was sick, but dying never came to my mind. He was sick like that before, remember?"

"Yeah, I forgot about that. Well, when they left here, Valerie said

171

they were going to a motel. She said she didn't want him going back to that house with you. Girl, she talked about you like a dog. She says you keep chasing after her man. She says every time she gets Jonathan back with her, here you come trying to pull him back."

"She said all that?"

"Girl yeah! She said that and more."

"Well, what about her husband? Jonathan said she put him out when her husband came back from rehab."

"Girl, that didn't last a week. Once he got back, her husband started the same mess all over again."

"Really? So why didn't Jonathan just move back out there to, to... that complex where she lives?"

"Oh, you mean out at the Sun Valley Lane Mobile Park. Well, Fred is so unpredictable. He told Valerie if he caught Jonathan in his house, he'd be a dead man. Valerie would get mad because Jonathan wouldn't go over there. Before she decided to go to the motel, the night you were here, they had a big fight. She said she couldn't afford a motel, and he said he couldn't either cuz you were spending up all his money. She said they fight, I mean fought all the time cuz he made her feel like a whore."

"Well, that's what she is."

We both laugh, but I feel the sting in Debra's words. Her glib remarks about me and her flippant attitude cuts deep, but I refuse to let it show. My laughter is only to keep me from crying and to keep Debra talking. Even in death, Jonathan's lies continue to have an effect.

"She sure is," says Debra. "She said Jonathan makes her dump those kids off wherever she can cuz they are too bad. If he wanted to be bothered with kids, he could be bothered with his own."

Suddenly Debra stops. She stops like somebody who almost divulged a top secret message. I look up, waiting for her to go on. She takes a few more drinks of her beer, seeming as though she realizes the mistake she almost made. I know Debra well enough to know that if she has a secret, it's a big one because Debra tells everything she knows.

As I listen to Debra, I find out the name of the hotel where they stayed. I know the cross-eyed lady's name and her husband's name, and, I also know the name of the mobile home complex where she lives. But,

I still need to get last names. Debra enjoys telling me how Valerie and Jonathan met, how long they've been together, and that they even spent the night at her house once, something that she says she's now sorry for. After an hour or so of this patchwork of a conversation and six beers, Debra is starting to nod off between every other sentence, and my patience is waning. As I sit waiting for her to regain consciousness, I look around her beautiful mini-mansion. I feel a wave of sorrow for her. Her husband, Tom, makes big bucks and hardly ever comes home. He travels between Benton Harbor and Detroit. He claims the distance he has to travel keeps him from coming home more than a few times a month. She has no children, only this house and her beer to keep her company. She's never worked a job in her life and doesn't stay sober long enough to make friends. Even her family, Jonathan's family, doesn't want to be bothered with Miss High-N-Mighty. I look down at her and hear her snoring softly. I feel for her. I realize how easily this could have been me. Actually, in my heart, I know that that was me before I decided to take school seriously and to find myself in the process.

I take a blanket off the back of the sofa and cover her up. I turn off the television and go down the short hallway to the front door. I decide as I walk to the door that I'll never be back. I am sure that Debra will never again be a part of our lives. I close the door softly behind me, leaving behind a prayer for Debra.

***

I get back to my room late in the afternoon; I still need to call the hospital about Jonathan and get in touch with Mr. Martinez. I also need to talk with Kathy and the pastor. I decide not to put off the call to the hospital any longer. When I contact the morgue about Jonathan's body, I find out it has not been released yet. A full autopsy has to be done to determine the complete cause of death. Also, I discover that his parents have arranged for Jonathan's body to be sent to A.J. Thompson's Funeral Home. I inform her of my right to select where Jonathan is laid to rest. After I tell her that, the lady is eager to share with me a few of the comments made by Ma Liberty regarding my status. I decide to make a point. My only experience with funeral homes is when Mom died, and I don't want Jonathan to go there, so I ask the lady which funeral homes are most often used. The lady on the phone gives me a short list. She tells me that I will have to come down and sign some papers before they will release him. I agree and decide on The House of Peace Funeral Home because it sounds just as phony as Jonathan really was.

On Wednesday, more than a week after Jonathan's death, the body will be released to the funeral home I selected. I get the number and address from the hospital and call to make the final arrangements. They are able to place Jonathan on the schedule for Saturday morning of the same week. The representative tells me over the phone about the different services they offer. I select the least expensive package. Everything will be held at the funeral home because I refuse to humiliate myself or my church by having Jonathan's funeral there. The burial is scheduled to follow the wake and funeral services. There will be no repast. Those who come will see, hear, and leave. Without leaving my room, the funeral is all taken care of because the hospital decides to fax all the paperwork I need to sign to the motel office, which I sign and fax right back.

My next call is to Mr. Martinez. This time he's in the office. I discuss with him my finances, Jonathan's insurance, his burial, my personal belongings, my new address, and my visitations with the girls. I also tell him about the private investigator, Mr. Tony, and the little investigation I did myself. I remind Mr. Martinez that I'm not the only person who had motive and opportunity.

This is a big case for this town. Mr. Martinez had attended Cornell University through a scholarship program designed to support minorities. That's where he received his law degree. He returned to Michigan passionate for justice and landed a job as a public defender. He has been in that position for 10 years now. This is the case he has been waiting for to boost his career right out of public defense into private defense, at least as a junior partner in Grand Rapids or maybe Detroit. His ambition shows. He wants to win this case, and I want him to win, too. He has me tell him all I know about Valerie and her relationship with Jonathan. My details are sketchy at best, but enough for him to investigate. He takes

174

down Kathy's number so that he can contact the private investigator. I also tell him about the whipping I gave Valerie when she sat waiting for me in my house with all the boldness of a fool. The last thing I say to him is how my ghosts watch out for me and are always on their posts.

Mr. Martinez tells me not to worry. He says that he'll get permission to enter the house to get me some personal items. He just needs a list from me. He also says he'll contact DCFS to discuss visitation arrangements with the girls and to get permission for the girls to attend their father's funeral along with me. He will talk with the insurance company and Jonathan's pension fund providers to try to get them to release some money so that the house can still be maintained for the children who are his beneficiaries in the event that I am not acquitted. He also says he'll ask the DCFS investigators to contact me as soon as possible. I hang up the phone feeling better. That sense of freedom comes over me again. Unfortunately, as I look around this small cubby hole that I call home, I'm left with overwhelming loneliness.

Finally, I get around to contacting my pastor. This will be our first time speaking since my arrest. I thank Pastor Johnny for paying my bail and supporting us with prayers. I confess how ashamed I am about some of my behaviors in this whole situation. It's clear that we are only human and that God stands between us and insanity. We talk for over an hour. I share my fears and concerns, and I even tell Pastor Johnny of some of the hardships my marriage has taken me through. I tell him how embarrassed I was to let anyone know. We talk about Ma and how she helped to hold things together in my life. We talk until I'm all talked out. Then we pray. It is one that uplifts God in the midst of the entire calamity. By the time I hang up, I feel renewed. I am relaxed, and I'm able to sleep.

I start work on Thursday night. That day, I am able to visit with the girls. We can't visit at Kathy's house; all supervised visits are held at one of the county buildings. It is set up like a playroom with small tables and chairs all over. There are toys, games, and a television in the room. Our visit starts with lots of hugging and crying from the two smaller girls, but Jonita has no expression at all. She comes over to hug me and whispers in my ear.

"I'm glad."

There is no reaction on my part. I wrap my arms around Jonita and hold her like a baby. Deep down inside I knew, and I let Nita know that I'm sorry I didn't protect her. I tell her so. She hugs me tighter and we stay embraced until they tell us our visit is over. Kathy has to pull Jonita away. I promise her that it won't be long. We'll all be back together soon.

Then, I remember that my court date is two months away. I hate that it's going to take so long. I want this whole thing to be over. I also remember Mr. Martinez saying when we first met that he hopes the court date will be extended. He says the evidence against me is pretty damaging, but it is circumstantial. We will need all the time we can get to prepare for our case. Now is not the time for me to lose hope. All of us will have to be patient.

The week passes quickly, and all the funeral information has been disbursed. The private investigator has set up two cameras in the small funeral home. There's one visible up front near the casket. The other camera is hidden back in the rear near the exit. I don't know what he's looking for, but I hope he finds it.

Saturday morning the funeral car goes to Kathy's house to pick up the girls and brings them to the funeral home. I drive myself so that the funeral car won't have to stop twice. I have gotten permission for the children and me to be together at the funeral without a chaperone. The girls have on their Easter dresses we purchased the day Jonathan died. They look beautiful. We all come in together and arrange ourselves on the front row, waiting for the wake to begin. This will be the first time anyone sees his body. My instructions to the funeral home are that no one is to see the body before the wake. My intention is for this to be done quickly and to get everyone to leave. I have explained to the girls how funerals proceed. They did not attend Ma's. They know that their daddy is no longer in that body. The younger ones want to know if Daddy is in heaven. I resist the urge to tell them that he has burst hell wide open and is doomed to eternal damnation. Instead, I say that we will have to wait until we face judgment before God, and then we will know. Of course, they want to know when that will be. I shush them because the service is starting.

176

Mr. and Mrs. Liberty show up. They refuse to look at me or speak to me. They do, however, pat the girls on their heads. As I sit looking at them, I'm glad I decided to do it this way. I'm imposing on no one, and when we get up and leave, there's no need to look back, no lingering memories that I must constantly be reminded of. Soft music is playing and people are coming to view the body. Some have just come to see the lady from their town who murdered her husband. I can see inside the casket from my seat. Jonathan looks like himself, not as gorgeous like when we first met, but there is still a hint of his good looks even in death. The funeral home did a nice job of filling out his face that had sunken in weeks before his death. I silently wish this ordeal might be over soon. The people trickle in slowly, one or two at a time. Quite a few of his co-workers come. Someone from the post office hands me an envelope with condolences and, I suppose, some money in it. I take it and smile, not hugging or reaching out to any of them. I can see it in their faces. They all know.

Finally, the funeral services begin. A few people from my church are listed on the program to sing a few songs. The songs they sing bring tears to my eyes. I let the people think what they want. I won't shed a tear for Jonathan. I grit my teeth as person after person rise and give testimony of what a great friend, son, father, husband, and employee he was. My eyes refuse to look at the hypocrites who smear the words "decency and honor" over his worthless carcass. But, I remain silent in my fury. One more hour and it will all be over.

I'm careful to keep the girls close. I don't want anyone saying things to them that might upset them. People love gossip, and I know Debra will be here leading the charge. Speak of the devil, she strolls in during the middle of the services. She waltzes right up to the front and tries to get a seat in the front row with me. She wiggles until she positions herself on the pew between Kathy and Jonita. Kathy and I were on either side of Jonita. I don't make eye contact with Debra. I don't have to; her breath reeks of alcohol. It seems to permeate the entire room. I turn my head the opposite way in an attempt to get some relief. I begin to pray harder than ever that the service will be over soon.

The final condolence is being read and the final review of the body is coming. The ushers come down to reopen the casket and line up people to process past him. That's when Mother Liberty begins her show. She wails loud enough to wake the dead. The girls are visibly starting to get upset. Mother Liberty then gets up from her seat and stumbles over to the casket. She begins draping herself over Jonathan, crying hysterically trying to call Jonathan back to life.

At this point I decide it is time for the girls and me to leave. I get Kathy's attention and stand. We gather up the girls. Mother Liberty is not too distressed to see me get up because that is her cue to really clown.

"Hold on there, missy," is how she first addresses me. From there, it goes downhill fast.

"Where the hell do you think you're going? You killed my son; now you want to run off with my grandbabies. I guess you want to kill them, too."

I do not respond. The condemning accusations feel very familiar. I only continue to move toward the aisle that will lead us out of the building. I pick Jovida up as Kathy ushers the other two girls up the aisle. My ignoring her has the same effect on her that it had on Jonathan. It makes her nastier than ever. She untangles herself from the casket and runs down the aisle to catch up with me. She comes from behind and grabs my arm so hard that I almost drop Jovida. She spins me around and screams in my face.

"How dare you run? You killed him! You planned this event; you need to stay and see this through."

It suddenly gets quiet enough to hear a pin drop. Even the organist stops playing. I feel years of anger rising in me. I'm ready to attack. I put Jovida on the floor, using that few seconds to control my anger. My lips are tight and my eyes narrow. I choose my words carefully because I mean for them to sting.

"Do not put your hands on me again, old woman. I have listened to all the lies I intend to endure. You have been the most wicked of all. You are the one who taught your son that it's alright to abuse me. When you could have spoken up for what was right, you didn't. In fact, you indulged him in his adulterous fantasies. You and the rest of these people know that he's not even worthy of a decent send-off. That's why I didn't humiliate myself and God by having his funeral in a church. I didn't want you and all these good people to have to lie in the presence of God. I'm leaving you and all who love Jonathan here, and as far as my children are concerned, it is my wish that neither they nor I ever lay eyes on you again."

I turn, grab Jovida's hand, and we walk away. I hear Debra start the chant of names that begin to ring out from Jonathan's family. I push Kathy on toward the door, keeping my body turned in such a way that I won't completely turn my back on this woman of treachery because I do not trust her. Before I can get to the door, my pastor, and several of our deacons have positioned themselves between them and me. I am past angry; I feel rage. I don't want my girls to see this. Everyone gets into my car. I start the car, still struggling to control my emotions. I point myself in the direction of Kathy's house. We travel in silence. Once we pull up in front of Kathy's house, I am able to find my pleasant voice. I turn around and speak to the girls.

"Mommy is sorry about what just happened. Your grandma is very upset about your daddy dying." Jolisa interrupts, "Mommy why were they calling you names and saying you killed daddy?" I knew the question was coming sooner or later. I have already rehearsed my answer.

"Baby, people think that mommy had something to do with daddy's death. Sometimes things look one way but they really aren't. Remember when I fussed at you because I found my favorite scarf all dirty, and it was on your bed?" Jolisa nods in the affirmative.

"Well, it wasn't until you explained to me that you found it by the front door and picked it up to give it back to me that I realized I must have dropped it when I was leaving and it got stepped on. That's when I found out I was wrong." Jolisa seemed to understand.

Then she asks, "When will they listen to you?"

"Mommy will have to go to court. My lawyer, Mr. Martinez, will speak for me and tell them the truth. Then people will know that it was not me."

All the girls wrap their arms around me and squeeze. Even Kathy gets in on it. Leaving them is painful, but I dare not stay alone with them any longer. I thank Kathy for her help, and she gets out the car with the girls. I pull off without looking back. It hurts like hell.

I hear later on that night that Ma Liberty continued performing for the mourners for another 20 minutes before she went back to draping herself over the casket again. Once she becomes the center of attention again and the epitome of the grieving mother, they are able to go on with the funeral and proceed to the burial.

I return to my room, undress, and go to bed for a few hours before I have to go to work. My shift starts at 11 p.m. I need to get a nap and relax before going. I only have to work tonight; then I'm off on Sunday and Monday night. I lie down looking forward to getting up. Having somewhere to go and something to do are the distractions that keep me sane.

***

After having worked in the morgue for a few days, I realize it is not nearly as bad as I thought it would be. I have never been down here before, so my impression was of a terrible blood-soaked, awful-smelling dungeon. On the contrary, everything is very clean. The coroner must have all the chemicals and supplies where they belong without any contamination in order to give reliable autopsy reports. Blood is drained either into a container, or it goes directly into a drain. The bodies are washed down and placed on stainless steel slabs to be rolled in a drawer. My job is to wash down all the tables, sinks, counter top, and refill chemical bottles that are low. I also need to use specific, proper dispensers for any contaminated materials, including needles, sponges, swabs, and dressings, which is similar to the process we used on the infectious disease ward. Sometimes the coroner is still working when I come. If that happens, he uses me as his assistant; I hand him instruments, help move bodies, or assist in tagging people if there is a backlog.

I'm usually finished with my responsibilities by 2 a.m. I spend the rest of my night reading my Bible or going over old nursing books so that I won't have forgotten any of my skills when this ordeal is over. But, I still miss the people; I miss my job.

CHAPTER TWENTY

The days are going by very slowly. I call Kathy at least five times a day. I talk to the girls almost every time I call. The social worker allows me to meet with the girls three times each week. Those are the highlight of my week.

There is just one month left before my court date. The district attorney is almost ready to start the jury selection process. This is when it finally sinks in that I'm in serious trouble. Mr. Martinez tells me that he has enough evidence to get me off, and assures me that all we need to do is create a reasonable doubt. He says we have enough evidence to do that. He is so confident that he makes arrangements to see the district attorney, Jack Aaye, to share with him what he's uncovered in order to expedite things and avoid a trail. Mr. Aaye agrees to meet us in his office.

Apparently, Mr. Martinez doesn't know how strong this small town, "good old boy" corruption really is. Even though we are in the year 2000, a new millennium, the minds of many in our town have not kept up. This case is as big for Mr. Aaye as it is for Mr. Martinez. The assistant district attorney has once again been pushed aside, while Mr. Jack Aaye soaks up all the publicity that has come with this case. Usually that means that a political office is in sight. Not only does Mr. Aaye not plan on losing, but he certainly has no intention of losing to a young, Latino public defender. Instead of allowing Mr. Martinez to show his evidence, Mr. Aaye tells him that this might be a good time for us to think about

182

cutting a deal. Of course, Mr. Martinez wants to know what he's basing his case on.

Mr. Aaye is terribly proud of himself; it shows in the way he struts around his office in front of Mr. Martinez and me. He offers Mr. Martinez pretty much the same evidence he showed me that day at the jail. He's basing everything on motive and opportunity. He thinks that his evidence of me calling the police on Jonathan for battery and putting him out of our house is motive. He uses the fact that I'm a nurse and know about chemicals as means. He believes this is enough to seal both his case and my fate. When Mr. Martinez tries to show him the new evidence we have, he refuses to listen. Figuratively speaking, he tells Mr. Martinez that he's playing outside of his league and to prepare for the beating he will get for taking on grown men, especially the white ones. Since Mr. Aaye's not a complete fool, he chooses his words carefully, but his meaning is clear. When he's all finished strutting and telling us what he's going to do, he asks me if I want to plead guilty to involuntary manslaughter. That's when Mr. Martinez gets to his feet and announces that we are leaving. He tells Mr. Aaye that we'll see him in court.

Needless to say, things did not go well today. Mr. Martinez is visibly shaken while he's telling me not to worry. He also seems slightly embarrassed. I don't find myself feeling very confident right at this moment. But, the one thing I am sure about is that Mr. Aaye has insulted Mr. Martinez on a level that will make him sacrifice everything to win my case.

When we leave Mr. Aaye's office, we go to see Mr. Tony, the private investigator. He has quite a bit of information and evidence to add to the case. When we meet with him, he has the videotape from the funeral. The front camera has the part I already saw, people coming in, sitting down, service starting, Mother Liberty clowning, Debra shouting, nothing unusual for Jonathan's family. However, the back camera reveals a different story. I am able to see for myself why they believe we will win. I'm starting to feel better, but at the same time I feel crushed.

***

During the next few weeks, Juan Martinez and I spend a great deal of time together. He has taken me out to eat a few times to discuss our case. These occasions have given me opportunities to know Juan better. Both his parents come from a place called Cuernavaca, Mexico. His explanation of how they got here is sketchy at best, but his Mom and Dad somehow make it to America, and Juan is born as an American citizen. His parents were initially illegal when he was a child, so Juan moved around a lot, eventually landing in Michigan just as he started high school. His parents worked hard, and whatever they were running from in Mexico motivated them to keep working hard and pushing Juan to get an education. It inspired them to eventually get their citizenship. For Juan, school was his top priority. His parents wanted so much for him to be American that they did what many immigrants have done. They refused to allow Juan to speak Spanish at home. I believe that's why he doesn't appear to have an accent when he speaks. Although when we are out, he speaks Spanish at restaurants like a native. In fact, the day we abruptly left the D.A.'s office is the first time I heard a hint of an accent. I guess anger must allow it to come through.

He is the first one in his family to finish college, and he shoulders the great responsibility of being a constant example for them, sponsoring some financially. He implies that sometimes the pressure to be the best and make his parents proud gets to be too much. The responsibility he feels for so many family members has also made it almost impossible for him to have a normal romantic relationship with anyone. This summary of Juan's life did not come easily. Whenever he found the conversation shifting to himself and his life, he quickly shifted it away from himself and back to me. I understand his struggle to be someone special. It reminds me of my struggle to be anybody. I think we are somehow connected in that way, but, I don't tell him that.

***

Four weeks have passed and my house is still being held hostage behind the yellow tape, so I'm still living in this motel. Somehow I've gotten used to it. I guess any place is better than jail. The insurance company has agreed to put a portion of the insurance money in a trust fund for the children, who are next in line as Jonathan's heirs. A trustee is assigned who can use the money for the upkeep of the house and the girls' needs.

In the meantime, the D.A. and my attorney are preparing to select the jury. Mr. Martinez tries to get as many female jurors as possible, while Mr. Jack Aaye sways towards male candidates. Mr. Martinez wins with seven females and five males. That is one milestone in our favor. Mr. Martinez says that he's submitted all the evidence he has to Mr. Jack Aaye, but he doesn't think he has looked at it. He blindly believes he's got the upper hand. Mr. Martinez believes it's that arrogance that might help us win.

The first day of the trial arrives, and I have to admit I'm extremely nervous. I didn't work last night; I asked for two weeks vacation. I only have a week's worth of time, but my supervisor approved it anyway. I'm sure he knows I may not be back, depending on the verdict. Perhaps he's considering looking for my replacement. I picked out what to wear to court almost a month ago. Now, I want to wear anything but that. My choices are limited, so it doesn't take long to narrow things down. I don't want to look like a frumpy housewife or a victim, but I don't want to come off indignant or arrogant either. I want to project who I am: a woman who has worked hard to find a place in this world only to have it ripped away from her due to circumstantial evidence. I keep telling myself that being right has to count for something, even in a messed-up world. Everything looks like it's working against me, but I refuse to give in. Mr. Martinez has shown me that he means business even if it is only to make a point to the district attorney and further his own career.

I park my car down near the street in the outdoor parking lot around the back of the building. Before exiting my car, I quietly wish that disappearing were an option. Since it isn't, I slowly mount the back stairs and enter the building from the rear. I enter the courthouse for the first time; it's not the same location where they held the arraignment. This building is on the square in the downtown area. The small town snoops are not out front waiting when I arrive. I'm not just wearing dark sunglasses because it's a bright summer day; it's also a feeble attempt to disguise my face from any of my neighborhood onlookers. I have spent the last few months being pointed out in the grocery store, at the mall, on the street, and any of the other places I go in this town. People stopped being polite over a month ago; they no longer whisper their disdain or their approval. They now loudly voice their opinions about what I have allegedly done, negative or positive. I try not to cringe. I know from firsthand experience that you can't change anyone's mind about anything if that's what they want to believe.

Surprisingly, there are no cameras or reporters either. My arrest took place over two months ago and from the looks of the outer halls of the courthouse, this is old news that no one cares to follow any further. I don't know how to react to that, but in a way, I do feel some relief.

I decide to climb the stairs instead of taking the elevator to look for Room 203. Once on the second floor, it is easy to locate. I peer through my dark shades into the windowed doors. It appears to be deserted. I feel myself let out a sigh of relief. I'm early. I want to go inside and wait alone, knowing that Mr. Martinez will probably come running in at the last minute. I pull the handle on the door and discover that it's locked. I don't want to just stand here looking out of place, waiting for the doors to be unlocked, so I decide to find a spot to disappear and wait. I remove the dark glasses and begin looking around the second floor. All I see near me are a few benches placed here and there. I decide to go down the hall to the right of the courtroom, away from the stairs, to find a place to wait. Then I notice the break in the line of wall. There along the hall, just as it begins to curve, is an opening where an office or room of some sort lies locked within the small break along the wall. By standing at the edge of the break, looking back the way I had just come, I have a perfect view of the courtroom door and the stairs. Here, I feel myself breathe again. Unfortunately, not much time goes by before I almost stop breathing altogether.

While spying on what, I don't know, there she appears. Once again, at the most unlikely place appears Valerie, the cross-eyed lady. I spot her as she mounts the last few steps. Her movements are familiar. They have that strange look. I reposition myself so that I can see her more clearly without exposing my hiding place. I know what's wrong with her, and it makes me feel faint.

I keep asking myself, *What is she doing here?* My suspicious mind tells me that she's here to finish hammering the nails into my coffin. Before I can come up with any clear reasons for her presence, my train of thought is interrupted when people start coming from every corridor, entering the courtroom. That's when I see a few cameramen enter the floor from the elevator, and stand around in the hallway. I was wrong. This looks like it's going to be the media circus I feared. My girls do not need to see their mother in the newspaper again, unless she is being acquitted.

With all the shuffling of the people coming onto the second floor, I lose track of the cross-eyed lady. I know her name, but I prefer using my name for her. That allows me to think of her more as a thing and not a person. I could say more about what I really feel about her, but I need to figure out why she's here.

A quick glance at my watch propels me back into my previous state of anxiety. I know I can't hide forever; it's time for me to go inside the courtroom. I have to leave the safety of my secret spot and subject myself to the eyes of the now crowded hall. While I'm trying to pull myself together, my in-laws come up the stairs and join the crowd. I haven't spoken or seen them since the funeral. Ma Liberty is wearing all black. She looks like the perfect image of the heartbroken mother who has a right to hate her murderous daughter-in-law.

I abandon my place of refuge and walk swiftly toward the courtroom doors. As soon as I enter, all eyes turn around. Ma Liberty's eyes are the first ones to meet mine. The expression on her face tells me exactly how she feels about me. Once she's sure that I have seen the evil eye she shoots at me, she turns back around and faces the front. Kathy says she hasn't called the girls even once in the two months that they have been with her. I guess I should be glad considering what a wicked, vile person she is. She and Daddy Liberty are sending me and the whole town a message by seating themselves behind the district attorney.

After I come through the courtroom door, I seem unable to move in one direction or another. I didn't expect this. While trying hard to make a decision, Attorney Martinez does his usual fast crash through the double doors and startles me. He takes me by the arm in one fluid motion as though he knew I'd be standing here. He ushers me to the front directly to the defendant's table. We haven't talked about specific strategy or what I can expect. I'm feeling completely off-balance. Mr. Martinez points to a chair, and I sit to his left. He sits down next to me and starts to arrange the papers from his briefcase. All the evidence he's presenting is labeled and already on the table by the court reporter. The D.A. comes in a little after we arrive. He is looking confident and smug. His table is to our right. He takes out his papers and sits, poised ready for action.

I don't want to look behind me because I am already nervous. I position myself in the chair, fold my hands close to me on the table, and fix my eyes forward. I can hear the people rustle and whisper behind me. Every few seconds I hear a group laughing softly. I want to turn around. I want to see what's so damn funny. I feel the muscles tense in my neck. Just being in the courtroom has drenched me with the realization that I could be going to prison. I can feel a small trickle of sweat run slowly down my hairline on the side of my face. I want to wipe it away, but I seem to be frozen. The urge to cry takes hold of me. I don't mean a soft whimper or weeping. I want to release a strong, violent, wrenching that takes control of all my being until it turns into convulsions. I want to fall out in the floor, the way an obstinate child might, and give back every suspicious stare and all the hateful words to the people in this room and this town have hurled at me. I want the courtroom to have all my beatings and disappointments. I can feel the breakdown coming as I sit trying to hold it back. It is easing its way up into my throat, and I can feel it rising. I dare not close my eyes. I am trying to focus when it's my eyes that save me. I catch a glimpse of a familiar figure just to the left of me. I turn my head slightly and I can see that it's Kathy. Sitting beside her is Jonita. When Jonita sees she has caught my eye, her smile gets bigger, and I'm able to feel her warmth and some of the tension release in my neck. Kathy and I hadn't discussed Jonita coming here. I am concerned about the effects this trial might have on her. Jonita has just had her 13th birthday and she's very mature, but this is stuff that I'm not mature enough to handle. I guess Kathy has her reasons, reasons I want to hear about later.

A door behind the judge's bench opens and breaks my train of thought. The judge comes in, and the bailiff gives an "All rise" call. He says a few other words, including the judge's name, Suzie Horne. The judge is a white female, medium build, and somewhere in her late 40s. She mounts the few steps adjacent to her elevated judge platform and sits. That same bailiff tells us to be seated. Everything starts out the same way that traffic court goes, but slowly things begin to change. This is a trial; and no other case will be heard but mine. The crowd of people in the courtroom today is here because of my case. Every seat is filled. One would think that people would have better things to do, like work. I guess that's not the case. I feel like Tom Robinson, Boo Radley, and Atticus Finch from *To Kill a Mockingbird*, but all wrapped together, watching and waiting for the townspeople to turn on me.

The jury is not present yet. The judge gives a few words of instruction, setting the ground rules for today's trial before allowing the jury to enter. Once she finishes, she has the bailiff bring the jury in. A door opens to my right and 12 people enter and sit in a boxed-off area close to the district attorney's table. We watch the seven female jurors enter, who the D.A. relentlessly tried to dismiss, in hope of eliminating the possibility of sympathy votes. Four of them appear to be about my age, while the other three are my mother's age. The five gentlemen remaining on the jury are only slightly older than me. Mr. Martinez was hoping for more father figure males, but the D.A. won out on the selection of the men.

The jurors walk in looking directly at me, sizing me up. I'm sizing them up, too. The seven women look just like me. I don't mean the same color or size; I mean they could be sitting where I'm sitting if not for the grace of God. The men, however, are a different story. I can't read them at all, but, I can see now that two of the five men appear to look older, which might be to my advantage. If the truth doesn't work, then I'll have to depend on sympathy to help me through this. After all, it could be or might be their daughters who end up in this same type of mess.

Everyone is now in place, and it's time for Mr. Jack Aaye to start. It is just like something out of a movie.

"Ladies and gentlemen of the jury, Mrs. Liberty may look like a sweet, heartbroken widow who would have you believe that her husband of 15 years mysteriously died in their home from poisoning. She not only has the knowledge of how to poison him, but she also has the means by which to poison him. This woman has committed cold-blooded, premeditated murder. I intend to prove beyond a reasonable doubt that she systematically poisoned Mr. Liberty to death. I will bring witness after witness who will testify that theirs was a volatile relationship. I'll also give evidence that Mrs. Liberty has tried poisoning her husband before and decided against it at that time for whatever reason. This time however, she was successful."

I try to look like myself and not let his words affect me. I look innocent because I am. Nothing he says should disturb me because I know that what he's saying is what some people think about me. But I feel myself squirming from the scrutiny of the jury members' eyes. The D.A. has deliberately drawn their eyes to me. Their stares are penetrating, but I have to keep my cool. Mr. Martinez pats me on the hand to get my attention. I look away from the jury to see what he wants, and I learn he just wants to distract me. The D.A. does a little more strutting like a peacock and finally sits down.

It's time for Mr. Martinez's opening statement. He doesn't hurry. He takes a long, disgusted look at Mr. Aaye before he stands. He gets up, shaking his head from side to side like he is sadly disappointed in what Mr. Aaye has just said, and he begins to turn to address the jury.

"Ladies and gentlemen of the jury, the prosecutor, my colleague, would have you to believe that Mrs. Liberty is a cold-blooded murderer. He bases his proof on the fact that Mr. Liberty was abusive to his wife. And that is true, but I will prove that Mrs. Liberty was not the only one with motive and opportunity who could have killed him. He didn't tell you that Mr. Liberty was not making his home with Mrs. Liberty on a regular basis. He didn't mention that there can be others who had just as much motive and opportunity to poison him. The D.A., like many other overzealous prosecutors, has made the mistake of focusing only on the spouse, making no attempt to investigate any others. Mr. Aaye has laid all his hopes of success, in the biggest case this town has ever seen, upon the conviction of Mrs. Liberty. I intend to present the information that the prosecuting attorney refused to review when I presented it to him weeks ago. I will prove that Mrs. Liberty is a victim of circumstances and should be set free by this court. Yes, she happens to live where the body was found, and yes, she happens to be married to the victim. That's where everything stops for her. As the jury, you are charged with the responsibility of acquitting Mrs. Liberty on a reasonable doubt once you listen and evaluate the information that I present to you …"

When Mr. Martinez finishes, he takes another long look at Mr. Aaye before taking his seat. He manages to do the same thing Mr. Aaye had done to me by forcing the jury's eyes to land on the D.A. It looks like Mr. Martinez has made a good start; he has planted the seed of doubt or at least piqued their curiosity. They now have to decide if Mr. Aaye is willing to railroad me into the gas chamber, electric chair, or whatever it is they use now, to further his own career.

Mr. Aaye feels the heat and turns a light shade of red, but recovers quickly. I guess right about now he's sorry that he dismissed Mr. Martinez so quickly. Right now, he has to make the jury forget what Mr. Martinez has just promised.

"Mr. Aaye, if you're ready to begin, you can call your first witness," said Judge Horne.

Mr. Aaye nods and quickly fumbles through his stack of papers and clears his throat. He calls the coroner as his first witness. I was expecting the coroner at the hospital where my husband was taken. This tall thin man comes past me from the audience and turns around ready to enter the witness stand. That's when I see his face and realize that he's the county coroner, Mr. Quincy, and my new boss for the past few months. I had no idea he had done the autopsy on Jonathan's body; he never mentioned anything to me. His testimony reveals that he was called in by the other coroner because he had more experience with poisons. My boss explains that Jonathan had been poisoned over a long period of time with ethylene glycol, commonly known as antifreeze. The coroner estimates the time to be anywhere between two days to two months before his death. It's too hard to tell. I thought to myself that the latter time is about the time that he left to live with you-know-who. He explains that Jonathan obviously did not realize he was being poisoned because antifreeze is hard to detect. It can be colorless, it's sweet, and it does not burn when it goes down, especially when it's mixed with something like sweet tea or coffee that already has a strong taste. Also, according to his medical records, Jonathan had been diagnosed before with a virus that causes similar symptoms. The coroner tells us that he read Jonathan's medical file and he believes Jonathan must have thought the virus had returned. Mr. Aaye asks him how difficult it would be to poison Jonathan without his knowledge. His response is that anyone who Jonathan spent time with regularly could have put poison in his food or drink very easily without his knowledge. He then asks if it were possible that what he described as a virus could have been a failed attempt at poisoning. Mr. Quincy said that the lab reports from years earlier show that there was definitely a virus. I don't know if that's the answer he wanted, but Mr. Aaye sits down after that.

Mr. Martinez gets up asking the same question.

"Are you saying that it would have been easy for anyone, or someone other than Mrs. Liberty to have poisoned Mr. Liberty?"

"Yes."

Mr. Martinez asks one more question.

"Could the affects of the antifreeze come and go over long periods of time if the poison were not given on a daily basis?"

"Yes. The poison could have been administered several times a week or only once every two weeks. Mr. Liberty might be sick for awhile with vomiting, headaches, and drowsiness and then feel better if he was not being given antifreeze for a while."

Mr. Martinez sits down after that response. He seems satisfied. Next, Mr. Aaye calls one of the EMTs whom I had called to the house. After the usual swearing in, Mr. Aaye asks about the condition of Jonathan when he arrived at my house. He says Jonathan was barely breathing when they carried him down to the waiting gurney in the living room. He asks the rescuer if I rode with them to the hospital.

The driver says, "No." That is all Mr. Aaye asks.

Mr. Martinez asks the EMT if he has any idea why I had not gone with the ambulance. The attendant replies that I told him I was coming as soon as I got someone to watch the children, and that I asked where they were taking Jonathan. Then, he quickly closed the door and left.

"What was Mr. Liberty's condition when you arrived?"

"Mrs. Liberty was administering CPR, but there was no pulse. We took over from there."

Mr. Martinez asks if I told him anything else while they were at my house.

He replies, "Mrs. Liberty said she'd been shopping and came home and found him like that. She called for help immediately. She told us she'd been trying to get him to go to the doctor, but he refused."

Mr. Martinez asks, "Did she say how long she'd been trying to get him to see a doctor?"

"She said she'd been trying to get him to go for several weeks before that day. She said she tried to take him when he came in that morning, and again he refused."

"Are you sure she said that she tried to take him to the doctor?"

"Yes, she said he refused to go."

"Thank you."

The D.A.'s next witness is the police officer who slammed me to the floor at the hospital. He didn't look at me, but I was free to stare at him with disdain. Mr. Aaye asks what prompted my arrest. The officer told how Jonathan was brought into the hospital and how the doctors ran a toxic substance screening and did not discover any poison in his system. However, they suspected foul play and notified the police that they felt something suspicious had happened to Jonathan. Mr. Aaye asks if there was anything unusual about the screening. The officer says that Jonathan was so sick that they were administering every test they could find to determine what was wrong. The officer is asked about his response to the doctor's preliminary diagnosis. He tells them that they decided to go to the house to talk with me, but I was already gone. They found the children there with a neighbor. They asked the neighbor for permission to enter the house. Once inside, they asked her where Jonathan had been when the ambulance came. She told them she didn't know. She assumed the bedroom. They went upstairs and found an over-turned thermos on the floor, wrapped it up, and brought it back to the hospital. Upon their return, Jonathan had expired, and they gave the thermos to the doctor for analysis of its content. That's when the poison was discovered and the proper test was done that detected what was in Jonathan's system. Once I arrived, they instructed the nurse to make me wait, even though they knew Jonathan was dead. The officer says they left me there until they had all the evidence. When they entered the waiting room, one officer asked the nurse about me. At first she seemed confused, but then she pointed me out to them.

Mr. Aaye asks another question, "Were any fingerprints found on the thermos?"

"Yes."

"Were there any you could identify?"

"Yes, there were prints belonging to Mrs. Liberty."

Mr. Aaye seems satisfied with the officer's response and takes his seat. Mr. Martinez walks over to the officer and looks him squarely in the eyes. The officer appears to be a little nervous. Mr. Martinez only asks one question pertaining to the thermos.

"How many sets of fingerprints other than Mrs. Liberty's were found on the thermos?"

Before he can answer, Mr. Aaye jumps up from his seat and objects. The judge overrules him. Besides, she's interested in the answer herself.

The officer replies, "There were three other sets of fingerprints." Mr. Martinez asks him what caused him to arrest me in the first place. He said it was the thermos.

The courtroom starts getting noisy after the last response from the witness. The judge has to use her gavel to quiet things.

Mr. Martinez asks him, "When you suspected that Mr. Liberty may have been poisoned, did you get a search warrant to enter the Liberty home?"

"No, sir. Well, yes, sir. The officers went there to speak with Mrs. Liberty, but she was not there, like I said earlier," the officer says nervously.

Mr. Martinez then goes in for the kill. "If she was not home, who gave you permission to enter, search, and remove anything without a warrant?"

"We asked the neighbor lady at the house who answered the door," he replies.

"OK, so you removed evidence without a warrant. So, when was the answer to having the warrant, yes?"

"Well, once we knew what was in the thermos, we acquired a warrant and took it out to the house."

"So what you are saying is that you entered the house without a warrant, searched the house, and removed evidence from the house and then brought the warrant back to the house later." Mr. Martinez waits for the officer's answer. The officer looks over at the D.A. with a look of apology on his face.

"Yes."

Mr. Martinez turns to the judge and asks that the thermos and all the evidence pertaining to it be disallowed since it was obviously obtained illegally. The judge orders both Mr. Martinez and Mr. Aaye to approach the bench. I cannot hear what she is saying, but she does not look happy. When they step back, the D.A. looks sick when he turns around. The judge announces to the jury that all evidence connected with the thermos is disallowed. Mr. Aaye walks back to his table and begins shuffling his papers. Then he stands and asks the judge for a short recess. The judge says that it's close to lunch and court will reconvene at 12:30 sharp. She hits her gavel down hard, and the jury is ushered out the same little door through which they had come.

I ask Mr. Martinez if he knew about the illegal search. He says he did, but this is an important case for the District Attorney. He says he's been around long enough to know that in a small town like this things can appear and disappear, so he didn't say anything when he saw that the search warrant time and their hospital report times did not match. It was better that the evidence be shown in open court among witnesses. Plus, Mr. Aaye was hoping for a plea instead of having to go to court. He thought we would accept a lesser charge, and that he'd get the "feather in his cap" without the work. I might be naive, but I'm amazed that he thought he could get by with illegal evidence. Mr. Martinez says Mr. Aaye has been the district attorney for more than 15 years, so he is used to manipulating things in his office to work the way he wants; we all saw how that worked with the officer on the stand, only answering parts of the D.A.'s questions.

But times are changing. In the past, this small town has not had to contend with black defendants who had competent representation. There are good lawyers now who don't subscribe to the old methods of prejudice and intimidation. Besides, Mr. Aaye has seriously underestimated Mr. Martinez, seeing him as a young foreigner, public defender, and no threat. Mr. Aaye has not kept up with the times. His small town is feeling the effects of big town liberalism flowing across from Detroit and up from Chicago. He has just received a devastating blow from his sloppy work and outdated arrogance.

Mr. Martinez may have counted on the thermos evidence being thrown out, but he isn't ignorant about the influence the D.A. still carries in our town. He fully intends to prove his case and I'm upset because he doesn't ask for a mistrial or dismissal. He says he promised he'd create a reasonable doubt and win fair and square, and that's what he intends to do. I don't know if that determination is for me or him. All I know is that I want to go home and get back to my children.

Mr. Martinez doesn't release me to have lunch with Kathy and Jonita. He wants to keep me close, so I still don't get a chance to talk with Kathy. We grab a quick sandwich and Mr. Martinez reviews some facts we'd discussed earlier about Jonathan and me. We discuss the beginning of our marriage breakdown. We discuss the cross-eyed lady. We go through each time she and I met. We discuss every detail I can remember, including my visit to Debra's house and the things Debra told me.

Mr. Martinez is so consumed with what he is figuring out that there is no time for me to ask about his strategy. I want to know if he plans to put me on the stand; I do get to ask that question. He says that he will avoid that. He doesn't think it will be necessary. He does say, however, that he is going to need me to be strong. I might have to hear some ugly things, and I will have to stay composed. He says that things may come out that I didn't know. If that happens, I am not to look shocked or surprised. His statements make me nervous, if it's possible to be more nervous with the charge of murder already nipping at my heels.

196

It's time to return to the courtroom. When the jury is in place, Mr. Aaye calls one of the city police officers as his next witness. He has him read the charges I'd filed against Jonathan several months earlier. He also asks him to read the statement the witnesses gave at that time. He reads what my ghosts told him about all the times that they'd seen Jonathan manhandle me and twist my arm, and the times they'd heard him yelling at me from inside the house, so loudly that it could be heard through closed windows and doors. I always suspected that others heard, but it is truly embarrassing to find out it's true by hearing it told in the courtroom. They testified that this abuse has gone on through the years until I started going to school and getting out of the house. They say they called the police this last time because this time they saw me fighting back. Mr. Aaye is happy with the last statement, "She was fighting back." He repeats and takes his seat.

Mr. Martinez ignores everything Mr. Aaye has brought out and asks a strange question.

"Do you have any other police calls or arrests for Mr. Liberty that didn't involve Mrs. Liberty?"

The officer hesitates at first and then answers, "Yes."

"Under what circumstances were you called?"

"Domestic Disturbance."

"You say that call did not involve Mrs. Liberty. Who did it involve?"

"A Mrs. Valerie Jones."

"When did this happen and what were the details of the call?"

"The call was about a month after the charges made by Mrs. Liberty. Mrs. Jones called because Mr. Liberty was drunk and becoming physical with her."

"What do you mean by becoming physical?"

"Mrs. Jones says Mr. Liberty pushed her, but then she says that it was a big misunderstanding and that she just wants him removed until he sobers up."

"What did the police do?"

"We escorted him off the property and warned him about returning in that state."

"Was that the only time you were called for Mr. Liberty?"

"No Sir. We were called to that address again the day before he died. It was late into the night."

"What happened then?"

"Mr. Liberty looked bad, like he had been drunk for a while. He kept saying he hadn't done anything. He said Mrs. Jones was crazy and that we didn't have to worry because he was leaving and Mrs. Jones wouldn't have to worry about him anymore."

"Did you escort Mr. Liberty out?"

"Yes we did."

"Did you arrest him?"

"No. No charges were pressed against him."

"Thank you, officer. That's all."

The officer steps down, looking at Mr. Aaye, then leaves the courtroom. This had been the D.A.'s witness. I look over at the jury. They are all alert and sitting up straight. Mr. Martinez has opened a door that now has their interest. I can see in their posture that they're hungry for more.

Mr. Aaye fumbles with his papers some more. Then he calls his last witness. He calls the director of the Infectious Disease Unit from the hospital where I work. I recognize him, but we've only spoken a few times when I was first hired. Mr. Aaye asks him what type of employee I had been. Mr. Douglas is singing my praises. I'm surprised when he tells how lucky they are to have me. He tells them about my patience with the terminal patients. Then Mr. Aaye changes his line of questioning. He asks about my knowledge of chemicals and drugs. He assures the D.A. that I have a thorough knowledge of how chemicals and drugs react to each other, especially poisons. That's what Mr. Aaye is after. He tells him that a superior knowledge of poison and drug interactions is required to work in his ward. I see a smirk on Mr. Aaye's face when he turns around to walk back to his seat.

That sick, sinking feeling is on me again. Mr. Martinez asks Mr. Douglas if he knew about any troubles I might have been having at home. He says he was not aware of anything. He asks about my work performance. He says my performance was excellent up until the day I was re-assigned. Then Mr. Martinez pursued the DA's line of questioning.

"You say Mrs. Liberty has a superior knowledge of poisons and drugs?"

"Yes, sir."

"Would you say her knowledge would enable her to poison someone without there being much evidence if any?"

"Yes, I would say that wouldn't be difficult for anyone with her knowledge."

"If that's the case, in your opinion, would you think antifreeze would be her, or anyone with her experience, choice?"

"Well sir, there is a warehouse of drugs that could kill someone without a trace of suspicion. That's common knowledge for nurses on her level. Antifreeze will do the trick, but there is a greater chance of getting caught when it's done long term."

"One last question, Mr. Douglas, is any special skill needed to poison someone using antifreeze?"

"No, sir. It's the method of an amateur."

"Thank you, Mr. Douglas."

Once Mr. Douglas leaves the stand, Mr. Aaye announces, "The prosecution rests."

It is time for Mr. Martinez to bring forth his witnesses. The judge grants a short recess, so that gives me a chance to speak with Jonita and Kathy. Jonita gives me a huge hug, and Kathy explains that she had to take Jonita out of school because Mr. Martinez intends to use her as a witness. Apparently, the subpoena was not served until this morning. Kathy had no time to warn me. A wave of anger shoots through me. Mr. Martinez had not informed me of this, and I do not want Jonita having to live with choosing between her dad and me. I'm seething. I need to confront Mr. Martinez, but I know there isn't time for the conference we need to have.

When I return to the courtroom, Mr. Martinez turns around and sees me enter with my arm around Jonita. He also sees the expression on my face. I know Mr. Martinez wants to win, but not at the expense of my daughter's innocence. I'm trying to control my expression, but, my anger has me breathing hard. I take those last few steps, concentrating on calming myself. I ignore the stares of those around me. I'm trying to focus on not doing anything that will hurt my case. Although I don't like what Mr. Martinez has done behind my back, I certainly can't complain about the results he's getting so far.

CHAPTER TWENTY-ONE

M r. Martinez begins his defense. His first witness is Valerie Jones. Everyone turns around when he calls her name, including me. Valerie raises slowly from her seat just a few rows behind my in-laws. Everyone looks surprised, but I knew she'd be here, so I'm able to keep a straight face that lacks shock. She apprehensively makes her way down to the front. She still has her hair fixed in micro-braids, she's dressed plainly, and she's still cross-eyed. There is, however, one change that I and everyone one in the courtroom noticed: she's not skinny. She takes the witness stand, avoiding eye contact with me. Every juror has his or her eyes fixed intently on her. I have a good idea where Mr. Martinez is going to go with his questioning.

"Mrs. Jones, how long have you known Mrs. Liberty?"

"Well, we really don't know each other."

"When did you first have contact with her?"

"Almost a year ago."

"What were the circumstances of your encounter?"

She hesitates, but Mr. Martinez is very patient. She shifts in her chair and finally replies.

"She called me one day accusing me of having an affair with her husband."

"Were you?"

"Not at that time." Mr. Martinez let her words settle for a moment.

"When did you have contact with her again?"

Again she shifts in her chair, looking very uncomfortable.

"A few months later, I was at a motel with Mr. Liberty."

With that answer, I can feel the entire courtroom lean forward, including the judge. Mr. Martinez makes them wait for his next question. It's so quiet that I'm sure everyone can hear me breathing. Finally, Mr. Martinez asks his next question.

"Why were you at a motel with Mr. Liberty?

"Jonathan, Mr. Liberty, was protecting me from my husband. He was trying to beat me up. That's when Mrs. Liberty showed up."

"When was your next contact with her?"

"A few days later, I was at her house."

"Why were you at her house? Had she invited you there?"

I almost feel sorry for her myself. She has to tell everyone that she is dumber than I am when it comes to Jonathan.

"No, she didn't invite me. Jonathan did," she replies with slight annoyance I'm sure she didn't mean to show, but it is just what Mr. Martinez wants to see.

"Let me get this straight. Mr. Liberty invited you to come visit with him and his wife."

"No, that's not how it happened."

"Then tell us Mrs. Jones, how did it happen that you met Mrs. Liberty at her home on your third encounter."

Again she hesitates, no doubt trying to answer without sounding like a complete idiot. Unfortunately, she isn't successful. She tells the court that Jonathan told her that I had run off and left him with the kids. He asked her to move in with him so that they could be one big happy family. She loved him so much that she agreed. She packed some things for herself and her children and brought them there to his house. She explains that I was not there when she arrived, and she had no reason to not believe what Jonathan had told her. When they went out that evening with all the kids to get something to eat, they returned home and found me there preparing for bed. She says she gathered up her children and left.

She stops talking, and I can see the pain twisting her face. I can also see that Mr. Martinez is not finished with her. He asks her how all this made her feel. At first she doesn't answer. She acts as though she doesn't hear the question. So Mr. Martinez asks her again.

"How did it make you feel?"

She narrows her beady eyes and looks squarely in his direction, as though she would hurt him if he got close enough. She tightens her lips and answers.

"How do you think it made me feel? It made me angry, and he humiliated me in front of his wife and my children."

"How many children would that be?"

"I have five, but only three were old enough to know what was going on with us."

"Were you angry enough to want to hurt him? I mean if you had some way to hurt him at that very moment, were you angry enough or humiliated enough to do it?"

Mr. Aaye objects, but the judge allows the question.

"I don't know," is her reply.

I think she is catching on. I think she finally realizes that she is that reasonable doubt Mr. Martinez spoke about earlier today. Before she can say more, Mr. Martinez asks his next question.

"Mrs. Jones, I can't help notice that you are pregnant. Is Mr. Liberty the father of your unborn child?"

Everyone in the courtroom is waiting for her answer. I already know the answer. That's what they wanted to prepare me for when they called me into the investigator's office to watch the videotape that covered the rear view of the funeral. I didn't notice her profile during that brief moment at the hospital when I was in the police car. But, apparently it was visible then, and during these past few months she has grown considerably.

She finally replies, "Yes."

I thought I was ready, but her words cut through me like a razor. I didn't expect to hear it said out loud. I thought I was past any more hurt or betrayal, but I was wrong. Even in death, Jonathan continues to land his sucker punches all over me. Her response sends everyone in the courtroom into a feverish frenzy. The judge has to hit her gavel down several times before she is able to regain control of the courtroom.

"Was Mr. Liberty aware of his unborn child?"

"Yes, we discussed it."

"What were your plans for this new child? I mean how was this new baby going to be raised? Was Mr. Liberty planning to move with you and your children or were you moving in with him and Mrs. Liberty?"

That last remark is nasty and uncalled for, yet I find myself curious about what their plans were.

Apparently, Mrs. Jones didn't like his remark either because her voice changes when she answers him. Her lips are tight again and it's clear that she's angry.

"We had not decided what we were going to do yet. It was still early in my pregnancy when Jonathan died."

"When was the last time you spoke with Mr. Liberty?"

"We spoke the day he died."

"When?"

"We spoke early that morning, before he left."

"Left? Left where and where was he going?"

She hesitates again and then says, "He left my house and he was going home."

"Let's me get this straight again. When you say home, do you mean to his wife and children?"

"That's where he kept his things."

"Did Mr. Liberty show any signs of illness before he left?"

"He said he'd been sick before and that it would pass."

"When did you expect Mr. Liberty to return?"

"He was just going to collect a few things and come right back."

"Had he sobered up from the night before when you called the police, or did you let him come back the same night?"

"I let him back in that night. He was sorry."

"Are you sure his plans were to come right back? Remember, you are under oath."

"That was what I thought he would do."

"Is that what you agreed upon or is it what you hoped?" I suppose that was a rhetorical question because Mr. Martinez does not give her a chance to answer before he moves on to a new question.

"Did you see Mr. Liberty after he left you to go home?" Mr. Martinez asking that question makes no sense to me. I see no point in exposing her presence at the hospital. That's not going to help my case.

"Mrs. Jones, you're under oath. Did you see Mr. Liberty again the day he died?"

"Yes."

"Under what circumstances?"

"He would not answer his phone when I called. I got worried, so I decided to go over to the house to check on him."

"The house you're referring to is the house Mr. and Mrs. Liberty live in, right?"

"Yes."

Oh my God! She was at my house again! She really has lost her mind. She was in my house before Jonathan died. I know I'm not supposed to show surprise, but there's no point in working on my face now. I know I look surprised and I'm not alone. All the jurors have their eyes focused on Miss "I'm having Jonathan's baby" and so does everyone else in this courtroom including me.

"Weren't you afraid Mrs. Liberty would be there and you and she would have another confrontation?"

"No. Her car wasn't there, so I figured she was out. I saw Jonathan's car in the garage. I rang the doorbell over and over, but he didn't answer."

"Then what did you do?"

"I had a set of Jonathan's keys, so I let myself in."

The entire courtroom lets out a sigh after her response.

"Had Mr. Liberty given you a set of his keys?"

"No."

"I see. Then what happened?"

"I called out for Jonathan but got no answer. I decided to go to his bedroom to find him."

"Was he there?"

"Yes, he was in the bed. I called his name several times and he still didn't answer me. I stood there a little bit longer looking down at him. Finally, I decided to leave."

"You said you were worried; why would you leave him without an answer? You had come this far, used a set of keys you either made or stole, and entered another family's house. Why wouldn't you get an answer?"

"Sometimes Jonathan was like that. He just wouldn't answer you."

"Are you telling me that you didn't suspect anything was physically wrong with him? You just thought he was ignoring you, right?"

"That's right."

"Mrs. Jones, did you have any further contact with Mr. Liberty after you left his house?"

"Yes."

"How did that come about?"

"I went to the hospital after the ambulance took him."

"How did you know Jonathan was in the hospital?"

"Ma Liberty called me."

"Do you mean Mr. Liberty's mother?"

"Yes."

"Did you see Mr. Liberty at the hospital?"

"Yes."

"How did you get in when he was in such critical condition?"

"I told them I was his wife."

There isn't a sound in the courtroom. I could not follow Mr. Martinez's instructions; my mouth is agape. She was in with my dead husband while I was left outside in the waiting room handcuffed.

"I only stayed a few minutes," she adds on her own. "I knew his wife and parents would be there soon. I couldn't leave the hospital. I needed to be close to him. Finally, when I was going out the hospital, I saw Ma Liberty rushing in. I hid myself and slipped out of the hospital once I thought it was safe."

"What do you mean, when it was safe?"

"I just didn't want anyone asking me a lot of questions like you're doing right now."

"Has anyone asked you any questions about Mr. Liberty's death? The police? The D.A.? Anyone?"

"No."

"One last question Mrs. Jones. When you heard that Mrs. Liberty had been charged with Mr. Liberty's death, did you offer to tell anyone that you knew he was sick prior to his death? Or did you tell anyone that you had seen him just moments before he died?"

"No."

"Thank you, Mrs. Jones, no further questions."

I almost smile when I see everyone in the courtroom lean back once Mr. Martinez sits down. It reminds me of a smooth, single motion that a choir makes when the director signals them to stand or to be seated. The jury, as well as the rest of us, has gotten an ear full. All eyes are now on the D.A., who sat looking dumbfounded during most of her testimony. I imagine he wanted to object many times, but Mrs. Jones is not his witness. Besides, the one time he did speak up was overruled by the judge. Furthermore, he is already in hot water with the judge for trying to submit illegally obtained evidence. He has, however, managed to scribble a few notes during the witness's testimony. He approaches the witness stand and clears his throat as though waiting for an idea to hit him.

Finally he says, "Mrs. Jones, according to your testimony, you and Mr. Liberty were planning to start a life together. Is that true?"

"Yes."

"No further questions."

Mrs. Jones steps down from the witness stand somehow seemingly pleased with herself. Her posture has changed and she appears to be pushing her belly out further as though she is proud of her illegitimate child. All eyes are on her, especially mine. I'm looking at her and grappling with my feelings at the same time. I have both loathing and sorrow for her. She should have run when we had our first conversation. While I'm staring and trying to separate my feelings, Mr. Martinez's voice catches my attention as he calls his next witness.

"Miss Jonita Liberty, please come to the stand."

My attention immediately switches from the cross-eyed lady to my baby. She gets up and walks confidently past me to the stand. I try to muster up a smile, but I'm worried for my baby. The court officer swears her in, and she is seated, ready for whatever is to come next. The jury is now focusing on what my baby has to say.

"Miss Liberty, how do you know Mrs. Jones?"

"She's the woman that tried to become my dad's new wife."

"How did she try to do that?"

"My mom was gone for a day and she and her kids came to move in. When Ma came home that evening, Ma Val, I mean Mrs. Jones, and Dad argued and she left."

"Have you seen her since that day?"

"Yes, she has come to my house again since then and my dad has taken me over to her house. I never told Ma."

"What kind of relationship do you think they had?"

"I think Dad liked her at first, but then he didn't. That's just the way he seems to be. He told me that he didn't think that baby was his. He said that it could easily be her husband's baby."

"Why would your dad have that kind of conversation with you? I mean it sounds like the type of things he would discuss with an adult, not his young daughter."

"My dad and I were very close before, uhh, Mrs. Jones came into the picture. She wanted Dad all to herself and used me to babysit her kids whenever I went over there. She was always complaining about my mom to my dad and wanting him to do one thing or another. At first Dad seemed to like her a lot. Then, he started complaining, and I was the only one there to listen. I wanted us to be close again, so I would listen. I guess he just forgot that I am his kid. Besides, I like being treated like an adult. Anyway, my daddy didn't want his old family or his new one. He didn't want any of us. And, he said he had found a new friend."

"Did he say who that new friend was?"

"No. He just said that Mrs. Jones would be mad at him."

"Why would she be mad?"

"Because he said he didn't want her anymore. He said those were not my brothers and sisters anymore, especially the new baby."

"So you're saying your dad didn't think Mrs. Jones was carrying his baby. Do you know if he told her?"

"Yes, at least I think he did."

"Why do you think he told her?"

"The last time we were over to her house they were arguing about something. Dad kept saying that Mrs. Jones was lying about something. He said he didn't believe her."

"Do you know what it was he didn't believe?"

"No. But Mrs. Jones was very upset. She was crying and saying that it was true."

"Then what happened?"

"After she stopped screaming, Dad came out the room angry and told me we were leaving."

"Miss Liberty, I want you to think carefully. Was your dad sick before all this happened? I mean before Mrs. Jones came into the picture."

"No."

"Once he got sick, did you and your dad go back to Mrs. Jones' house?"

"Yes. We went a few times together. I don't know if he went other times, but when he was gone days at a time, we all just assumed that's where he was."

"Think back to the argument between Mrs. Jones and your dad, did Mrs. Jones seem angry enough about the situation to become violent?"

"Her voice sounded harsh and hard like when Daddy would be angry with Ma. I didn't worry though because I knew she wasn't strong enough to physically hurt my dad."

"Thank you, Miss Liberty."

"Your witness, Mr. Aaye," says the judge.

The D.A. makes his usual strut to the witness stand.

"Miss Liberty, did you see any violence between Mrs. Jones and your dad?"

"No."

"Did you see any violence between your dad and your mom?

"Yes."

"That's all. Thank you. You may step down."

My baby steps down and walks back to her seat looking much older than when she went up there. Mr. Martinez doesn't waste any time moving on. Mr. Martinez calls his final witness. He calls Debra Liberty-Smith.

"Mrs. Smith, have you seen Mr. Liberty and Mrs. Jones together?"

"Yes, many times."

"Did they always appear to be the couple in love the way Mrs. Jones portrays them?

"Well, at first when Jonathan left his wife, he was all over Valerie. But later things changed."

"How do you mean?"

"Well, Valerie started complaining to me that Jonathan made her feel like a whore."

"How did you respond to her concerns?"

"I told her that's what you get when you steal another woman's husband. And that's about all there was to say."

"Was she angry about Jonathan's change?"

"Yeah, she was furious the last time they were at my house. Jonathan refused to go to her house. So, she would have to rent a room if she wanted him to spend the night. Jonathan would lie and tell her that his wife was taking all his money. She just didn't know that Jonathan wasn't doing much for her either. Jonathan was using her like he used most anybody he could."

"Did you get the impression or did she say she was going to get even with him?"

"She didn't have to tell me. She hated Jonathan's wife because she seemed to be the cause of all her problems. And she hated Jonathan because he only complicated her life by getting her pregnant and then trying to weasel his way out of her life. She was a woman scorned in the worst way. And you know what they say about a woman scorned."

"Your witness, Mr. Aaye."

This time the D.A. doesn't do his usual stroll to the witness stand. He simply stands and asks his question from the table.

"Mrs. Smith, did Mrs. Jones discuss any specific plans with you to hurt Jonathan?"

"Sir, you do the math. She's pregnant by another woman's husband with baby number six. She has no financial support from her lover. Jonathan is running back and forth between her and his wife. Finally, he refuses to claim her unborn child, and probably has started another relationship with someone else. What do you think?"

"Please just answer the question. Did she say she was going to do anything to Jonathan Liberty?"

"No."

"Thank you. You may step down."

With Debra's testimony completed, the defense rests. It's now almost 4 p.m. The judge decides to let each of them make his closing statements and says the jury will begin deliberating in the morning.

Mr. Jack Aaye goes first. Basically, he repeats all that he'd said in his introduction. He said I had motive, means, and opportunity. He then has the jury look over at me to recognize me as the cold-blooded killer he knows me to be. Once he sits down, Mr. Martinez begins his closing argument. He focuses on all the things Mr. Aaye had addressed. Regarding motive, he tells them I was not alone. He asks the jury who would have more motives: a woman being left by an abusive husband or a woman who finds out she's stolen someone's abusive husband and who will not claim their unborn child? He also reminds them of the police's reports pertaining to Mr. Liberty and Mrs. Jones, saying that she too has had Jonathan removed for violence. When addressing means, Mr. Martinez reminds the jury of the coroner's and infectious diseases director's testimonies: no degree or special knowledge is needed to administer antifreeze. In fact, a child could have done it because it's so simple. Also, anyone can purchase it. Finally, he addresses the fact that Jonathan was found at my house—opportunity. He has the court reporter read back to the jury Mrs. Jones's testimony where she admits that she used a set of Jonathan's keys to enter my house while I was not home. He adds, for their consideration, that no one knows how many other times Mrs. Jones may have entered my house without anyone's knowledge. Before Mr. Martinez finishes, he returns to his promise to provide a reasonable doubt. He tells them that it was convenient for the police and Mr. Jack Aaye to lay Mr. Liberty's death on the wife. They never looked for anyone else; even though his evidence shows that someone else may have had a stronger motive. As he spoke, some of the jurors nodded their heads in agreement. Once Mr. Martinez concludes his closing remarks, the judge briefs the jury of their duties, and they are led back through that small door. Now, all I can do, is wait.

CHAPTER TWENTY-TWO

The people in the courtroom linger after the judge and jury leave. I don't want to talk to anyone except Jonita. But before I can get to her, she and Kathy are cornered near the door by a couple of newspaper reporters.

I can hear Kathy saying "No comment," but they persist in badgering Jonita.

Mr. Martinez is trying to say something to me while I'm intent on getting to the door to rescue my daughter. There was no more niceness in me. The next "No comment" they hear is clear, forceful, and given with a promise. They look up at me with surprise. Then, they decide to move away, without asking any more questions. Mr. Martinez comes up behind all of us and pushes us out the door before anything else can be said.

Outside the building, I follow Kathy and Jonita to Kathy's car. I tell Jonita what a wonderful job she did. I tell her how proud I am of her and how grown up she looks. She doesn't respond. She just gives me a sheepish smile. It's as though she knows something that I don't know. I want to ask her what's going on, but I decide that this is neither the time nor the place. Besides, waiting for the verdict is all the drama I can handle right now. I open the door for Jonita and promise to call Kathy later. I step away from the car as Kathy starts it and puts it into gear. As she pulls off, I look across the street, and I'm surprised to see Mr. Martinez standing at the curb; I'm so accustomed to his disappearing acts. I walk back across the street in his direction. Most everyone is gone now.

"Thanks for everything, Juan. I'm not sure that I like everything you did in court, but I do appreciate all your hard work. Now, tell me what you think. Do you think it's going to pay off?"

"I created a reasonable doubt. I even gave them a different suspect. And, the reality is that Jonathan could have been killed by just about anyone. He didn't make a lot of friends along the way."

I don't respond to what Mr. Martinez said. Even though I know it is true, his comment hurt me. I start walking toward my car, not angry because he is telling the truth, but angry at myself because I still care. After all I've been through, I still can't get rid of him. Juan walks alongside me, escorting me to my car. The sun is just beginning to set, and an orangey shadow is cast in the sky. I'm not in a hurry as we stroll toward the rear of the courthouse to my car. Suddenly, all the events of the day hit me. The weight of it all causes me to stumble. Juan reaches out to me before I meet the pavement. It is as though all my life energy is leaving me. Tears are flowing and I can barely keep my balance. Juan helps me to my car and leans me against it, taking my keys from my hands. He opens the door and puts me in the car on the passenger side. I don't really know what's happening to me. I just feel exhausted. Juan gets in on the driver's side and starts my car. I lay my head back on the headrest and close my eyes.

When I open my eyes again, it is morning. I'm in my small room in my bed under the covers. I hesitate to raise the blanket and look beneath it. Thank God! The only things missing are my shoes. I'm able to get myself together and pull myself up enough to see the digital clock. It flips to 9:30 a.m. When I prop myself up higher, I see there is a note on the mirror.

Mrs. Liberty,

I have left your car out front. Your keys are on the table. I will call you as soon as the jury is in. Until then, try to relax.

Juan

Try to relax. That's not as easy as it sounds. There's nothing for me to do but worry. I can't eat anything, so I just lie back down and try to take

Juan's advice. Just as I close my eyes and begin sliding into twilight sleep, the phone rings. It startles me into an upright position. It's Kathy checking on me. I promised to call the night before. She tells me that the girls are fine. She says Jonita was up all night worrying about today. She's keeping her home from school. I don't object. In fact, it's probably for the best. Kathy says that Jonita wants to be in court when the verdict is read. To that, I do object. I wouldn't even go if I didn't have to be there. Kathy is in agreement and promises me that there won't be any more surprises.

"Hold on, Kathy, I have another call… Hello?"

"Mrs. Liberty, this is Juan Martinez. We're being summoned back to the courtroom. You need to be there by 1 p.m." I don't respond because I can't breathe.

"Mrs. Liberty?" asks Mr. Martinez. I finally catch my breath enough to answer.

"I'll be there."

"Good-bye, Mrs. Liberty."

I switch back to Kathy and tell her what just happened. She wants to come down to be with me. I don't want her to leave Jonita, so I tell her not to come. I promise that someone will call her either way the verdict goes. Before I hang up, I ask Kathy to pray for me. It feels like God has forgotten me. However, it is more likely that it is I who has forgotten Him. I know that I need to feel the strength of God to help me face what is ahead. I need His support in accepting his will.

Kathy prays a powerful prayer. She asks that we all be delivered from this terrible tribulation. She asks for God's favor for me. She prays that my family be mended and that hearts be strengthened.

"Amen."

"Amen. Good-bye."

After hanging up, I continue to pray in my head that God is all forgiving. I know that there are consequences and that I will reap what I have sown. My seeds have not always been good ones. So, I continue to pray for God's mercy as I dress. I'm moving, it seems, in slow motion, sitting down as I do each task to prepare to leave.

I make coffee with the small pot that comes with the room. Today, I'll drink it black. I need the strength of the bitterness that it freely offers.

215

It is noon now and there's no more time. I've stalled long enough. It's time to go. I park in the same spot as before and again enter through the back door. I take a deep breath before entering the courtroom that holds my destiny.

Mr. Martinez and Mr. Aaye are already here waiting. It is only about 12:30. I expect this to be the longest wait of my life. I ask Mr. Martinez if it's a good or bad thing when a jury deliberates for such a short time. He says it's hard to know, and that he doesn't want to speculate. That's not what I want to hear. I am too nervous to sit down and wait. I keep getting up and pacing the floor. At first, there is no one in the courtroom but the three of us. Mr. Aaye is busy shuffling through papers in his briefcase and totally ignoring us. Mr. Martinez is seated with his briefcase closed and his hands folded on top of it as though he were a schoolboy waiting to be dismissed. He looks over at me pacing every now and then and then looks forward toward the judge's podium.

Finally, the court officer enters, followed by the court reporter, and the judge. "All rise" is called again. The spectators who entered the courtroom in the past 30 minutes all rise to their feet. The jury starts to enter from the little door again. I make my way to my seat. I try to make eye contact with a juror, any one. I try to see their faces, but not one of them will look up. I feel that sinking feeling again. It is me the DA wanted for Jonathan's murder; and it looks like that's what they have given him.

Something's wrong with my hearing and everything seems to be slowing down.

I'm trying to fight it off.

I'm trying to control my breathing and focus.

The room is getting smaller.

The judge is speaking to the jurors, but I can't make out what she's saying.

They are all looking at her.

No one looks at me.

Now she turns to me and starts talking.

I can't make out what she's saying.

Mr. Martinez is pulling at my arm helping me to stand.

A juror starts reading from a paper.

I don't know what he's saying.

I'm fighting the spin of the room and forcing back the bitter taste in my throat.

I look to Mr. Martinez for help.

He's smiling. They're all smiling, all except Mr. Aaye.

Mr. Martinez says to me "Not Guilty."

I lose my balance and land in my chair.

The words start to penetrate the fog that envelops me.

I repeat the words Mr. Martinez just said, "Not Guilty."

CHAPTER TWENTY-THREE

The police finally release my house. The yellow tape is taken down and I can move back home. Juan is working on having the girls returned home, and they are scheduled to be here at the end of the week. The insurance company has released the funds they were holding back. My vacation doesn't end for another week, and I've been reinstated to my old position. I decide to spend time getting things together for the girls.

I collect all my belongings from the living room and move them back into my bedroom. Juan helps me get all of Jonathan's things folded into trash bags, and he takes them to a church donation box near his home. My pastor has come by with a few of the mothers to help me clean the house. We have tea and we pray to rid all the bad spirits that might linger in my house.

I am able to spend quite a bit of time with Juan, talking about what direction I want to take with my life with the girls. The first thing I do is give Jonita her own room. I realized in the past few months that she has matured greatly, and she needs to have her own space. I turn the spare bedroom into her room. It's the smallest room, but it's big enough for her.

While the kids are in school, Kathy and I go to a local furniture store and buy Nita a canopy bed and all the furniture that goes with it. We decorate her room up like a young princess; everything is a lovely pink and lavender. We have to move quickly to have it done by Friday. I don't stop until it's all perfect. I feel deep down inside that she needs something of her own. I know there is emptiness inside her that I can't fill. This is just my attempt at trying to make things a little better. I also spruce up Jolisa and Jovida's room. I add a few stuffed animals, disassemble Jonita's bed, and take the bunk bed down to make two twin beds. They get new comforters and pillows. Everything looks clean and fresh. I want them to feel like this is a new beginning.

Juan tells me that the police did not arrest Mrs. Jones. That's right: Mrs. Jones. I can call her by her name now. I really am trying to put all this behind me. The police don't believe they have enough evidence to get a conviction on her either. Jonathan was disliked by many and there is no way of telling who decided to act on it.

Anyway, I guess we'll just have to wait and see if Mrs. Jones tries to claim any of my dead husband's estate or benefits. Juan says she will have to provide proof that she's had Jonathan's baby to get anything, and I'll have to deal with that reality if it happens.

***

The girls are coming home today. I don't know why I'm so nervous; I drank a pot of coffee already and it's just 10 a.m. I guess it's going to be new for all of us. Daddy won't be here as usual, but there won't be any more surprise visits either. My brothers and some of our church family wanted to come over for the welcome home, but I want my girls all to myself. I want this moment to be special and private. I want a chance to talk to them and to give them a chance to talk with me. They didn't go to school today. The social worker came yesterday to inspect the house. She says it is just a formality. She is supposed to be back today by noon with the girls. I still have to have visits from social services every three months for the next year. That is a small price to pay to keep my girls, even if I didn't do anything wrong.

The doorbell rings, and it's them at the door. I am so excited I can barely get it unlocked. Jovida and Jolisa jump into my arms; they almost knock me over. They are visibly happy to be home. Jonita, on the other hand, passes by me and heads upstairs. She doesn't say a word. The social worker notices her behavior, too.

Once Jonita is out of earshot, she tells me not to worry. Sometimes it takes the older children longer to adjust to the loss of a parent. She says Jonita has been through a lot and that maybe counseling is a good idea. The other two girls have released me and run up to their room. I can hear them squealing from upstairs. They are arguing about which bed is whose.

I don't get to show Jonita her room because I am still downstairs with the social worker, but when I enter the living room I can see upstairs and that she has found it on her own. When she sees me looking, she closes the door—not hard, but firmly. I feel a knot in my throat when the knob snaps shut. I try not to react while the social worker is still here. I divert my attention by helping her get the girls' things out of her car. I pile them all on the kitchen floor, intending to call them down later to get them. Kathy has splurged on each of them. They had only taken a small suitcase, but a lot more than that has found its way back.

The social worker leaves me with her card and tells me to call if I need anything, even if it is just to talk. I thank her and assure her that everything is finally going to be all right. I lock the door behind her and take a deep breath. I hope my words of assurance are true.

Lunch is ready, so I call the girls down to wash their hands and eat. The two little ones chatter throughout the meal. Jonita barely says a word. She helps me get the dishes off the table as she has done before, but she still doesn't speak. The girls retire to their respective rooms and seem to be content while I finish the dishes. My intentions are to take the girls out to dinner tonight. They used to love to go to the pizza place with all the dancing bears; even Jonita liked going there. I know it'll be different today without Jonathan, but we might as well get used to it.

Everyone collects their things from the kitchen floor, and I help the younger ones put their belongings in the right places. After I finish with them, I go to Jonita's room. She has the door closed, so I knock before entering. She is lying on the bed looking up at nothing in particular. I ask if she feels like talking. She sits up, so I pull out the chair at her new desk and sit down. I ask if she has something on her mind she wants to talk about. Jonita gets up from the bed and leaves the room.

When she returns, she is holding the three thermoses that had been missing months earlier when I was trying to fix Jonathan some soup. You can imagine my surprise. She extends her arms out toward me and says, "I thought that I should hide these. What do you think I should do with them?"

I get up from the desk and take the thermoses from her. I wrap my other arm around Jonita and again whisper in her ear,

"It's over now, and I'm sorry Mommy didn't protect you."

Breinigsville, PA USA
29 November 2010
250253BV00001B/5/P